CHRYSALIS

Gilded Love # 2

KILBY BLADES

To Mr. Blades, my beta hero, for indulging my passion to write.

PROLOGUE

I 've got to stop this.

It's the one thought that's repeated itself in my mind since I walked into the suite. That I can't let this be the end. That I shouldn't put her through a scene like this. What right do I have if I can't even bring myself to say it out loud? "Snapdragon" is the safe word either of us can say to instantly end our arrangement. Instead of speaking it, I've gotten us the Presidential Suite at the Drake, crystal vases on every surface, overflowing with hundreds of snapdragon blooms.

I've got to stop this, I think again. But I'm paralyzed, staring inertly at the general manager's card on the nightstand while my hand palms my phone. I'm keystrokes away from making the call that will put this all in reverse. What we're doing still has to end but it doesn't have to be like this. I can find a different way.

My mind hurtles to think it all through. First, I'll have the hotel disable her key, and I won't answer the door when she knocks. That way, she'll be forced to go back down to the front desk. When I'm sure she's back in the elevator, I'll leave the suite and meet her downstairs. I'll stall her with a drink at the bar for an hour or however long it'll take. That's when I'll have the staff remove all traces of snapdragons from the room.

We'll make it back up here eventually and have the romantic weekend getaway she thinks she's walking into. I'll call Dale with my resignation on Monday, extricating myself from the job transfer I've just accepted and the promotion I've worked tirelessly to achieve for more than two years. I'll still have to travel to Sydney for a while—long enough to wrap things up. In the meantime, I'll figure out how to have a different talk with Darby, about a different ending for us.

Then I hear it. The door closing. And I know she's arrived. A look back at the clock on the opposite nightstand confirms that I've let time slip too far. I close my eyes for just a moment, half steeling myself for the inevitable, half ruing the day I ever dreamt up this plan. A clean ending to our arrangement was what she said she wanted, but nothing about this feels right.

When I hear a dull thud, my stomach plummets. But I have no right to be gutted. I agreed to this, too. Friends with benefits with absolutely no strings. So I stand on legs far braver than my heart and walk from the bedroom to the grand entryway of the Presidential Suite. A lump forms in my throat as I see her first tear fall.

"When do you leave?" She asks it so calmly that I know she knows about Sydney. Though, by the rules of our arrangement, I needed no excuse. "Snapdragon" was our exit hatch. I hadn't actually said it, but a room full of snapdragon blooms was my not-so-subtle means of invoking it, the safe word either of us could use to put a stop to us.

"Tomorrow...how did you find out?"

"Andrew. He didn't mean to tell me. He thought I knew."

I'm walking toward her when another tear falls. I begin to apologize, because she deserved better than to find out the way she did.

"It's better like this." She shakes her head, sniffling some of her tears away.

All I want to do right now is hold her, but I can see she doesn't want to break down. Neither do I.

No messy breakups. That's the shitty part, right?

She'd spoken those words over a year ago. This whole scene was about sticking to them. I hate this, but I owe it to her.

"So we have tonight?" I can see her try to strengthen her resolve.

I nod as I take her hands in mine.

"I missed you when I was gone," I choke out. I've never spoken these words to her before.

"I missed you too."

"I miss you every time I go," I say, because if the agreement is really over, I'm throwing the rules out the window.

"So do I."

I tuck her under my arm and pull her close as I coax her inside. I don't let myself think about how different things could be if we hadn't lied to each other for so long.

Five minutes later, we're in the bedroom and Darby's undressing me. The imperative is unspoken, but somehow, we both know. If these are our last hours together, we should spend them intertwined. She's walked me backwards until my thighs are up against the edge of the bed. I look between us, watching her hands as they disappear beneath my shirt. When her warm fingertips fan out above my navel until they settle on my waist, I feel it all begin.

My eyelids lull as her palms slide their way up either side of my torso, her thumbs tickling my armpits before skating upward until I bend my elbows to let her pull off my shirt. My eyes are back on her the second my head is through, but she's not looking at my face. Her hands are back on my chest, and her fingers are taking their time as they explore my skin. Her thumbs skim my nipples seconds before her palms settle over the muscles between my neck and my shoulders. When her fingers fan upward once again to caress the base of my skull before grazing behind my ears, I nearly purr.

She knows how much I get off on this. She hears the helpless sounds I make and notices my stuttered breathing. To her, this is foreplay—a quirk of mine that she indulges—a sexy, teasing gift. She still doesn't understand how much I need to be touched for reasons that have nothing to do with sex. She has no idea that no woman's hands on my body have ever bound me in rapture like this. I'm on the brink of whimpering in ecstasy and I'm barely even hard.

That changes the second her hands slide down my shoulders and she leans in to bite my ear. Her teeth on any part of my body always goes straight to my dick. By the time I feel her nipples graze my chest through her sheer dress, my hands are already sliding around her middle. With one hand cupping her waist and the other palming her ass, I roll her sex against mine. I could lie and say I do it because I want her to feel how hard she makes me, but she needs no reminder of that. I do this once, twice, three times because the friction feels so, so good.

She still has me in the in-between place—my skin tingles from the touches she is delivering to my shoulders, my neck, my back. But my kitten is getting frisky and I know she wants to play. Now her every calming stroke is punctuated with a hint of sex—her nails on my back as she traces my tattoo, a rough grab to the back of my neck as the pad of her bare foot snakes beneath my jeans and sneaks up my calf. These hybrid sensations are the ones I love most of all.

But it doesn't last. She's awakened my baser instincts—and my primal being wants to use every part of me to claim every part of her. My balls are getting heavy and my pants are getting tight and it's all I can do not to rip off that hot little dress she's wearing, but I finally get both of our clothes off. The second we're naked, she jumps up to wrap her legs around me, and I know what she wants.

With my hands holding her up by her ass, I walk her to the

wall. Her wet heat makes me throb and I can't wait to be inside. We both moan as I enter her in one long stroke. She craves me doing her like this. It's been more than two weeks since we've seen one another, and our reunions always carry fierce urgency. We have a rhythm—slow and constant and oh, so deep. It's as natural as breathing to us. Coming together like this is so perfect. So desperate. So right.

But her tightness around me isn't even the best part—the best part is the magic that passes between us. Our eyes say everything we won't. Truths that we know better than our own names are easily exposed in this sacred space. The agreement has never existed here. That some of these truths have been whispered aloud a time or two may not be my imagination.

And, God, her kisses. When her lips find mine for the first time, I whimper at the contact, the softness of her mouth mixing deliciously with the hard intensity of our screwing. When I feel her coiling tighter around me, it spurs me to bite her lip. She moans helplessly and digs her nails into my bicep. I dip down to bite her neck and she curses. We love to one-up each other like this.

Somewhere inside me, my heart is broken. But I'm miles away from that place. Nothing exists right now but us. Not the snapdragons in the other room. Not the red-eye I'm out on tomorrow. Not the out we said we'd give to each other if one of us walked away. Right now, there's only togetherness—a divine intertwining. In this moment, we are what we were always meant to be. We are one.

Part One

ORDINARY WORLD

Chapter One

LEAVING ON A JET PLANE

"Can I bring you something to drink, sir?"

I recognize the flight attendant. I know them all by now. She's never offered her name, but I've heard the other one call her Kim. Everything about this flight is a facsimile of the same leg I've taken a dozen times before. Flight 187 from ORD to YVR. I'm seated in 3A. Left side window. The last row in first class. I usually decline Kim's offer, content to wait until dinner is served before I order a beer.

This time, I do need something before takeoff. Though, it will be a lot stronger than a beer. This flight is different from all the earlier flight 187s out of O'Hare. This time, my ticket is one-way.

"Just water, please."

Her face falls a little when I barely make eye contact. I've always gone out of my way to be warm with people who others treat as nameless, faceless help. But I've been dismissive. I fish the pill bottle out of the pocket of my jeans. If I don't take a valium soon, I might get off this plane. And what would that achieve beyond doing more to fuck up this already-fucked situation?

Talk is cheap.

My mother's mantra repeats itself in my overcrowded mind. This time I believe it. What good would it do for me to tell Darby what I really want for us if sacrifices are out of the question? She'd never stand for me giving up my promotion in Sydney. And she's just been through hell to earn Chief of Psych. So I'd traded a pointless confession for an open-ended goodbye.

"Thank you," I say to Kim, and this time, I make eye contact, but I waste no time after she sets down the glass to pick it up and swallow my pill. This may be unwise. The flight to Vancouver is only four hours and I need to be coherent if I want to make my connection. I hate medication. But I need something to quiet the cacophony of thoughts inside my mind, something to stop the voices screaming that I'm making the biggest mistake of my life.

It's too early to recline my seat, so I slip my padded headphones over my ears. I start to queue up the Iron and Wine album I usually like to listen to—the songs play like whispered lullabies that soothe me to sleep—but Darby loves this album and it's more than I can handle. Unable to think clearly enough to choose an alternative, I flip the music off but keep the headphones on and pull a black mask over my eyes. I'll settle for noise-cancelled silence instead.

Sleep comes quickly, and is mercifully deep, and I might have slept for hours had Kim not coaxed me awake with instructions to place my seat upright for descent. I'm dazed as I walk through the Vancouver airport, absently content that the valium is keeping me numb.

I take another half a pill after boarding my flight to Sydney, even though you're only supposed to take one at a time. I'm still out of it when I meet my driver at the airport, but the winter air outside baggage claim sobers me. By the time I let myself into my apartment, it's midnight, I'm lethargic but not tired and I feel the dreaded stretch of a sleepless night.

What I should do is work. I've been ignoring my job for days. As shitty as the past forty-eight hours have been, I worked hard to make them perfect. It may not have been the right time to tell Darby the truth, but that didn't mean I couldn't leave her clues. I gave her as much as I could handle of the ending we agreed to, but made absolutely sure she knows this isn't over.

We both know what this is, even if we've never said it. But what kind of dick would I be to say it a second before I walk out the door? It needs to be confessed in its own time. Not because of some job transfer. Not like this. And when it comes, it won't come easily. We each kept secrets. We both told lies. And each of us knew the other one was doing it.

It's beautiful, are the only words written in the text I awake to on Wednesday morning. The vibration of my phone on the marble countertop my cheek lays upon rouses me. Her text is accompanied by a photo of her wearing the necklace I had made for her, an exotic mixture of rubies and yellow diamonds that make up the leaves of the pendant. Set in platinum on a delicate white gold chain is the bloom of a multi-colored snapdragon.

The photo doesn't show her full face. Somehow, she's framed herself from her nose to her décolleté with the butterfly painting I gave her in the background. I drink in her slender neck, her elegant jaw, her kissable lips, her soft hair falling in waves over her shoulder, and the necklace, quite beautiful, as it sits just below her clavicle.

Girls love shiny things, too. They're called diamonds.

I text back the words she'd once said to me offhandedly when we'd been talking about men and their cars. Even then, I'd thought about a ring.

You're never getting the painting back.

She thinks I gave it to her because I know she loves it. Darby can't yet comprehend what the gesture of giving it away means to me.

It's been yours since the moment you laid eyes on it.

Do you work today?

I have to be there in an hour. I stayed in Chicago for as long as I could.

I'll let you go, then. Have a good day, she returns simply, with an emoticon of the sun.

Have a good night, baby.

I want to say something more, but "I love you" is out of the question and everything else I think of sounds lame. So I drag myself off of the bar stool in my lonely kitchen, knowing I have to hustle if I want to make my first meeting.

Chapter Two

IT'S NOT EASY (SUPERMAN)

I catch a glimpse of myself in the mirrored back wall of the elevator as I step inside. The worn boots, distressed jeans and fitted jackets that Michael likes to wear have been traded for the custom-tailored suits of Mr. Blaine. Beneath today's navy jacket is a slim-cut herringbone shirt in ivory, and cufflinks that match the fastening on my Italian leather shoes. The suits have always felt like a costume, but I wear them well. I excel at looking the part.

Everything skips a few beats when I stride into the office. Five years ago, so much attention would have made me uncomfortable. Dale's mentorship has been key. He taught me how to master the art of charming intimidation—of doling out rations of the sex and charisma that draw people in, but sheathing it in a layer of gravitas thick enough to warn them not to get too close.

My training has served me well. I've metamorphosed from an introverted collaborator to a quietly effective leader. I love the complexity of managing so many things at once. I spent most of my life catering to the shy comic book geek, but this has been inside me all along.

Not that leadership hasn't come at a price. The higher I climb, the less time I get to spend on meaty problems. Apart from an astonishing number of HR issues, there's ass-kissing and political posturing now that I'm the boss. I remember what Darby said to me when I told her about the strange new feeling of everybody looking to me.

"You know what they say," she'd said. "Climbing the corporate ladder is like monkeys climbing a tree. When you're on the top looking down, all you see are a bunch of smiling faces. When you're on the bottom looking up, all you see are a bunch of assholes."

I spent so many years as a monkey, forcing my grimace into a smile as I clambered my way up. And I'd started lower than any other monkey I'd ever met on that tree. I'm grateful for where I came from—few people understand the gifts that come from growing up poor. But I didn't want to stay that way. For as long as I can remember, I've been driven to achieve.

And I'd done it. I'd hand-washed the one uniform at a time my mother could ever afford every single night. Each morning, I'd put it on a little damp before I took two buses and a train to reach my posh private school. I changed the way I talked, depending on which world I was inhabiting. By the time I got to college, I sounded like a prep school kid al the time.

It wasn't cool to be younger, or smarter, or to be on scholarship, but I made it through. I got what I needed in terms of book study, but the real calculus I'd learned was getting people to like me. The difference between what I came from and what I've become is hard to fathom. But the saying is true—you can take the boy out of the South Side, but you can't take the South Side out of the boy. Even now, in $6,000 custom-tailored suits, some part of me feels that I don't belong.

"It's nice to see you, Michael." Alicia smiles hopefully as I walk into my private conference room. As always, she's on time. She looks to be in her late twenties, wears her blonde hair in a smart, shoulder-length cut, and is the object of many an office crush.

She's been cold to the advances of other men but she's interested in me. She's offered to show me around the city four times in the nine months since I started spending more time in the Sydney office. I politely decline each time, but she's not taking the hint.

"Morning, Alicia."

I pretend not to notice how she's pulled out the seat next to her at the conference table. She has her laptop open, and papers out, but I don't take the bait. I sit across from her and pick up the TV remote.

"Why don't you put what you've got on the monitor?"

Experience has taught me not to sound like too much of a dick when I'm trying to give off the "don't even think about it" vibe. Acting like a pompous jackass is a turn-on for some women.

"I'll just lower the lights, then, so that we don't get glare."

Alicia hits the button that lowers the blinds a second before she turns down the dimmer on the overheads. She then closes the door that I intentionally left ajar.

You've got to be kidding me.

Before the door clicks shut, my finger is on the speakerphone button of the Polycom and I've dialed my assistant Kat's extension. She transferred from Chicago, too, though she's new to working for me.

"Would you mind coming in to take notes, please?" I ask evenly while avoiding Alicia's questioning eyes.

Kat sails into the room a moment later. She sits silently but gives Alicia a look that says she's got her number before training her eyes to the TV. As the supervisor of the admins, there's nothing Kat doesn't know.

We spend the next ninety minutes poring over Alicia's designs. She's talented, and normally I would be thrilled to work with her. The project we're talking about is exciting, and, professionally, this has been a good move. The aesthetics of architecture in this part of the world are different, and I'll learn a lot, even in a role as hands-off as mine.

The rest of the day is more meetings, more feedback to give to juniors, a call with a client, and a late afternoon call with Dale, the firm's founder, my boss and the Managing Partner in the Chicago office. I've been open with him about having affairs to settle back in Chicago, and he knows this is the first day I'm in the Sydney office for real.

Because he thinks he's hilarious, he's sent me an enormous welcome basket full of nothing but Vegemite. There are jars, tubes, and even single-size mini-servings of this abhorrent spread and a huge yellow ribbon that matches the label. The first time I was here, we had breakfast together and he lightly recommended that I try it. I actually gagged a little. And he's never let me live it down.

By the time I get home, my lack of sleep has caught up with me. The housekeeper has stocked my fridge, and I whip up some chicken and vegetables to bake in the oven while I slog through a run. Running feels better than it should for someone so tired. I'm exhausted by the end but running five miles actually makes me feel normal.

I watch the news channel that I've taken a liking to, still not totally understanding or caring about all of Australia's current events but watching just the same. It's the only sensible thing to do while I eat. I shower again, don't bother to attempt reading, and stare at the photo of Darby on my phone for a full fifteen minutes before drifting off to sleep.

Chapter Three

ANGER MANAGEMENT

"Randy."

I hear the guilt in my voice as I say my friend-slash-publisher's name. He's been trying to get a hold of me for weeks. He knows how busy I get, but this is the first time I've been so slow to respond.

"You're alive! I was starting to worry."

"I know. I'm sorry. Things have been nuts. I should've at least texted."

"Cringer was ready to put out an APB," he says, speaking about his ten-year-old tabby cat who is named for He-Man's shapeshifting battle cat in *Masters of the Universe*. Randy lived, ate and breathed comic books.

"What are you doing up? It's, what, 6AM there?"

"Early flight. Sac Comic-Con is this weekend. Seems like you've got quite a fan base in Northern California."

Getting up from the sofa where I was having my dinner, I walk into my office and fire up my Mac. A nudge on my mouse causes the huge screen to light up and it doesn't take me long to navigate to my Andrew Dufrain e-mail. It's the account Randy uses to send me stuff about the graphic novels I draw.

"I'm weeks behind," I admit. A quick scan of seventy

unopened messages shows that at least ten are from Randy. I've ignored this account for so long that I have a backlog of fan mail, too.

"You're losing your edge, kid," he says. "What kind of hack can't juggle a high-powered job, a non-profit, a bestselling graphic novel series and a hot-as-Violet girlfriend?"

I can't even bring myself to tell him to shut the hell up and quit ribbing me about comparing Darby to Violet. The second he met Darby, he knew.

"Me, apparently…" I mutter, sweeping my hand over my face. And I do feel like a failure. I hate the feeling of letting people down.

I know he's just giving me shit—trying to get me to quit being such an overachiever just like he's been doing for the better part of twenty years. But he's more right than he's ever been. I have too many balls in the air and, one by one, they're starting to drop.

"Think we should delay the launch?"

"No," I say reflexively. "We're already pushing a year since *The Architect* came out."

"Yeah, you're right. Your asshole publisher will probably drop you if you don't deliver on time."

The asshole publisher Randy is referring to is none other than himself.

"You know I work best under pressure. Nothing would ever get done if I didn't have a deadline."

"You have a deadline now, and nothing's getting done. If I had to decide whether to spend my time with a fake girl and a real girl, I'd make the same choice."

"Yeah, well, that's no longer an issue. The real girl is 10,000 miles away."

There's no point in concealing the misery from my voice.

"How'd she take it?"

"I don't know. I haven't talked to her. much"

I don't say that I'm starting to worry. She's texted me, but it's not the same thing. I've been resisting the urge to call her all day.

"Why the hell not?"

"It's only been four days."

"Have you learned nothing from my life?"

"I know, I know. Clarine. The only woman you ever loved. The one you let get away."

I still remember the day Randy got the invitation to her wedding. I'd been about thirteen. It was the only time I'd ever seen him cry.

"I still see her at Cons sometimes," Randy mutters, and now it's his turn to sound miserable. "The first thing I look at is her left hand. Every time, that ring is still there. I put it there. Because I was the idiot who was so busy building a future for us that I didn't remember to make sure there would be an us to enjoy it. At least I needed the money. What the hell is your excuse?"

I swivel around in my chair. I'm not looking at the monitor anymore anyway. Instead, I look down at the city.

"It's not the money."

"Then what is it? Any idiot can see you two are in love. Why did you take a promotion you don't need?"

I don't gratify his sarcasm with a response.

"Sometimes it's hard to believe you have an IQ of 157," he says with some reproach.

"Not helpful."

"You should have gone with Plan A."

Plan A had been half-baked, but I'd liked its simplicity, and the movie reference would have been apropos. I still would have done the thing with the flowers and presented her with the necklace. But I'd have told her it didn't have to be over. From there, I'd have given her a choice.

I'd wanted it to be a nod to her favorite movie, *Before Sunrise*. In the movie, two strangers spend a single night walking the streets of Vienna together and fall a little bit in love. But they each have their own lives to get back to, and things to work out if they decide to be together. So they agree to meet again in the Vienna train station in exactly one year if they still want something more.

What I would have told Darby is that if she wanted a different ending for us, she could meet me in the Vienna train station, on Platform 7, just like in the movie. A year would have killed me, so I'd have given her three months. I would have told her that *I* would show up, because I already knew what I wanted —that part would have been true. I also would have told her that if she didn't show I'd be okay—that part would have been a lie.

"Plan A is off the table. I'm focused on Plan B."

"Plan A had a nice romanticism to it."

"Knowing about the transfer kills the sense of possibility. If she thought choosing me meant choosing a long-distance relationship, she'd feel like I was already too far gone."

"She already thinks you're gone."

"She knows I had to go. There's a difference."

"Which is..."

"I want her to know that me being called here is separate from what happens with us."

"Yet instead of showing her a path for the two of you to be together, you left her in limbo."

"No. I laid the first stone on the path. I killed an agreement that neither one of us was sticking to. One that can't possibly work from so far away."

When Randy doesn't fire back, I know he's letting up a little.

"So what does she think your status is?"

"Undefined."

"Says the man who hates ambiguity."

"In order for something better to live, the agreement had to die."

⁊

Noon in Sydney means that it's nine at night in Chicago and if Darby didn't have to stay late, she will have just gotten off of her shift. I calculated it all six weeks ago. My lunch hour will be the ideal time to drop her casual calls, at an hour that's decent for both of us.

Except this doesn't feel casual. We rarely talked on the phone when I traveled, always saving ourselves for our next rendezvous. Except there is no next rendezvous. And it's been four agonizing days since I left her with tears in her eyes.

Hold my calls, please.

I message Kat, but it's redundant. I've already blocked time off on my calendar. So I dial, not knowing what I'm going to say, but hoping she'll pick up. I'm shocked to discover that my usually flawless planning overlooked the possibility of being sent to voicemail. Rather than rattling off an unscripted mess, I hang up when she doesn't answer. It only makes me feel like we're farther apart.

By that time, I'm drawing. Sometimes my fingers cramp from how often my pencil is in motion. I can sketch while doing nearly anything, and when I'm alone, I do. Sometimes, they're random things, sometimes they're scenes for my graphic novels. Darby hasn't mentioned reading *The Architect*, and I haven't pressed it. I'm dying to know what she thinks—but I'm not eager to talk about how the heroine, Violet, bears an unmistakable resemblance to her.

I'll never admit it, but the line between Darby and Violet was once blurred in my own mind. They're both my ideal woman, though one I created and the other materialized. Seeing the woman I had invented personified was what prompted me to speak to her that first night. If there had never been a Violet, there may never have been a Darby, or an *us*.

But what I'm sketching now is Darby. In my drawing, she is in her room, lying in bed—her hand is touching my side of the bed—now empty, with a nearly imperceptible imprint of where I've once been. From behind her, a ghostly figure has wrapped her tightly in his arms. Even though he's barely visible, he is holding her. Her eyes are closed, and it's not clear whether it's from the anguish of being alone or from the comfort of feeling held from afar. The entire drawing is done in graphite pencil, but only the butterfly painting, the snapdragon necklace, and the blue of his eyes glow in subtle color.

I have never—not once—drawn anything expressly for her. In this moment, I don't care that this will be a dead giveaway as to how I feel. The compulsion to connect with her in some way is strong, and I'm just lovestruck enough to take a picture of the drawing and send it.

Since I can't be there, this'll have to do. XOXO

Chapter Four

IT AIN'T OVER 'TIL IT'S OVER

W hen my phone sounds with the first bass guitar notes of *Sex and Candy*, I startle awake. A look at the clock tells me I've only been out for a few minutes. I grab the vibrating phone off of my nightstand faster than I've ever grabbed anything in my life. My thumb rushes to hit the green button that will allow me to pick up the call

"Heyyyyy."

"Oh, no...were you sleeping?"

I blink and rub my eyes. "Even if I was, I'd wake up to talk to you." I'm smiling in spite of the uncertainty that has plagued me. "I was starting to get worried."

"I'm sorry...I didn't want to call at weird hours. But I texted you..."

"Which I appreciated."

And after our first words comes our first silence. If our chemistry doesn't translate even a little to talking on the phone, I'm screwed.

"I loved your drawing," she offers. It's adorable and shy and above all else, her voice is a welcome sound to my ears.

"I think I drew it more for myself than for you."

I hear her let out a shaky breath, but I'm still holding mine.

"Your gifts are...astonishing, Michael. The necklace, the butterfly, *The Architect*, and now this. They're all exquisite."

"You read *The Architect*?"

"Parts of it."

"Do you like it?" I try to sound casual.

"Michael. Are you kidding? You're an amazing storyteller."

The hero, Keith, is a modern-day prince masquerading as a commoner. When his engagement to Violet is threatened by her disapproving father, he goes on a quest that will help him win Violet's hand.

"How far into it are you?"

"I'm taking the ending kind of slow..."

That's code if I've ever heard it. Last year, I pulled every string I had (and some I didn't) to get her a signed copy of the *Before Midnight* screenplay from Richard Linklater. When I'd implored her to read it, she'd insisted that it was too precious to handle, claiming that it was a collector's item. I'd given her hell over it that day.

"What is it with you and endings?"

"The part before the ending is full of possibility. But the end is just...the end."

But I can't let her keep thinking this way. If I want to get her back, she has to see hope.

"What if the ending is better than you could ever have imagined?"

"Every once in a while, I get so invested that I just can't handle having my heart broken."

I want to tell her that my story gets its happily ever after and that ours can, too.

"Can I ask you a question?"

"Of course." I don't like how hesitant she sounds. I don't want distance to mean *distance*.

"How does a guy who doesn't believe in love write such a beautiful love story?"

"I never said I didn't believe in love," I answer carefully. "I said I didn't think I could be a good partner—and I was right. I was barely around. Now I've moved halfway around the world. And it feels like shit. And I left you feeling like shit too."

"Don't be stupid," she says with a bit of her fire. "It only feels like shit because you were a good partner."

Neither of us speaks for a minute.

"So it's not..." Why is she struggling to ask me questions? "...autobiographical? Like, Violet isn't based on somebody?'

"I wrote Violet before I met you."

"Yeah, but I thought that maybe Violet was based on somebody else, and that I just happen to look like both of them."

"There is no real-life Violet. But when I saw you that night on the patio, I nearly tripped over my own feet for how much you looked like her."

More than a year has passed and I've never mentioned it before.

"That night...I stared at you for a long time before I walked up to you. You were different from her in so many interesting ways. I wanted to memorize you and go home and draw you—not her. I'm really good at observing people without them knowing—but something different happened with you. I wanted to meet you. I told myself that I'd let myself talk to you for just a minute. But you know what happened next. I couldn't stay away from you, Darby. I haven't been able to since." I don't know why I can't stop spilling my guts. I'm saying far more than I planned. "Does that bother you?"

"No. It feels special. Kind of...extraordinary."

We don't say anything for a minute.

"So, *The Architect* has a happy ending?"

"I don't know. What do you think? Should Violet accept Keith in spite of his flaws?"

"Everyone is flawed, Michael. Even Violet."

"He doesn't care. He worships the ground she walks on."

"And she idealizes him. Each one idealizes the other."

"So that's the question. Does love survive because two people choose to focus on what they have together, or because they focus on what's missing and decide to take a chance regardless?"

She sighs. We both know I'm not going to answer her question. But I will tell her something I've been repeating to myself.

"There's something my mom used to say to me. 'Everything will be OK in the end. If it's not OK, it's not the end.'"

"This feels like the end." Her voice quiets and I let mine quiet, too.

"It's not."

"Sometimes two people who drift too far apart never find their way back together," she says finally.

"They do if they're meant for each other. Time and distance won't change that."

"So what do they do...in the meantime?"

My heartbeat quickens. Everything rides on whether she likes my answer.

"They become the best friends they can to one another. Because they were meant to be that, too. All the rest is just a matter of time."

She's silent for a long time—so long that I wonder whether the call has disconnected. Pulling my phone back from my face, I see the call timer is still ticking away.

"You make it sound like a fairy tale," she says finally, her voice even softer.

"Real fairy tales are scary, and feed from things that are dark. What they have together has its shadows. But when their light shines bright enough, it will chase their shadows away."

"What if their light burns out?"

"His never will. His light for her is brighter than the sun."

I hear her take a shaky breath.

"It's late there." she whispers. "You should get some sleep."

I don't bother protesting that I'm not tired anymore. I know it's time to hang up.

"Have a good day, baby," I murmur.

I love you, I think, but don't say aloud.

I don't sleep a wink that night.

Today is a coffee day. I worked through the weekend and pulled an all-nighter on Sunday. Landing the Kensington account would be a major win for me. It's unusual for a firm with a new in-country presence to even be considered for a contract this big. But, last week, I got a call from Lucas Kensington, CEO of Kensington Hotel Group and the architect of a billion-dollar empire.

He was familiar with my work—said that once he found out I was now at the helm of the Sydney office, he was eager for Dewey and Rowe to put its hat in the ring. That was on Thursday, which had given my team three-and-a-half days to put something together for the Monday pitch. Afterward, I took the team to dinner and finally got some sleep, but it's Tuesday and I'm still dog-tired.

When I step off the elevator, I see that I'm the first one here. It's only seven-thirty but there's a ton of stuff that needs doing. A lot of people—mostly people who've been in line for longer—think I don't deserve this promotion. The first guy Dale hired to run the Australia office fucked it up. I can't let that be me.

I prefer the office when it's this quiet. Most people can tune out ambient noise. Even with my office door closed, residual noise overstimulates me. Instead of fading into a neutral roar, everyday commotion feels to me like a clamor of conflicting sounds.

Things that other people take for granted, like getting work done in a coffee shop or sitting in an open floor plan, send my stress levels through the roof. It's like wearing a hearing aid I can't turn off. Sounds from ticking clocks, televisions, and other peoples' conversations irritate me.

In my neighborhood, they used to call me Radio Raheem,

like the character from the Spike Lee film. I never went anywhere without headphones on. I still use them a lot and put on white noise more often than music. But, when it comes to relationships, my need for controlled quiet worries me. If Darby has some noisy habit that ramps up my anxiety, that will create problems of its own.

"Hey, it's Michael," I say at eleven on the dot when I hear the beep through the line that confirms I've joined the call. "Who else is on?"

One by one, my other Board members chime in. Ronnie, Darnell, and Isaac are the other officers. I'm Executive Director. Five other general board members are also on the call.

The Tara Foundation funds youth arts organizations in Chicago. A new class of students started a couple of weeks ago. We provide them with art supplies, pay for their independent classes, and run our own curriculum that they take with other artists their age. My staff is top-notch. They love the kids and they love our mission. There is nothing I am more proud of in my life than having built this.

"Andre Spence dropped out," Darnell says gravely after sharing news of otherwise strong attendance.

"*Dropped out,* dropped out?" I ask with alarm.

"Joined the Disciples," he continues. The Gangster Disciples are one of the fiercest gangs on the South Side. At fourteen, Andre's at the age that they recruit. "I've been by his house twice. He's been out running the streets. His mother doesn't know what to do."

Andre is more than just another kid in the program. He started in our first cohort and he's been with us for four years. He reminds me a lot of myself at that age. He's a kid leading a double life, the talent that will launch him toward something better is forcing him to straddle two worlds. He's too street for uptown, and too uptown for the streets. There is no place where he belongs.

I think about the bathroom at the McDonald's on Garfield.

By the time I was Andre's age, I carried a change of clothes. A uniform for school and plain clothes for my neighborhood. McDonald's was where I changed. I walked the long way to the El so I could stop there on my way to and from school. But my clever disguise didn't do much. For years, I took a lot of beatings designed to remind me that I wasn't the same.

I'm terrified for Andre right now. If we don't get him out of there, he'll end up dead. But I understand his decision. They're giving him the one thing he wants the most—something that feels like love. For a teenage boy whose real father has abandoned him, finding people who will stand by you and make you feel like a man is worth a lot.

"Is she still on night shifts?" I ask. His mother is a clerk at the Walgreen's on the northern edge of Hyde Park.

"I'll find out," Darnell says.

"I want to give her a call. Meanwhile, can you call Corliss Eversley at Hood to Stable? Tell her we have a kid for her. Tell her I'll pay his way."

Hood to Stable is a program that moves kids in gangs to rural areas to get them out of the lifestyle and help them escape retaliation. If he tried to leave the Disciples but didn't disappear from the neighborhood, that would land Andre in a coffin faster than anything else. No doubt, he's witnessed crimes and has probably committed a few by now. Gang members who leave are a liability. No one wants to get ratted out.

I wrap up the meeting efficiently enough. Given how good our numbers are, we're finally ready for the real estate buy that will get us into our own facility. The team confirms that they've scheduled the charity gala on the weekend I'll already be home for my niece Ella's birthday, so I'll be able to kill two birds with one stone. I should be ecstatic. But I can't stop thinking about Andre.

When I walk back into my apartment that night, I'm exhausted. It's only six-thirty, but I'm seriously considering crashing. I drop my bag on the floor next to the elevator, untuck my shirt and start to unbutton it as I make my way to my bedroom. Dropping my jacket and leaving it on my dressing bench instead of hanging it up makes me feel like a slob, but I'm that tired, and I feel kind of grimy and in the short distance between the elevator doors and my closet, I decide I want a bath. I turn on the spigot, rummage around for some Epsom salts, and squeeze in a dropper-full of an oil I found in an apothecary in London that I am pretty sure was run by a witch. When the water is ready, I ease myself in slowly. I hope I don't fall asleep in here.

I haven't been in the tub for two minutes when I hear my phone chime. It's the special tone I hear whenever Darby sends a text. But my phone is on the sink all the way across the room. I'm so warm and comfortable that if it were, literally, anyone else —even the twin sister I shared a womb with—I would let it go. But it's Darby. So I pull myself out, walking gingerly—I don't want to slip on the marble floor.

When I look at the screen of my phone, my face melts into a grin. The picture she just sent me is totally worth it. It's a close-up of her holding my book. She's hugging it to her chest and the back cover faces the camera. Her eyes are cut off, and the picture shows her from her nose down. Her lips curve in a contented smile. She's in her bed—I can see her sheets around her—and I realize it's four o'clock in the morning in Chicago. After I slip back into the water, I swipe the screen so I can view the full picture. That's when I see her text.

You've restored my faith in endings.

Chapter Five

WICKED LITTLE TOWN

I t's been two weeks since I left and the first time I wake to a text from Darby. It came in at about 3AM. It's a selfie—she and Andrew sitting at her desk with mostly-eaten sushi in front of them. Seeing both of their faces makes me smile. Andrew is my assistant-slash-friend who works with me at Dewey and Rowe on the Chicago side. He's also been my year-long accomplice in having sumptuous lunches delivered to Darby at her job.

I'd ask you to guess who stopped by, but I think you already know, the message says.

You didn't think I was going to stop making sure you ate, did you? I shoot back from where I'm lounging in my bed. I'm groggy, but grinning like an idiot. I've never been more grateful for Andrew than I am right now.

Honestly, I did.

Her text comes through as I'm putting on my workout clothes. It's mid-afternoon there, now. She still doesn't get it—how devoted I am to her. I need little gestures like this to prove to her that I'm still very much in the game.

Nobody likes you when you're hangry.

I send that one with an emoji that is frowning with steam coming out of its ears.

I'll give you that. And it was sweet of you to ask Andrew to keep me company.

I'm stepping on the treadmill when I text her back.

I didn't. That was all him. He's your second biggest fan.

Andrew likes everyone, but Darby's high on his list. And he's convinced that Darby loves me. He's begged more than once to have first dibs at planning our wedding.

Headed to work, I presume? she texts back.

About to go for a run.

Isn't it still cold there now?

Sydney winter isn't Chicago winter. It's warm enough to run but my neighborhood isn't great for running outside.

I take a quick picture of my home gym, which is really a guest bedroom with a lot of exercise equipment in it, and I send it to her.

Wow! Is that your place? Your view looks really nice.

I wish I'd gotten something smaller. It feels too big for me. Kind of empty.

Maybe you should get a cat, she replies a second later.

I shake my head. *Do I seem like a cat person to you?*

Haha! That was a test. And you passed.

I'm grinning when I send back a smiley face emoji and a thumbs up. Apparently, Darby has turned me into the kind of man who sends emojis. But I'm too giddy about talking to her to care. So I write her back.

I've always wanted a dog.

Me too. My mom was allergic, so I never had one.

And my mind flashes to me presenting her with a puppy in the entryway of the house I want to build. Before I get carried away and consider what breed would be good for us, I ask about her hermit crab.

How's Consuela?

Fabulous, as always. And a lot easier to take care of than a dog.

Her emoji is a sad smile.

One day, cupcake.

And I'm back to picturing her puppy and our house.

Oh! I keep forgetting to tell you, you forgot your Tufts Crew t-shirt at my house. What's your new address? I'll send it to you.

I chuckle. It's cute how she thinks that anything I do when it comes to her isn't deliberate.

I didn't forget anything. I put it in your drawer.

It's your favorite t-shirt.

You wear it more than I do. Keep it warm for me, alright?

It's Friday night and I'm still in the office. Not that I have anything better to do. If it were during the week there may have been a few stragglers, but I've been the only one left for hours.

We got the Kensington account. It's a whale of a win. The office is still buzzing with excitement. The deal is huge—ten luxury hotels across the region over the next three years. I've been here for less than a month and I've already made my sales goal for the next five quarters. I feel victorious about hitting the pitch. Now I have to knock the projects out of the park.

I'm friendly with Vitiana, the cleaning lady. She's the only one I see in the office when I'm here this late. She looks to be in her sixties, but she may be younger. She speaks with a heavy Fijian accent, but she has a kindness about her and a beautiful smile. She has two sons—one in Fiji, and one in the U.K. When she talks about them, her face lights up. I hear her cart as it makes its way down the hall and know when she's getting close. I've come to look forward to our chats.

"What'chou doing here so late?" she grills me, pausing as she stands in my open door.

Her hand is on her hip and she's pinning me with a

reproachful look. "Didn't anyone tell you it was Friday night?" she fusses.

She shuffles into my office, because she isn't young, or thin, and I can tell she's had an injury somewhere along the line. She doesn't have a pronounced limp, though she clearly has some sort of difficulty in walking. It's backbreaking work—bending hundreds of times a day to grab trash cans under the desks of many tiny offices and cubicles—running heavy industrial vacuums, pushing mop buckets filled with water from place to place. When she walks in, I do as I always do: walk around my desk to pull the visitor chair out for her.

The first time I did it, she spent half a minute staring between the waiting chair and my eyes. So I'd turned on the charm.

"Come on," I'd said. "Everyone has time for a five-minute break."

That day, when I'd sat down, I'd opened my drawer—top right—where I keep the candy and spread out a feast that was too delicious to resist. Ever the phenomenal assistant, Andrew had kept me rich in American sweets. I'd watched as Vitiana's eyes swept over my Nerds, my Kit Kat, and my Atomic Fireballs. When she chose a pack of Twizzlers, I knew we'd be friends.

By now, she knows the drill, and she sighs as she sits down, eager to take a load off of her tired feet, I assume. I spread out an array of candy—she tries a new one every once in a while but has developed a liking for Mike and Ike's. We chat for a good twenty minutes—about the scandal of an unscrupulous businessperson that made the news today, and a little about her sons.

Before she leaves, I pick up my own wastebaskets and walk them to her cart, dumping them into her bigger trash can.

"You need a good woman to get you out of this office," she scolds, stopping to look at me before she walks out my door.

"I've got a girl back home," I say, smiling at my own phrasing. It makes me feel like a soldier who's gone off to war.

"She coming here to live with you?"

"She's got her own career back in Chicago."

Vitiana tsks and shakes her head. "In my country, we have a saying: 'Each bay has its own wind.' Have you ever heard it?"

I shake my head, already turning it over in my mind in an attempt to deconstruct its significance.

"The winds in Sydney will steer you in one direction. The winds in Chicago will steer her in another. If you want to find the same sunset, you need to sail in the same wind."

I smile a sad goodbye, but instead of sitting down and continuing my work, I'm rooted to my spot. I'm still thinking about what she said long after I stopped hearing her cart making its way down the hall.

By the time I finish my work, it's ten-thirty and there's no point in going home. I have a call scheduled with Corliss Everly. She's made room for Andre in her program—even though her waiting list is a mile long. I want to thank her, and we said we'd talk this morning. Eleven at night for me will be nine in the morning for her.

"Heyyyyy!" she greets with a 1000-Watt smile a few seconds after we connect. I see myself smiling back in the thumbnail-sized video. "It's good to see your face. How long has it been?"

"Too long."

She nods, still smiling, but appraising me a little with her eyes.

"It has been," she agrees a bit saucily, and quips, "and you still look good..."

I laugh. And it feels nice. "I could say the same about you."

Corliss is beautiful. I had a monster crush on her when I was eighteen. We met at a Gulf War protest. She was holding up a sign that said, "Real men pull out on time". I was instantly and completely infatuated with her. She had fierce determination, cinnamon skin and eyes ten times more dangerous than mine. A soft look from her conjured a contented joy, a reassurance of all the good in the universe. A hard look could make a grown man cry.

She'd planned to become a diplomat. That's what she was doing in the International Relations program at Tufts. Once she'd figured out that infiltrating some of the more corrupt institutions was useless, she'd gone grassroots. Now, she advises a number of Chicago non-profits, but Hood to Stable is her creation. Like The Tara Foundation is to me, it's her baby.

"I can't thank you enough for what you did for Andre," I say in earnest. "You saved his life."

"It's getting worse out there," she says. "You wouldn't believe the drugs. And it's not the stuff that was on the streets even a year or two ago. It's pharmaceutical shit."

"Who's supplying it?"

"That's what we've been trying to find out. Whoever it is, they're stirring shit up. They're moving product, but they're not playing nicely with the other boys."

Gangs are like little countries. And when an outsider tries to do business in your territory without negotiating terms, it's war.

"Amateurs?" I ask.

"Not with what they've brought to town. The gangs that have the connect are making bank. The ones that don't are losing money. I think they're gearing up to take the new guys down. That's why recruitment is so high right now." Her face changes, and for the first time, I see despair in her eyes. "We can't keep up," she says. "Too many kids to extract and not enough places to take them. And last month, our city and state funding got cut."

"You should've called."

"You've got your own shit."

"And I've also got time and money for the worthy causes of my friends."

She smiles wryly.

"How much do you need?"

She actually laughs at that, but I don't.

"I'm serious. How much?"

"More zeroes than your bank account can handle."

"I've got friends."

"More zeroes than theirs can."

She's a proud woman, and I appreciate that she doesn't see dollar signs when she looks at me. But I believe in what she's doing.

"I can't help if you don't let me."

I see her defeated look once again.

"I've got thirty-three kids who need placement. But our program is designed for small-scale living. We know the success formula. The more kids in a setting, the lower the rehabilitation rate."

"So you need more safe harbors."

"The real estate would be a start. Then we need qualified staff to run them. And more security teams to handle the extractions and to keep the facilities safe."

"So, what's your number?" I prod again. "Spit it out. I can take it."

"Two point five."

She's right. It is more zeroes than my bank account can handle. I don't hoard money. I give to what matters to me and keep everything else pretty lean. But I do have friends. And I'm nothing if not resourceful.

"Let me see what I can do."

"Thank you." From the way she says it, I can see how this is weighing on her.

"I'm going to help you with the other stuff, too."

"The other stuff?"

"Finding out who the big Kahuna is," I say. "I have a guy."

She laughs and shakes her head.

"Of course you do."

"His name is Avi. I'll have him give you a call." I know she can't do half the shit she's talking about with company funds. If she's trying to find the kingpin, she's financing it herself.

"You are a force, Michael Blaine."

"I learned it by watching you," I say. "Let me know how it goes, alright? And, next time, don't wait so long."

Chapter Six

KING OF PAIN

I *can't believe you did this.*

The text comes in as I'm sitting at my desk, waiting for my sister Bex to call. Between school and an early bedtime, there's a very short window to work with when it comes to talking to Ella. I wonder which of the dozen items I hid in her brownstone Darby is talking about. Apart from my Tufts Crew t-shirt, some pixy sticks I left in her nightstand, an Anne Taintor flask and a blank Liechtenstein journal, there are eight more she still hasn't found.

What did I do this time?

When the image comes through on my phone, I see the brightly colored art. The author and title are barely visible on top of the splash of painted images—lush palm trees, a rising goddess and neon dots. It's a first edition of *100 Years of Solitude*, her favorite book. The simple paperback on her shelves is a worn Penguin Classic that I know she's read a dozen times.

Thank you seems inadequate, she writes.

Every bibliophile should have a first edition of her favorite book.

I'm ashamed that I don't know yours.

The Picture of Dorian Gray.

Oscar Wilde...Interesting...

Uh-uh. No psychoanalysis, Dr. Freud.

Fair enough, she concedes. *But, seriously...I will cherish this.*

She's back to thanking me now. I think of how she won't touch the *Before Sunset* manuscript.

You can thank me by enjoying it. No collector's item bullshit, okay? Great works are meant to be read.

❧

"When are you coming home, Uncle Michael?"

It's been a month since I've seen her and the sadness in Ella's tiny voice nearly does me in.

"Your birthday, sweet pea. It's only six weeks away."

With Bex's husband Alex gone for weeks at a time, I've been like a second father to my little niece and her question reminds me that Darby's not the only one I've abandoned.

"And then will you stay?"

This kid is killing me. Her question ties my stomach into tighter knots than it's been for the better part of a month, but I make myself sound reassuring.

"Just for the weekend...but I'll be back again for Christmas."

"Good! Then you can meet my new baby twin sister."

I perk up at that, still too far gone to smile, but amused all the same. "Your what?"

"My twin sister. That's what I'm asking Santa for."

I don't bother reminding her how the twin thing works. It's a conversation we've had before. She thinks that since me and Bex are twins, all siblings are. "Did you tell your mom that?"

"Uh-huh."

"What'd she say?"

"She said Santa can only bring baby brothers and sisters if the elves don't spend all year knock-blocking him when they're supposed to be taking a nap."

I smile for real then. "What's knock-blocking?"

But before Ella can answer, I hear a "Time to tell Uncle

Michael goodbye!" in the background and next thing I know, Bex has the phone.

"What's knock-blocking, Bex?"

"Duh, Uncle Michael!" she mocks in an Ella voice "Knock-blocking is when the elves make too much noise cobbling together the toysc."

"Joke all you want," I snark back. "She thinks she's getting a baby sister for Christmas. You might want to handle that."

Now it's Bex's footsteps I hear along with the sounds of cartoons fading in the background and I know that she's going to find some privacy. I know what she's going to say before she says it.

"If I get pregnant, you'll be the first to know."

It's a joke between us and I don't miss the irony in her voice. Most people think that twin sense is bullshit. Believe me when I tell you it's not. When Bex got pregnant with Ella, I knew it before she did. I was the one who called her out of the blue and told her to take that pregnancy test. It was a formality. She knew that if I knew it, it was true. We've always known things about one another. I've heard of twins who don't feel bonded, but I don't understand it. My bond with Bex is stronger than steel.

For us, conversation is superfluous—a show we put on for other people. When it's just the two of us, what we say out loud is choppy at best. Even when we're thousands of miles away from one another, it's like this. I'm grateful for this strange little piece of supernatural that's helped us stay close all these years.

"You settling in alright?"

The question is about three weeks late, but she's only asking because she knows I'm not. I'm not fooling her, or even trying.

"So when are you going to do something about it?" she prods. "Before or after you break another pencil tip?"

"After."

I feel my frustration bubbling up. I'm not mad at her. I'm mad at me. I deserve an Academy Award for how well I'm acting my part. But, inside, I'm lovesick and homesick and stressed out about work. And I've lost my best coping mechanism—Darby.

The time apart is making me edgy. I'm working the plan, but most days I'm impatient and insecure. Talking to Darby always buoys me, but I'm often riddled with doubt. It doesn't help that I've discovered a jealous streak. A few days ago, Darby had after-work drinks with Rich. I know they've been friends for years, but I don't fucking care. Every time he looked at her at that Christmas party, I thought I was going to have to scrape his eyes off of her boobs.

"Don't make a liar out of me. I told her you were worth waiting for."

I knew she said something to Darby that day at her house. My pencil tip does snap again. That's the second time since I got on the phone.

It's not that simple, I think.

"It is that simple." Bex counters aloud. "Come back to Chicago. Tender your resignation. Figure out what you really want to do with your life 'cause we both know this isn't it."

Bex thinks I focus on work for all the wrong reasons. She thinks I have a misplaced need to seek external validation because we never got it from our dad. She's pretty much the opposite of Darby when it comes to diagnosing me. She is a clinically trained social worker who's all too happy to be my shrink.

"I'm not going to trade one mediocre situation for another. I'm going to wait until I have something to offer her that she actually wants."

"How do you know she doesn't want the same thing you do?"

When I don't answer, I know Bex is shaking her head. My mind's eye can see the expression on her face.

"You should give her more credit. A woman knows her own heart."

And I do know. Some part of Darby's heart wants me too. "Hers is fragile."

What I don't say is that I know I've already broken it a little and I don't want my actions to damage anything more.

"She's not a bird with a broken wing, Mikey. She's a grown-ass woman who deserves the truth. That bullshit man logic will fuck you over every time."

I drop my pencil. I honestly don't know whether I can deal with this right now. She doesn't know how much of a trigger the man-logic thing is for me. Growing up, all I had were my mom and Bex to give me advice about love. What they never understood was how differently men think about these things. As one thought of my father leads to another, I wonder what I always have: how many mistakes could I have avoided if he had ever bothered to teach me anything?

"I know what I'm doing." I'm only half lying. "And I'm not treating her like a bird with a broken wing. I'm showing her what I couldn't show her before and making sure she knows what she'd be getting into."

This quiets Bex.

"Are you back on your meds?"

I rub my hands over my face. I haven't been on anti-anxiety meds since my mother was sick, and that's been damn near ten years. "I'm not sick, Bex."

"You know how dangerous stress can be for you."

"I'm working it out." Debating Bex is like debating with myself. I've been having the same conversation in my head for the past two weeks. On the surface, I'm holding it together, but Bex sees the part of me that's spinning out. "I'm not going back on my meds." I say it more gently. She's only pushing so hard because she's worried.

"Then do the other thing."

"You know I don't do psychiatrists."

"That's not what Darby said."

And in the middle of this sparring, I actually smile. "Shut the fuck up."

"Don't make me worry about you," she scolds lightly. And, in that moment, I sense her fear before I hear it. It holds the memory of things that happened a long time ago. "I can't take care of you like I did last time. Not when you're so far away."

I know she's not guilting me. But more guilt is what I'll feel if I fail her.

"Do you remember that thing Dr. Dan used to have you do?" she asks softly. "Don't try to do it all at once. Solve one problem, or admit one feeling each day. Whatever you do, get it out of your head. That's the part that'll kill you."

She doesn't have to mention that, once upon a time, that simple act may have saved me. It's a good idea. And, not just for Bex, I know I'll do it.

"You're gonna be okay, Boo-Boo. I've got you."

Hearing her call me the pet name my mother once did feels special. She's never called me it before. I wonder what my mom would tell me to do right now. "Love you, Bex. Tell Ella I love her, too."

"Love you too, Mikey."

"Bex..." I choke out a second before she would've hung up. It takes a thick swallow and another deep breath before I can utter the words. "I'm afraid that if she ever sees this side of me...she'll run."

Darby Christensen is now online, the alert on my phone reads. Taking a quick glance at the clock, I see that it's evening in Chicago.

Hey, baby, I quickly tap out. *Just get out of work?* I'm trying to filter myself less, and that means not being shy about reaching out when I want to talk. The dancing dots on my Facebook message app tell me she's writing a reply.

Yup. What are you up to?

Drawing.

Want to hop on the phone?

Always, I reply. I dial her number and put her on speaker, planning to keep drawing while we talk.

"I loved the last one you sent me." She doesn't bother to greet me when she picks up. "I love all of them, Michael."

Yesterday's sketch featured an issue of the American Journal of Psychiatry on a newsstand. On the cover was a picture of Darby in a white coat with a stethoscope around her neck. The headline read, "Revolutionizing Opioid Addiction" and the sub-header said, "Meet the woman behind the Christensen Method".

She was so delighted by the first drawing I sent her that I've taken to drawing for her daily. It's helping me channel my anxiety into something more productive. Art is the only language I've ever really spoken fluently.

"I like sending them to you," I admit.

"I look forward to them every day."

Something in her tone makes me optimistic.

"It makes me feel closer to you," she admits.

That's all I've wanted—to show her pieces of me, and to give her a little romance. I'm more optimistic than I was even a moment before.

"How are you really doing?" I ask.

It's been three weeks since I left Chicago and we've had a few more tentative, but hopeful conversations. From our last one, I know that she's nearing a critical point in her research and that hunting down her breakthrough has been taking its toll.

She's on the brink of a milestone that has the markings of a major discovery. My girl did what nobody has ever done—identified a set of chemical reactions in the brains of opioid addicts that changes their ability to respond to therapy. Developing ways to neutralize this reaction will revolutionize treatment. Right now, she's scrambling to have validated results before her grant review.

But she doesn't answer my question right away, and in that moment I'm not above begging. There's such a thing as being too driven, and I worry about her.

"You've got to help me out," I say. "When I was in Chicago, I always knew. All I had to do was look at your face."

She sighs. "I'm tired and restless all at the same time. I'm working too much already, but whenever I'm not there, I feel like I'm in the wrong place."

"Are you still doing your weekly movie?"

"That pretty much dried up when I made Chief. Besides, I miss seeing movies with you."

"I miss that, too. I've been thinking...we should go to another film festival together."

"Most of them are in January, but I'll be in Australia then, remember? That is, if you still want me to come."

"Of course I want you to come. So, you're serious?"

"Why wouldn't I be?"

"I don't know," I say, feeling insecurity creep in. It's been a rough week. "It's beautiful here. I think you'll like it."

Her pause unsettles me.

"I'm coming home in November." I infuse lightness into my voice.

"Thanksgiving?" she asks.

"Ella's birthday. It's November 4th. My charity gala is that Saturday night. Do you want to be my date?"

"Sure," she replies easily, but something about it rubs me the wrong way. She says it in the same tone she used to use when I was asking her to a function I had to attend. I'm not asking her out on a serious date, but I'm not asking her out as a friend either. It's been bothering me. I've put myself out there in a dozen different ways, but I can't figure out whether her feelings for me are fading. For every moment she gives me hope, there's another to make me worry. I'm paranoid that she's easing me into the friend zone.

"You don't have to come," I say in a joking-not-joking kind of way. "If you're not into it, I'll just ask one of my other ex-non-girlfriends."

"Oh, yeah? How many of those do you have?"

"Nine or ten. I like to rotate, but if you don't want to take your turn, I guess I could let you skip."

"And miss ogling you in a tux? That doesn't sound like me. You know how I like you in black tie."

"So you want to come, then?"

"Of course I want to come with you, you idiot. I'm crashing Ella's birthday party, too. I need my Michael fix."

Finally, I relax a little. I'm almost calm when she throws me for a loop. "So, when are you going to tell me how you're really doing?"

"Am I that transparent?"

"No. But you're not gonna tell me unless I ask." I'm trying to fix that. And I'm about to tell her so when she repeats my words.

"When I was in Chicago, I always knew. All I had to do was look at your face."

"What did my face tell you?"

"Whether you were fighting with yourself."

"I'm always fighting with myself." And it takes guts for me to admit.

"I wish it were easier to pick your battles," she says.

We only talked about it once—my overactive brain. Not being able to control all the inputs I try to process. It's at the crux of my anxiety.

"It's not just at night, is it?"

And I think she may know me better than I've given her credit for. When I first told her about it, it was in the context of my insomnia. I haven't told her about my sensory processing disorder, or how I have to manage my anxiety all day.

"No. It's bigger than that."

"How bad does it get?"

"I manage," I say vaguely.

She sighs and I know she's thinking about what I told her once before—that I don't want her to be my doctor. I know I need to get over myself. It's dumb luck on my part that I've fallen in love with a mental health professional. If she weren't one, I would have told her more by now.

"There's nothing I can say right now that won't make me sound like a shrink."

"There's nothing more I can tell you that won't make me feel like a patient."

"It's worse when you don't talk about it, babe."

"I know."

Chapter Seven

EYE OF THE TIGER

I have a routine. Treadmill first. A fast four miles of 1-2 intervals that take exactly thirty minutes to complete, and another five to cool down at a walk. For a full ten minutes, my feet never touch the floor as I work my abs. I go five, five and five on push-ups, chin-ups and dips. Even though I'm alone in my apartment, I prefer my earbuds to surround sound.

My showers are long. I spend half of them catching my breath and enjoying the ritual of water hitting my body. I went all out with the master bath remodel—a fully-installed rainfall ceiling with nine surrounding body jets. I've had a thermostatic mixing valve put in so that the spray comes out as a combination of hot and cold water. The temperature differentiation is rapid and distributed enough to give most people the sensation that the water is simply warm.

But I'm not most people. My hyper-sensitive skin feels both temperatures acutely, and I'm calmed by its dynamic delivery. It reminds me of when I was little—me and Bex sitting side by side in our ancient tub—feeling the water from both spigots hit the surface to swirl and blend.

When I need to relax, I use this with the soft rainfall, standing for minutes that slow to hours as I let myself enjoy the feeling of each water droplet hitting my body. The other new feature—the sprayers—will give me something different from the rainfall. Hard jets of water assaulting me from nine different angles will stimulate my senses in ways I have yet to fully explore.

I've long since gotten over my guilt over the colossal waste of water this is. When I discovered how much of a regulating effect the right shower could have on me, I started taking as many as I could. Darby thinks my fancy showers are just an obsession. But it's more than a guilty pleasure for me. I need the sensory input. My body craves these routines to manage my anxiety.

I take my time soaping every crevice before massaging my scalp with a conditioning shampoo. As usual, my dick begs for attention. It's been two weeks since I've jerked off and my cock is starting to ache. The act has been too fraught with emotion and I rarely let myself indulge. This time he isn't taking no for an answer, so I cool the water temperature and soap my hands before wrapping them around myself. It feels amazing and I fill my mind with luscious thoughts.

But this pales in comparison to what the real Darby feels like around me. Her pussy is so good. I had to sleep with a lot of women before I knew what that really meant. It's not about how tight she is—it's about how it feels when her excitement builds. The way she coils ever-tighter with every few strokes, the effort it takes close to the end to keep pushing inside her, the final thrust that triggers her release...I live for that moment—the moment when all she needs in this world is me to fill the tiny space inside her. It's not my hand stroking myself desperately, but the memory of that, that catapults me over the wall.

❧

Breakfast is an egg white omelet with plenty of butter, salt and sautéed onions. I pour a whole milk hot chocolate in a travel mug—I'll drink it on my way to work. That's when I have my call with Avi. I talk to him most mornings on my drive to the office. He's my friend—the one who conducted the investigation that took down Darby's ex-boss Huck, the one who tried to give Darby's promotion to a doctor he was sleeping with but not before taking credit for Darby's killer idea. Officially, Avi's a private investigator, but the truth is, he's a fixer. The computer hacker kind of fixer, not the hit man kind of fixer. He fixed the Huck situation by delivering a file to the hospital board exposing his shenanigans. He's helping me keep Darby's father, Frank Christensen, in line and making sure Charlie Sweeney gets what he deserves.

I've known Avi since I was in the second grade. He lived down the hall from us in the building where I grew up. His mom was addicted to crack. When things got bad at his place, he came to hide out in mine. We've been there for each other through thick and thin. Apart from Bex and Randy, he's my oldest friend.

He was always into computers. Knowing how to hack networks was his ticket out of our neighborhood. A string of lucrative Internet security jobs in his twenties found him making six figures a year. By thirty, he had graduated to seven. He still makes crazy money, but he traded corporate America for a job that lets him live out his spy fantasy.

Monitoring Frank Christensen isn't as easy as it sounds. Now that he's on the presidential ticket, there are scores of articles that mention him every day. A Google alert would have been useless. I need to know what the gentrification projects he's been trying to push through are doing to hamper our neighborhood projects on the South Side, and what he's doing that might mess with Darby. He needs the appearance of a perfect family to help his chances of getting elected. Just because Darby wants nothing to do with him doesn't mean the press are off her back.

"It's a slow news day for politics," Avi is saying. "Everyone's talking about the game last night. The Patriots are going to the playoffs. Again."

I only follow sports to the extent that knowing about them helps me make small talk in work situations, and nobody in Sydney cares about American football.

"How's everything else?"

"We're closer on Sweeney," Avi continues. "That intern—Lisa Sherbourne—she's agreed to talk."

"Good," I remark gravely. "How much more do we need?"

I don't plan to ever give Darby the play-by-play on how I've conspired to take down Charlie Sweeney, her father's longtime crony and current Chief of Staff. He's also the man who assaulted, and nearly raped Darby when she was fifteen. It still makes me murderous to think about how she wouldn't have gotten away if her housekeeper hadn't walked in. Investigating Charlie Sweeney is ugly business and disturbing as hell. But I do look forward to the day when I can tell her he's behind bars and will never hurt another young girl again.

"Any news on the kingpin?" I ask.

Avi's been in contact with Corliss. I've tapped my network and raised half the money she needs already. But the real problem won't be solved until she attacks it at the source.

"She was right. It has all the markings of somebody big. Whoever it is, they want control over a big part of the South Side."

"I don't get it." I've been thinking about this. "How can someone brand new, who nobody knows, just swoop right in?"

"My guess is, white-collar crime."

I chew on this for a moment. "So, you think it's the drug companies?"

"It's someone with access to them. From what I've been able to find out, the product is authentic."

"What else?" I ask.

The fact that Avi pauses for a beat sets off alarm bells.

"She had a run-in with a pap." He's talking about Darby, and the paparazzi. "Got caught off-guard outside her house. I sent the video to your private account."

Nothing related to Darby and Frank comes through my work e-mail and I won't even do so much as Google Charlie Sweeney on a company computer. Even now, I'm talking to Avi on my second, secret, cell phone.

I ask about Jasmine after our briefing is done. She's still a sore topic, but if I don't force him to talk about her, no one will. The hurt doesn't just go away when the love of your life leaves you at the altar. I've given him time to lick his wounds—tried not to be the dick who swoops right in to tell him that letting Jasmine walk away was the biggest mistake of his life. I need to say it at some point, but not today. I'm still hot over Sweeney. And I know I haven't been myself and that it hasn't been pleasant for people around me. I'm still always an angel with Darby, but I need to chill the hell out with everyone else.

The freak-out happens after I hang up the phone. Cursing loudly while hitting my steering wheel does nothing to appease my frustration. Biding my time until I figure out how to make it so that Darby and I can be together is one thing. Being halfway across the world when my woman is being assaulted by the paparazzi is another. This fucking sucks.

I look at my watch. It's three in the afternoon there. She'll be in the middle of her shift, and I have no idea what I would say. "I've been monitoring you and wanted to make sure you're okay after your encounter with that reporter" would just be too creepy.

"Darby called," Kat informs me apprehensively as I walk broodingly into my office.

I stop in my tracks and take a step backward to speak with her. "At what time?"

"You just missed her."

I take the time to thank Kat and even muster a small smile before I close my door. I'm dialing before I sit down and am hanging my suit jacket in my closet when she picks up. My shaded glass wall office is enormous, and I have to close the space between my closet and my phone if I want to respond to her greeting, even though I'm on speaker.

"Hey, cupcake. I just got into work. Are you in the middle of your shift?"

"I never made it to work today," she admits. "I wasn't in the mood."

"That sounds like a good idea," I praise her gently. "You've been working so hard you deserve a day off. You gonna watch some movies?"

"I dunno. I haven't decided yet."

She's trying to keep her voice light, but I know what happened to her. Even if I hadn't, I would've sensed the tension. I slip an earbud into one ear and navigate to my e-mail on my secret cell. I want to see the video Avi sent me of Darby.

She is clearly startled as she exits her house, not having expected anyone to be there. Immediately, they're questioning her about the way Frank voted on a bill that would expand access to opioid drugs. With so many experts speaking out against the senator's position, they're trying to get Darby to oppose him. It would be a big story if his own daughter—herself an opioid expert—admitted that she didn't support his stance.

Darby quickly puts her poker face on and politely declines to comment, but one persistent little fucker won't leave her alone. He's in her face and when she won't say more, he baits her with offensive questions and comments, hoping to get a rise out of her. That way, even if she doesn't say what they want her to, it becomes its own story.

Darby's a pro. She doesn't bite, but when she realizes she can't get past the wall of paparazzi, she retreats into her house. She makes her reaction look natural—carries herself with class and grace. To an outsider, she seems confident, but I can see beyond the mask. She's surrounded where she lives. The vultures are circling and she's all alone.

"You should go to my place," I say casually. "My movie collection is better than yours. Plus, I have a waterbed." She loves my apartment. It's been her sanctuary many times and the paps will never get up there with the building's security.

"I have an extra parking space," I say. "Keeping your Range Rover there would be no problem." Also, if her house is still surrounded by paparazzi, she can leave through her own garage. Her back alley is gated, which makes it the perfect escape.

"Haven't you closed up your apartment?"

"Bex and Alex use it sometimes. And the cleaning service still comes twice a month. I'll call in some groceries for you. Use it today, baby. Use it any time you want."

"Thanks." Her voice is soft.

She still hasn't said why she called, and I won't ask her. I know why she called. I hope she got what she needed.

"Michael?"

"Yes, cupcake?"

"Why would I want to take my car? It's a ten-minute Uber ride away."

She knows I won't admit that I know. Just like she won't admit that it even happened.

"Sometimes it's nice to go for a little drive."

Later that day, I send her a drawing of my Chicago apartment building. I've added subtle detail to the basic construction that replaces the reflective windows with imposed blockades that make it look like a medieval fortress. Instead of city streets at the base of the building, I've drawn a moat and a drawbridge is being lowered. It's ready to let in the old Range Rover that awaits.

Chapter Eight

MY PHILOSOPHY

Darby's still at my house after yesterday's fiasco with the reporter. When I found out his name and who he was with, I gave Ben a call. Ben is the reason Darby and I met. He was my college roommate. She was his boarding school friend. Happening upon Darby at his wedding last summer had started it all.

The New Yorker is owned by Condé Nast, which is also the parent company of Ben's magazine, *Vanity Fair*. I showed Ben the video and he was livid. He sent me a text this morning to let me know that all of the Condé Nast publications will leave her alone, and that the reporter had been fired.

She and I have been on the phone for an hour and I'm relieved that I've convinced her to spend the whole weekend at my place. She surprised the hell out of me by mentioning what happened the day before and admitting how much it rattled her. But I've had zero success in convincing her to move some place more secure.

"I'm not moving out of my house, Michael."

"Just 'til the end of the election," I say.

"The election's not for another year."

"Exactly." What doesn't she understand about this?

"I said I was rattled—I didn't say I couldn't handle it," she says.

"Sure you can. But why would you want to?"

When she doesn't say anything, I know that my objections are trying her patience. At the moment, I don't care. Darby has cried on my shoulder about this. She's been stalked, had death threats and survived a kidnapping attempt. Why she's acting like this is an annoyance rather than a risk to take seriously is beyond me. But she presses on.

"Finding a new apartment is not easier than dealing with what happened today a few more times."

"You don't need to find a new apartment. You can move into my place."

It's a sensible suggestion. She's comfortable there. I'm not using it. And my building houses enough of the Chicago elite that security won't be an issue. Still, it feels strange to say it because I have ulterior motives. If Darby agrees to move into my apartment under any circumstances, I'll do everything I can to make sure she never leaves.

"It was just a reporter, Michael."

Yeah, this time, I think but don't say.

"If something else happens, will you at least consider it?" I know that I've been beaten—at least for now. And there's no reason to push her if she won't be swayed.

"If I'm in any real danger, yes."

"Alright," I relent. "Let's talk about something else."

Not thirty seconds later, my phone makes a flat beeping sound.

"Shit...My battery's dying. Wanna switch to video?"

"Yeah. Lemme get my computer. Hang on..."

I hear her footsteps against a hard floor, and I know she was in my bedroom. I hear the scrape of the barstool where she always left her purse as she drags it away from the island. I'm opening my own laptop by the time she walks back into my room. It's taking her a long time, and instead of initiating our video call, she tells me to hold on again. When it finally comes through, my headboard is coming into view and she setting her computer down on her lap. Her hair is over one shoulder the snapdragon is around her neck, and she's wearing one of my button-down shirts.

"What took you so long?" It's a miracle I manage to say anything. Because I already know the answer. Darby's in my bed looking hot as hell in my clothes.

"I wanted to put on something decent."

I might be gaping.

"What? I'm completely covered up." She looks down at herself.

I swipe my hand over my face as I let out a pained chuckle. "You're killing me, cupcake."

She shakes her head a little and rolls her eyes. Reaching her hand toward the bedside table, she picks up a glass of red wine. "Where were we?"

"We were about to agree on a dress code for video calls."

She laughs in that cute way of hers. "Oh, yeah?"

"Yeah. You're gonna have to wear something about ten times frumpier than that. Like, turtlenecks and corduroys frumpy, and put on a Snuggie on top of that."

"Don't you think I'd be too hot?"

You're already too hot.

"I'll pay your air conditioning bill."

She rolls her eyes again.

"I'm serious," I say.

"Alright. I'll dust off my granny panties."

I adjust myself discreetly as she takes a sip of her wine.

"It's weird being here without you, you know. This morning I woke up in your bed and, for a second, I forgot that you were gone. I rolled over to look in toward the bathroom. I figured you were taking a shower or something. I used to spy on you, you know. I always loved to watch you dress."

I hate the sadness I see in her eyes, but I've come to crave these tiny morsels of validation. They're few and far between, but I survive on these little gifts for days.

"I miss waking up with you," I confess quietly. "When I go to sleep, I start out on my side of the bed, but, by morning, I've migrated over to yours."

"Your place looks like it's missing something without the painting. It's strange...how perfect it looks hanging in both places."

Her voice is wistful, and her comment is innocent enough. She still thinks it's just a painting we both like.

"I painted it when I was fifteen."

I suppose that now is as good a time as any to bring this up.

"It's so good, Michael. Like, museum good. Did you ever show it or consider selling it?"

My words are measured. "It's always been too special to give away. I painted it when I was going through a tough time."

She blinks slowly and I see a stain of pink color her cheeks. But I don't want her to dwell on the fact that I've given her one of my most prized possessions. I want to spit this out. "Do you want to see a picture of me at that age?"

She nods.

"Go into my office. There's a yearbook on one of the shelves. The spine says 'Legacy '96'."

She nods. "Hang on."

And as she puts down the laptop facing the other direction, the view from my windows comes into focus. It's strange for me, too—that she's there and I'm not. And in that moment, a wave of pure homesickness crashes over me. I want to be back in my own house, sleeping in my own bed, with her.

When she settles back onto the bed and repositions the laptop back so that it's facing her, I see the cover of the familiar book.

"Turn to the Juniors," I say, and I see her flipping pages. I can tell the moment when she reaches the page that has my picture.

A small smile graces her face, and she touches her finger to the middle of the page."

"You were adorable," she gushes, and it makes me smile, even though I hate that picture.

She hasn't met my eyes in a full minute, and as she drinks in the thumbnail-sized image, I conjure up the picture in my own mind—me in my prep school uniform, a maroon V-neck sweater over a collared shirt and tie. My head is cocked slightly to the side and I'm smiling at the camera just like they tell you to do.

"Did you even have an awkward phase?" She finally looks up at me. "I expected a pimply-faced kid with braces and dated glasses. But fifteen-year-old you is kind of hot. If you and I had gone to school together, I totally would have had a crush on you."

It's my turn to smile sadly. "Now look on my side of the bed, in my bedside table. You'll find a different picture there.'

She gives me a questioning look, not knowing what I'm hinting at, but doing it all the same. She puts down the laptop again, and I hear the drawer open just before I hear her rummaging. "How many Pixy Stix does one person need?" she calls out.

Under any other circumstances I'd come up with a clever retort. But I've never shown anybody—not even Bex—the picture I've held on to for so long.

When she places the laptop back on top of her legs, I can see the picture in her hand and in just a few seconds, her face has sobered. "Wow. You look really different."

In this picture, I'm dressed head-to-toe in black. It's the first time she's seen my natural hair, which is thick with loose curls. It's a big difference from the crew cut in my school picture and the buzz cut I wear now. What people never guess on their own is that I'm half Black—my mother was light-skinned, and my dad is white—but seeing me with my hair grown out and an end-of-summer tan makes it more obvious.

People who don't know a lot of mixed-race people don't get the skin tone thing. They see the coloring of two parents and figure the kid's coloring should be right in the middle. It's a common misconception, and a false one. Genetics are more complex than that.

In the picture, I'm sitting on the sidewalk in front of Randy's comic book store, Heroes and Villains, looking into the camera, unsmiling. My face is blank—almost dead-looking. Even someone who doesn't know me could see the ocean of pain behind my eyes. I remember that kid, and how tired he was from trying to fit in. A round peg in a square hole nearly every place he went.

"At school, I made sure to blend in," I begin. "Buttoned-up. Clean-shaven. They thought I was just another white kid from a low-rent part of town. I let them believe what they wanted to believe. But that was me over the summer. In my neighborhood, it was smarter to play up the part of me that was half Black. So, I grew out my hair and did everything I could to get a tan."

She looks up at me with pain in her own eyes.

"There were other mixed kids, but I was the pretty boy with the blue eyes. I must've gotten into ten fights that summer, between not letting shit-talkers push me around and keeping guys away from Bex. For her, the light skin and blue eyes made every guy want her. The other girls hated her. She got her ass kicked a lot, too. But she learned to hold her own."

"That must've been terrible…" Darby says. Her eyes are shining, and it tugs at something inside to see her compassion for me.

"That summer, it all came to a head. I don't know what did it, but something inside me broke and I couldn't take it anymore. My mom thinking I was ashamed. My dad not being around. Getting shit from people in my neighborhood all summer after a year of getting it twice as bad at school. No one understanding how crushing it was for me there—not even Bex. The locker room talk at a school like Kensington Prep? It was vicious."

"Will you tell me about it?" The voice she uses is patient—

the voice of somebody who's trained not to react. She's slipped into psychiatrist mode, but I'd rather have her stoicism than her pity. I remind myself again that being more open with her is part of the plan.

"I remember the first time I really got it. There was this one time, before swimming practice. I don't even think I was in high school yet. They were talking about a kid in their class. A kid who was like me in every other way. Poor neighborhood. On scholarship. Really smart. Except he was obviously Black. I wasn't friends with the kid—he was older than me. But I knew who he was and that he was kind of...solitary."

"What did they say?"

I shrug. "Exactly what you'd expect. Shit about charity cases and all the affirmative action kids ruining their chances of getting into the good schools and keeping the riffraff out. I'll spare you the rest. You get the gist."

"I want to know."

"You already do know," I point out quietly. "You know how they talk about Black people when they think there are none around."

She sighs. But she doesn't look away. And I respect her for that. She probably knows the kids who said it. She'd have met them at country clubs and cotillions.

"I'm sorry."

"By the time Ben met me, I looked more like I do there," I say, referring to the second picture I showed her—me with the grown-out hair. "I stopped caring about passing. I spent a lot of college figuring myself out. Growing my hair out made less of a difference than I thought. Most people never thought I was mixed. People still don't."

I think about other friends who are obviously mixed race. People are always prying into their ethnicities, asking 'what are you?' and other insensitive questions that are none of anyone's business. Now that I'm older I'm glad that I dodged this bullet. It's exhausting work.

"Who took this?" Her eyes sweep over the image over and over again.

"Randy," I say. "He was worried. He wanted me to see how bad I looked every day."

"Was this before or after you painted the butterfly?"

"Before," I say, and I know what she wants to ask next. But this is progress for me, telling her the toll it took on me to always feel like I was straddling two worlds. So I shake my head before it can go any further.

"I'll tell you about it, I promise. But not now."

Chapter Nine

BAD REPUTATION

"**A** package came for you today, Mr. Blaine."

I usually nod hello to Stuart, the night doorman, as I pass, but this news interrupts my stride. Something has come for me. I don't recognize the return address. It's from a company called Muse. But I can see that it's come from the states. I wrack my brain trying to figure out whether I had Kat order something for me that I've forgotten, but I come up blank. I'm eager to get back into my apartment and see what's inside.

Sitting atop the inner package that is wrapped tightly in layers of bubble tape, I see a printed note.

Dear Michael,

Shut up. I don't want to hear a single complaint about this. I've heard good things about it. It's a meditation tool for people with wandering minds. I think it could help you. So try it, okay? And not just once. Long enough to see whether it makes a difference.

Love,

Darby

With a mixture of curiosity and caution, I tear open the bubble wrap and study the box. They're meditation headphones. A quick read of the explanation tells me that it detects the brain waves of the person who's meditating. Apart from monitoring brain activity, the headphones will tell me when I'm getting distracted with conscious thought and monkey mind.

Before I let myself deconstruct the concept behind this product, I think of my girl. I know she's just trying to help. Trying to give me coping strategies based on what she understands. It's sweet. The truth is, I trust her. And, because she asked me to, I'll give it a try. I know I've given her every reason to believe that I'm hostile toward her knowing about this part of me, but I'm trying to turn that around.

I got your package. Thank you. I text her, even though it's the middle of the night in Chicago. She's on late shifts this week, so she probably just went to bed. I'm surprised when my phone buzzes a few minutes later.

You're not mad?

No, I'm not mad. I promise, I'll try it. What the hell are you doing up?

I see the dancing dots. She's composing a response, one that is taking a long time. She starts and stops and then does it again at least five times over the course of several minutes. But the long response I expect never comes. The next message I get from her says simply:

Can't sleep.

And I wonder what's really going on. Before I can ask, a photo comes through. It's a picture of a pint of Ben & Jerry's in her kitchen recycling bin. *Pistachio Pistachio* is her favorite flavor. I hid two pints of that and two pints of her second favorite flavor, *Coffee, Coffee. Buzz, Buzz, Buzz!* in her kitchen freezer before I left.

Took you long enough, I text back. *You're slower than molasses.*

It was behind, like, ten other things! You could've made it easier.

I could've...but what fun would that be?

I'll give you that...this is better than a scavenger hunt.

I'm beaming.

You just made my night.

You made mine. I so needed this today.

Sometimes ice cream is the answer to all of life's problems.

Amen to that. I'm going to crawl into bed and read now. This guy I like just gave me a really great book.

An hour later, I've showered and am about to do the same when something tells me to call Bex. She picks up on the first ring and doesn't bother to greet me.

"Dad called. He wants to meet Ella."

The hair on the back of my neck stands up. I wait for her to keep talking. This is killing my Darby buzz.

"Said he tried as long as he could to respect us not wanting to see him, but that once he found out he had a granddaughter, he couldn't do it anymore. He said he hoped that, after so many years, there had been enough water under the bridge. And that kids need their grandparents."

"Did you tell him that kids also need their fathers?"

I've always been against the idea of letting him back into our lives. The last time either of us talked to him was ten years ago. Bex stopped being angry at him a long time ago. I think she was never interested in a relationship because she had truly left him behind. I know without having to ask out loud that Bex has changed her mind.

"How can you even consider this?" I demand.

"Back then, I wasn't thinking ten years ahead," she says in her defense. "Kids ask about these things, Michael. They have Grandparents' Day at Ella's school. Every year she has more questions about Mom and Dad."

"It's not like she doesn't have grandparents. Alex's parents live half an hour away."

"And Dad lives half an hour away in the other direction. When Ella grows up, she'll want to know why she wasn't allowed to meet him. I'll be the one she blames for keeping her grandfather away from her—not you."

I flop onto my bed and stare up at the ceiling. I miss my waterbed. Flopping down on a spring mattress just isn't the same. I know Bex is right about Ella's curiosity. I remember us having questions about our own grandparents and resenting how little we were allowed to know.

"She's six, Bex. She thinks grandparents are made out of sugar, and spice and everything nice. Her only frame of reference is Mom-Mom and Pop-Pop." That's what Ella calls Alex's parents. "But you're forgetting something. We don't know him. Are you willing to present a total stranger to Ella as a person she's supposed to love and respect?"

This silences Bex. The truth is, we have no idea whether our father is a decent human being. The fact that he left us is evidence to the contrary.

"If you do this, you'd better figure out what he's about before Ella ever lays eyes on him. And you'd better be sure he's not gonna disappear."

Bex is still silent, but as soon as I figure out what she's thinking, I grind out a determined "No."

I don't want any part of this. But Bex wants us to do this together.

"If she does meet him, she's gonna want to know why Uncle Michael doesn't talk to grandpa."

"I'll tell her the truth."

"You'll also be teaching her that instead of forgiving someone, you should hold a thirty-year grudge."

Fuck.

"Look, you don't have to decide now. I'm not even totally decided. Just thinking about it, okay?"

Before we hang up, we agree to talk about it when I come to town. I'll add my father to the long list of people who Avi is checking out. With my chances at sleeping shot, I unbox the headset Darby sent me and read the instruction manual. Now's as good a time as any to take it for a spin.

Chapter Ten

PEACE OF MIND

Saturday mornings are my favorite. I always sleep late, go for a long run, and most weeks, I'm able to talk to Darby before she goes to work. On weekends, she typically goes in at around 8PM, which gives us plenty of time to talk.

I smile when I see her on my laptop screen. The other thing I love about Saturdays is that, since we're both home, we can do video. I sit in my kitchen, where the light from outside and above are always bright enough to show my face. She sits on her bed facing the window, so I can see hers.

"How'd the fellowship review go?"

Yesterday she met with the committee. She had her findings peer-reviewed just in time to present it to the board. With validated results in her pocket, she's in a different position. Instead of asking for more money to prove her hypotheses, she can proceed with a new kind of testing and zero in on a treatment option.

"Not as expected." She cringes a little.

"Tell me what happened." I study her face for clues. This is why I prefer video. I've gotten better at hearing the nuances in her voice, but her face tells me what I need to know. She doesn't look crestfallen, which is a good sign.

"The review board part went great," she begins, brightening. She's looking at the image of me on her screen, which gives the illusion that she's not looking into my eyes. I miss this part more than I thought I would—miss seeing her look right at me.

"If their reaction was any indication, they'll fund the next phase of the project."

"Congratulations, sweetie," I say, reining my alarm in long enough to give her a warm smile. "I'm so proud of you."

She returns my smile.

"So, what's the problem?"

Her face falls a little. "Rich dropped a bomb."

"He quit?"

"Worse. You were right. His feelings for me are definitely not platonic."

She shakes her head and gestures her arms in a way that puts me on alert. My body tenses as I begin to suspect that Rich has made his feelings known in a way that will make me want to do him harm. I command myself not to lose my temper. If I freak out every time she tells me something I don't like, she'll stop telling me things.

"How'd you find out?" I ask as neutrally as possible.

"After the review board...we headed to the bar. That's nothing new. We've done it every single time. If things seem like they went well, we celebrate. If things seem like they went badly, we cry into our beer and promise one another we'll write each other reference letters once we need new jobs."

She talks about their friendship casually, and I have to suppress a wave of emotion. I know it's ridiculous. Of course I want her to have friends. Still, it doesn't stop me from wishing that I were the one doing things with her that her other friends take for granted.

"What was different about this time?"

"He was just...talking differently, you know? About what a great team we are, and how our research is going to change the

world, about all these things that we'll do together—professionally, after we finish the project—in the future tense."

I'm impatient for her to get to the part where he makes a
pass at her, and I bite the inside of my cheek to stop myself from
saying something I'll regret.

"At some point, I got tired, and he was being so weird I
figured he'd had enough to drink. So I called an Uber and he
waited with me outside. The Uber was still a few minutes away.
And, he kind of hugged me but I thought, whatever, he's drunk."

I grit my teeth.

"Then, out of the blue, he just kissed me. After I got over the
shock, I pushed him away. I told him that he was drunk and that
he ought to go home. So the Ubers came, and we went our separate ways and I thought it was over."

It's taking a huge amount of effort to appear calm. "It wasn't
over?"

"Oh, no, it wasn't over," Darby says, still caught up in telling
the story. She has no idea how tense this is making me.

"Three o'clock in the morning, someone's pounding on my
door. I go downstairs, see it's him, and he seems more sober than
he did before, so I let him in. He immediately apologizes, and I
accept. I make him a cup of coffee and he just pours his heart
out to me. It was actually kind of sweet."

"Isn't he married?" I ask, knowing that, to some men, this
isn't a deterrent, but having to point it out.

"Not anymore. The divorce was final a few months ago. I
thought he was dating, but he said he'd been nursing a crush on
me for years. Said he never considered acting on it until he was
sure about the divorce. He said he couldn't hide it anymore."

I feel better now that I know that Rich barely touched her,
that he took 'no' for an answer even when he was drunk, and
later apologized. I almost feel sorry for the guy, and kind of
admire him for putting it all out on the line, which is more than
I've ever done. I still don't like that he showed up at Darby's
house at three in the morning, though.

"So, what did you tell him?"

"That I think of him as a friend, and that even if I didn't, I couldn't start a new relationship with somebody who is so intertwined with my career. That I was flattered—"

"Ouch." Now it's my turn to wince.

"I know...it's so bad," she moans, letting her head fall into her hands. "But I didn't want to lead him on, you know? Male egos are tricky things. Some of them can get over rejection, no problem. Other ones can't handle it.

"And you think he's the latter."

"I don't know. But if he is, I don't want the drama to play out on my research stage. I feel like a jerk even considering finding a different neurologist. But if I'm going to fire him, I should do it now. Since we're in a new phase, nobody would ask questions."

I nod, but she still looks agonized.

"What should I do?"

"I'm extremely biased."

"I still want your opinion."

"I'm not kidding, Darby. Maybe you don't. I don't like thinking about other men touching you, and I don't care how this turns out for him or anyone else."

"You don't like thinking about other men touching me?"

When she smiles coquettishly, I mumble, "He's lucky I wasn't there."

"Michael," she starts over, "You may be biased but you're also the savviest person I have ever met when it comes to work bullshit. Remember how you handled Huck? You get the politics, the optics, the human element. I know you'll have the right perspective."

She knows that I know she's right.

"There's a woman at work who's interested in me," I begin. I've never told Darby a story like this. "She's never fallen out of line, but she's been after me for months. I've politely declined at least a dozen overtures, but she won't let it go."

"You've never told me about this before," Darby says, her voice tinged with the slightest drop of jealousy.

"I don't spend a lot of time thinking about her." I want to make it clear I'm not interested in Alicia. "Anyway...I realized it wasn't about me. It was about how much I trusted her judgment. I had to make the same decision you did—whether I thought she would drop it and move on, or whether it would keep getting in the way."

Darby seems to accept this comparison. "So, what did you decide?"

"That I had worked too hard to let anyone put my job and my reputation on the line. I didn't have to be a dick about anything, but I didn't have to give her more chances to back off than she deserved, and I definitely didn't want to wait for something to happen."

"Did you fire her?"

"I'm transferring her to the London office. She won't lose her job or have an HR claim filed against her. I'm taking her out of a situation in which she's showing judgment that could have bad consequences for both of us."

"So you think I should find a new neurologist?"

"I think that, if you were completely surprised by his confession, you don't know him as well as you think. And if you're not sure what his boundaries are, he's a liability."

She smiles and shakes her head at me and for a second the screen resolution is so good that I forget she's not right here. My body reacts to this look I've seen from her before—the one that is a cross between flirtation and admiration.

"Maybe you should've been the shrink."

"You asked for my opinion," I point out.

"No, you're right. And I knew you would be. I knew that whatever you said would make sense. Thank you."

"Turns out I'm beautiful *and* wise," I quip.

"I just feel so stupid. You and Anne both called it on how he felt. She's been telling me that for years. I'm clinically trained at reading people. I can't believe I'm so bad at figuring out when a man is in love with me."

I can, I think but don't say.

Chapter Eleven

LOVESONG

D ale picks me up in a pretty sweet Jag—a sport coupe I don't recognize. One cool thing about living in another country is that all the carmakers manufacture region-specific models. Whatever he's driving, I've never seen it in the States. I know that by the end of the weekend, I, too, will drive it.

Dale has been in Sydney since Wednesday and he'll stay the weekend for the leadership retreat. He's flown in all of the managing partners from every office all over the world. It's an annual gathering—last year at this time, I was in Buenos Aires—Australia was chosen this year because it's our newest and fastest-growing market.

The other partners have been rolling in for the past two days and it's been my job to show them around. I'm losing my voice from how many gatherings I've hosted—I've given speeches at site tours and all-hands meetings during the day and shouted over the music in loud bars at night. I've barely spoken to Darby and I get the sense that she feels a bit blown off. Last night, I stayed up sketching her some drawings that had been in my head. I don't want her to think I've forgotten her. I'll send them one by one each day I'm on the retreat.

Most of the other partners have grouped up to drive to Crescent Head in carloads of four, but I recognize Dale's insistence that I ride with him for the invitation that it is. I'm the youngest managing partner in the history of the firm. He's placed incredible confidence in me. I know he wants to check in.

"I ran into Kat yesterday," he says casually as he speeds down mostly empty streets. It's too early for rush hour traffic—Crescent Head is a five-hour drive and we're due there before lunch. "She sang your praises up and down the hall. You're a big change from Ross. Seems like things with him were worse than I thought."

"That's the understatement of the year," I reply candidly, referring to my predecessor. "But you know how it is. Everyone wants the boss to fix what's wrong, but no one wants to rat out their friends."

"Welcome to leadership," he replies drily. "It's lonely in the ivory tower."

I smile.

He pulls his eyes off the road long enough to study me for a second. "But you seem to be handling it well. You've unloaded the dead weight, hired some great new talent, and made the HR complaints dry up. All on top of closing a major deal within your first two weeks. You know you're making everyone else look bad, right?"

"All in a day's work," I say, with the lightness that is always present between us

"They like you, Michael," he says then, turning more serious than I expect. "That's no small feat. Partners who clean house as soon as they arrive don't usually have this many friends. But they're rallying behind you. You were more than ready for this."

I've spent more than a year trying to achieve exactly this— making partner, being sent to an important office, and exceeding everyone else's expectations. For all that I've given up to be here, some part of me takes pride in knowing that my bittersweet victory wasn't for nothing.

"From what I hear, there's one employee in particular who really likes you." His suggestive expression makes me cringe. "And she doesn't like anyone."

"Her attentions are unwanted," I say in no uncertain terms. "Besides, you know me better than that. Subordinates are off limits."

"Somebody should've told that to Grasso." He gives me a look and makes a slicing motion near his throat.

"You canned him?" Grasso is, or should I say *was*, the partner in the Los Angeles office. Come to think of it, I don't remember seeing him this week.

"Three weeks ago," Dale confirms. "So what are you gonna do about Alicia?"

"Her transfer will be complete next week," I answer smoothly. "I've found her a position in London. She's talented and we should keep her. We just can't keep her here."

"You should've just told her you have a girlfriend."

I don't mention that saying that would have been equally inappropriate. Alicia has never directly propositioned me. "I don't have a girlfriend," It's accurate, but saying it feels wrong.

"Darby Christensen?"

"It's complicated."

I've been making an effort to open up, and have held to my promise to Bex to relieve myself of one small burden each day. I told Dale several months ago about my friendship with Darby, and how it could complicate what we're doing on the South Side, but, at the time, I hadn't admitted to more.

"Chicago is 10,000 miles away," I point out.

"I know how far away Chicago is," he says. "Before we officially opened Sydney, I did all the Australia business by commute. It was the nail in the coffin of my marriage."

I look out the window. "That's why I don't have a girlfriend," I say. Eager to change the subject, I ask a question that's been on my mind. "What's happening on the South Side?"

Since I resigned as chair of the Corporate Responsibility

Committee, I have no idea what we're seeing from inside the company, though Avi's intel is showing that Frank is as determined as ever.

"You were right. Christensen's doubling down. I got a visit from his Chief of Staff."

"Charlie Sweeney?"

"That guy's a real piece of shit."

"I've met him." The mere mention of his name makes me want to punch something.

"He wants us to shift our focus to the West Side instead. Said he'd hand us a set of builders who could beat the prices of the ones we use. They'd run a press campaign to make sure we got big coverage and give Dewey and Rowe the key to the city."

Unbelievable. Not only does Frank want us to leave the South Side alone—he wants us to give business to his cronies. I stretch my fingers when I noticed my fists are clenched. "What'd you tell him?"

"I thanked him for letting us know about the needs on the West Side and assured him we would expand our efforts there." Dale gives me a sidelong glance. "Then I told him the last time I let a bully push me around was in the third grade. I said I'd see him on the South Side and showed him the door."

I swing my angry gaze back to Dale. He had my back. I figured he would, but didn't expect him to give Sweeney the finger. My voice is gruff when I speak. "Thanks."

Dale's attention, which really should be on the road right now, is focused on me. "You don't have to thank me for doing the right thing. You and I know what this work means."

I don't know Dale's whole story, but I've gleaned that he also comes from modest beginnings. I was initially surprised by how well he took to my ideas around building out our community practice. Over time, I've discovered that he shares my sense of purpose. He seems ready for a fight that's already getting ugly. I'm more worried about this than I've let on to Darby and I'm glad that Dale is in my corner.

We spend the rest of the drive catching up on other stuff. He tells me all the Chicago office gossip and gives me the dirt on what's really going on in the other markets. He tells me who's sleeping with whom and who's fucking up which accounts. He tells me things are getting serious between Andrew and his boyfriend, which I already knew. I tell him that, for all the time he spends at the water cooler, it's a miracle he gets any work done at all.

Crescent Head turns out to be a gorgeous little gem of a place. The town is pristine, with small but well-kept houses near the center and a well-planned downtown that is full of quaint little restaurants and shops. We're headed to some sort of retreat center, but already I know that when she comes to Australia, I will bring Darby here.

Winter is ending here so we're off-season for beach activities, but this coast is off the Great Barrier Reef. When Darby comes, the weather will be perfect. It's been years since I've had a beach vacation. I've never looked forward to time off like I'm looking forward to my time with Darby.

As we pull onto the property, I start to put all my stuff in my bag—my empty travel mug, the chewing gum I've taken out, and my bottle of water. But when Dale parks and turns off the ignition, he doesn't move to do the same.

"You know you've proven yourself, Michael, don't you?" he asks.

I'm not sure whether it's a rhetorical question.

"I never have to hound you for deliverables or get on your case. I know you know the work and that you'll get it done."

"I'm just doing my job."

"No." He shakes his head. "You're not. Epstein...Rodriguez...DiAngelo...*they're* just doing their jobs."

I frown a little, unsure of where this conversation is going.

"Talent is only half of it." He says it meaningfully. "You have that in spades, and the three of them have that too. But they don't come close to getting the results that you do, because they don't put in the time."

"And that's a bad thing?" I ask. Because it sounds like he's calling me to the carpet for having a strong work ethic.

"None of them steps foot in the office, or answers a single e-mail, over the weekend. But, along with you, they're still my top guys. I'm not running a sweat shop, Michael. I want you to work hard, but not at the expense of the important things in your life. Slowing down a little will do nothing to jeopardize your standing at this firm."

I don't mention that my life is in Chicago, that if I didn't work on weekends, I'd go insane in addition to falling behind. Instead, I say the only thing that should ever be said in response to feedback like this. "Okay."

"The corner office at headquarters still has your name on it. I'll leave it to you to decide when you need to manage Sydney from Chicago vs. when you need to be here. I trust your judgment. So, do what you need to do."

How's your day going?

I held off on texting her for as long as I could. It's been three and a half hours since Andrew confirmed that the flowers had been stealthily delivered. This is the riskiest one I've pulled yet.

It started out kind of shitty, then I found a surprise on my desk...

Oh, really? What was it?

You tell me.

New stapler?

Better than that.

A jasmine bouquet from a not-so-secret admirer?

Good guess.

My phone rings then.

"I can't stop smelling them," she says.

I chuckle. "That's exactly the point."

Darby is obsessed with the smell of things. And I know she likes jasmine. A lot of her bath salts and other girly things in her house carry this scent. Red roses seemed too obvious, but if she knows about the deeper symbolism, she'll have picked up on the traditional use of jasmine. For centuries, it's been given as a token of romantic love.

"These are so rare, Michael."

"In the U.S. they are, but they're more common here. When you come, you'll smell them everywhere."

"No one's ever done anything remotely like this for me."

"What kind of two-bit suitor do you think I am?"

Yeah, I slipped that in there. She quiets at my use of the word.

"It's just...I don't know what all of this means."

"You're a smart woman..." I return softly, "I think you've figured it out."

When she remains quiet, my confidence starts to wane. Me doing this from 10,000 miles away is ass-backwards. By shying away from asking her for anything official, I've confused the hell out of her. When she doesn't speak for a minute, I can tell she's having trouble with all of this.

"I know it's all fucked up—me here, and you there. I don't want to make you uncomfortable. I'm just a guy doing everything I can to impress the girl I like."

But she's still not talking, and I consider that I'm missing the mark, that my attempts to woo her are failing. If she doesn't want this, I have to give her an out.

"You can tell me to back off, you know..." I say quietly. "It's only fun if you like the attention."

Heavy heartbeats punctuate my breath. She's taking even longer to respond this time. When the wayward thought occurs to me, it hits me like a ton of bricks.

"If you met someone...you would tell me, right? I mean, you wouldn't feel like it was weird to tell me..." I blurt. "My fragile ego can take it."

I would pay money to see the look on her face. Her expression alone would tell me the truth. But I'm glad she can't see mine, because she'd know, too. I'm lying through my teeth.

"It would be totally weird to tell you." She says it like I'm crazy. "And if you were seeing someone, I wouldn't want to know. I couldn't handle it if she had a better body or if she sucked dick better than me."

"Not even the gay boys suck dick better than you," I deadpan.

I'm hoping that made her smile.

"I'm not seeing anyone, cupcake."

"Me neither."

"I haven't wanted to."

"Me neither."

I decide to drop it. Enough has been said for today. A second later, an alarm on my desktop tells me I have a call with a client.

"I've got a meeting," I apologize. "But I'll call you soon, okay?"

"I'm on doubles for the next two days," she complains.

"Just text me when you're around."

"I will. And, Michael? Don't back off."

I yawn as I stand in the high-speed elevator, hearing the whoosh of vertical gain as I rocket to the forty-fifth floor. It was an early morning. I toured a job site for the first Kensington hotel, which was far enough on the outskirts of the city that my driver had to pick me up at five in the morning. Australia's topography is more diverse than Chicago's, and beachfront property comes with complexities. Projects like this have to be planned in ways that withstand winds and take other circumstances like storms, erosion, and salt air into account. I like thinking through these kinds of issues and am already learning a lot since I've been in place.

I smile at Kat as I approach her desk. I'm in a better mood since I started the relaxation therapy. She didn't call or text this morning, which means that nothing is on fire, but I figure I'll check in anyway.

"Anything good?"

"Nothing work-related." I wonder why she's smiling so widely. "But something came for you. It's on your desk. And, Michael— Happy Birthday."

My eyes widen in embarrassment as I realize that it is, indeed, my thirty-second birthday. "Thank you." I muster an appreciative smile before I proceed to my office.

My birthday means it's also Bex's birthday and I'm grateful for the flower delivery I scheduled a month ago. I wonder what Bex has sent me now.

When I see the pink pastry box, I try not to hope. A white card sits on top, and as I approach, I recognize Darby's elegant scrawl. I can't stop myself from smiling and staring for a moment before opening the envelope, the contents of which I care about far more than whatever is in the box.

It's one of the gaudiest greeting cards I've ever seen, and I laugh suspecting from the abundance of glittery cupcakes that completely covers the front that it's been designed for a six-year-old girl. I admire it for a long moment before opening the card to see the note she's written within.

When you're home, I'll make you my red velvet. In the meantime, these will have to do. Happy Birthday, babe. XOXO, Darby

My face hurts from smiling so hard. Finally, I open the box. The smell makes me weak in the knees and I sit down then, dipping a shameless finger into the delectable pile of cream cheese icing on the cupcake closest to me.

A moan spills out of me, but I don't care. I snatch an entire cupcake from the box and remove the paper as quickly as possible while giving the cupcake its proper respect. It's not a tiny cupcake, but I eat the whole thing in three bites.

"Holy hell," I mutter, smiling again.

This feels better than anything—literally, anything—I've felt since I left home. Moments later, one hand is holding a second unwrapped cupcake, my mouth is chewing a bite, and my right hand is on my phone, finding her number.

"I fucking love you," I say around a mouthful of cupcake as soon as she picks up, too far gone to realize what I've said.

She laughs in response, harder and more genuine than I'm used to hearing lately.

"I'm fucking awesome. I take it they meet your standards?"

"You don't even know..." I don't bother to mind my manners as I continue eating. "Hang on..." I dial my intercom.

"Kat, would you please bring me some whole milk?"

Darby laughs again. She's really enjoying this.

"Whatever. It's my birthday. I can have whatever I want."

"So, what are you up to tonight?" Darby asks, clearly wondering whether I have anything special planned.

"Something amazing." I lie in a way that isn't meant to be convincing.

"Uh-huh." She doesn't believe me.

"Alright, you caught me. I forgot it was my birthday."

"I didn't," she sing-songs, a smile in her voice.

"No, you didn't, cupcake. You did good. I didn't know how much I needed this."

Kat slips in with a quart of milk, and I thank her before turning my attention back to Darby.

"What are you up to?"

"I'm at work. Busy night, so I've actually gotta hop."

"Alright, sweetie. Thank you so, so much."

"Happy birthday, baby. And don't eat them all. Kat helped, so give her one, okay?"

Chapter Twelve

THE CATERPILLAR

or real?

Her text comes in right after she sends me a picture of the small movie popcorn machine I sent. It's amazing how much can be achieved with one-day shipping and Amazon Prime.

You love movie popcorn. It was supposed to come with the butter.

"Butter" may be a stretch. The label says "buttery-flavored topping"

Whatever. You love that shit.

It's sweet.

You have no time to go to the movies, so I'm bringing the movies to you.

Her reply is an emoji that is blowing a kiss. It emboldens me to move to phase two of the plan.

I thought maybe we'd watch a movie together.

I've thought through the logistics. We can queue up the same movie and press play at the same time. When it's over, we can drink a bottle of wine and talk like we used to.

When?

Friday night. You pick something, I say.

I've been wanting to watch Kill Bill *again...*

I'll get it on my DVR. Bring wine, okay?

I'm grinning when I see what she returns.
It's a date.
Mission accomplished.

✌︎

I return from my morning run to the news that I have a package. Andrew's been forwarding my mail from Chicago, but it comes weekly through inter-office post. The only mail I've been getting through my apartment building here is the occasional drawing from Ella. The box that the doorman hands me is small and light. It's from Amazon so there's no telling yet who sent it. The impulse to shake it to guess what's inside makes me feel like a kid on Christmas morning. I wonder who's sent me this.

I'm sweaty as hell and I don't want to be late for my movie with Darby, so I prioritize taking a shower, queuing up the movie and getting everything ready. I've got four minutes to spare before I return to where I've deposited my box on the kitchen counter. Slicing open the seams with a steak knife, I pull open the flaps. Five King Size packs of Reese's Peanut Butter Cups lie loosely among the padding. A typewritten gift note reads "Don't eat them all before the movie."

I'm still grinning a minute later when our video call connects and I've already on my second pack of the candies. I know she can see me eating and she laughs the minute she sees the peanut butter cup in my hand.

"How many are left?"

I shrug. "Three-and-a-half."

She's still smiling when she brings the wine glass to her lips.

"What'd you pick?" I ask. I left a few nice bottles of red in her wine refrigerator, but I'm not sure whether she's noticed them yet.

"A really nice Amarone that I don't remember buying."

"I hear they pair nicely with popcorn."

Watching the movie together is nowhere near as awkward as

it had the potential to be. I'm lying on my side on my sofa with my laptop on the coffee table and the camera on me. She's mirrored the same posture on her side—half-sitting-up, half-lying as she munches through her small snack and drinks her wine. Her eyes are on the movie, but my eyes are on her. I've muted my TV because we're a few seconds out of sync.

The lights are low, so I can't see her as well as I'm used to, but the blue light from her television reflects in a way that illuminates her face. I drink in her every expression—her subtle smiles at the clever parts, and her cringes when it gets too violent. As the movie nears its end, I know that if I don't want to get caught staring, I need to tear my eyes away.

"Did I ever tell you I saw it three times when it came out?" she asks after she puts down her remote.

I smile as I pour myself another glass of wine. I don't care that it's barely noon here. I've taken the day off of work and I'm determined to enjoy my time with my girl.

"I used to play hooky from work...go to the Loew's on water to take a long lunch for an afternoon movie."

"Ballsy for any Tarantino flick," I point out. "That's a pretty long lunch."

"I used to go shopping, too...why do you think I picked a hospital on the Magnificent Mile?"

"Cushy lifestyle," I murmur.

"Yeah, well, it used to be." She smiles sadly.

"Don't worry. It will be again."

⚘

"Morning, baby."

I know the second she sees my image appear from the way her lips melt into a lazy smile, and from the pillow at her back, I can see she's taking her video call from bed. It's Sunday morning for her, Saturday night for me—it's become our usual time—though it's clear she' just woken up. Her hair is slightly wild, her eyes are still sleepy, and I can see the hint of her nipples through her sheer camisole.

"Go back to sleep, sweetie."

My cock has already sprung to life. He remembers this look. He also remembers the dozens of times he'd laid into her for having the nerve to look so delicious the first thing in the morning.

"But I want to talk to you," she pouts, which only makes me harder.

"I'll still be here in an hour," I insist gently, my hand already moving down to adjust myself. "Call me back when you wake up, beautiful. I'll be here."

"Alright..."

"And, Darby?"

"Mm-hmm?" She yawns in that cute way of hers.

"If you don't put on a robe or a bra or something by the time you call me back...I'm not gonna hear a word you say."

A second before I end the call, I see her face flush red and watch her look down at what she's wearing in alarm. I might laugh at her surprise if I weren't in such a rush to get off the phone. Closing my laptop, I flop back on my sofa, one arm flying up to cover my eyes as the other hand reaches down to my fly.

The way she looks this morning makes me think of the way she used to like to wake me up—with my dick down her throat while her fingers stroked my balls. The sexiest thing about it had always been watching her before she realized I was awake. Whenever I did, her attention shifted away from whatever she was getting out of it to bring me into the mix. She didn't get that the hottest part was catching her unaware and getting to see the love affair between she and my cock.

God, she got off on sucking me. I've met a fair number of women who like it and do it well, if not from a sense of obligation. But Darby loves it. Before my pants are fully removed, my hands are gripping my dick, and I'm recalling the vision and the feeling of her lips sliding down my shaft.

I groan with the first pump of my fist. My memory greedily holds on to the deftness of her lips and the darkness in her eyes. Soon, my thoughts carry me to the sounds of agonized pleasure she makes when my hand is on the back of her head and I'm driving into her mouth. When she sucks me so good I can't stand it, I like to pull her into a sixty-nine. Every time I do, she's dripping.

I cry hoarsely as my orgasm hits, pulling my shirt up just in time for the first ropes of semen to arc over my navel. My hips are off the sofa as I ride the wave. Eventually, my breathing slows and I sweep my other hand over my face again. Three minutes later, I'm stepping into the shower and waiting for my erection to subside, but it's still standing proudly, and I'm still horny as hell. I'm thinking about burying my face between her legs when I jerk off again.

When I call her back half an hour later, I'm feeling more relaxed. She, on the other hand, looks more alert. Her hair is tamed and she is nursing a cup of coffee. She's put on a robe over her camisole, but the front is open, and it covers nothing.

"Better?" The flirtation in her voice is unmistakable.

"Much," I smile as my dick stirs again.

The subtext in our interactions is becoming more frequent, and more intense. It's thrilling and dangerous all at the same time. It makes me believe that things between us are going in the right direction. But I have to accept that she may not be as ready as me. I don't want to saddle her with expectations, or have her think that whenever I blow into town, I expect us to fall right back into some version of what we were. That doesn't mean when I see her two weeks from now it'll be easy for me to keep my hands off.

Not much is going on, so we talk about a little bit of everything—what's happening on the show we're bingeing together on Netflix, what Anne's new girlfriend is like, and what's going on with my non-profit. She tells me she's been to the Art Institute twice since I left and admits to something I've suspected: that the large, anonymous donation that was made to my foundation six months ago came from her.

She slips it in casually a moment after I've told her that I'm debating over whether to bring in a different Executive Director. It will be difficult for me to implement the new programs we'll be able to develop given our budget windfall. It's my baby, but I'm in Sydney and I don't want it to suffer because I'm gone.

"Back then...I thought you'd be mad. At this point, it's stupid for me not to tell you."

"Did you do it because it was me?"

"I did it because I love the work you're doing," she says earnestly before her face takes on a playful smile. "But I'd have supported any cause you were involved in—even if it was stupid."

I chuckle. "Define stupid."

"You'd be surprised," she murmurs in that dry way of hers and I don't care about her answer. I just love that things between us right now are so light. This is the happiest I've heard her sound in weeks. "Money makes crackpots come out of the wood-work. Last month, some doomsday preppers tried to get me to fund a non-profit that was trying to build underground colonies in silos. Their mission was to save the human race from the zombie apocalypse. I have no idea how they got their 501(c)(3)."

"So, if my next cause is the end of the world, you'll finance it?"

"Believe it or not, yes."

I smile at that.

"The for-profit ideas are even worse." She regales me with stories about ideas people have pitched to her. Someone wanted five million dollars to finance a glass bottom airplane, another wanted her to invest in toilet paper gloves, and a third was developing a breathalyzer test to keep people from drunk dialing. I'm loving this conversation. It feels good to laugh, and gives me hope that when I see her, we'll still be *us*.

"You never talk about your money," I say. It's a weighty observation but it flows easily.

"What do you want me to say?"

"Nothing, maybe. But I've always wondered whether you had some master plan for how to spend it." Maybe I'm off base with this. Maybe people who are born rich, and who stay as rich as Darby, don't bother to think about this. But people who grew up poor like me always know the answer to that question. We've fantasized our whole lives about what we would do with a big pile of cash.

"You're the master planner, Michael."

"And you're the one with dreams and big ideas."

She looks mildly bewildered, as if this indelible fact is foreign to her.

"You've really never thought about it?"

She shrugs. "I do a lot of surviving and not a lot of thinking. I'm trying to turn that around."

I get quiet then, knowing that if there's ever been a perfect time to say more, it's now." I'm trying to turn that around, too," I say.

"What's that big brain been thinking about?" she asks with a tentative smile.

"The future, I guess. You know...what the next thing might be for me."

When she straightens a bit, I know that she's sensed something serious in my voice.

"I thought you were gonna keep living the dream for a while."

"I'm working the plan," I say. "But plans change."

She knows we've entered delicate territory and I wish I knew whether the apprehensive look on her face came from wanting me to say more or wishing I wouldn't. Sometimes things between us are so easy that bringing up the heavier stuff feels like it would take us back to the awkward place.

"Are you unhappy at D&R?"

"Unhappy, no, but up to my neck in twice as much administrative bullshit than I bargained for."

"You and me both," she admits, and the cloud of worry that's followed her for the past few weeks shadows her face a little. "Nowadays I'm lucky if I see ten patients a week."

Come on, baby.

I'm leading her, for sure, but I want her to step back and think. To come to some of the same conclusions I have.

"Short term, it's fine," I say. "I, mean, you can get through any shitty situation as long as it's temporary, right? But longer-term...I don't know. I just think I can figure out a way to focus on the parts of the work I love."

"What do you think you'll do?"

"Hire a Chief of Staff at Dewey and Rowe? Go to a smaller firm? I'm not sure. Bex has been suggesting for years that I open my own shop..."

"But?"

"But sometimes I think I'll get out of architecture alto-gether...maybe go off somewhere and save the world."

"Wow."

"You sound surprised."

"I guess I am a little. Not at the save the world part. At the others."

"I got what I thought I wanted, and it wasn't what I thought it would be."

"Are you still thinking about Paris?" She's remembering a conversation we once had. Apart from Chicago, it's the only place I've wanted to live.

"I think I'd still like an apartment there, and maybe some project work," I say. "But being here has made me realize how much unfinished business I have in Chicago."

She seems to digest this for a moment. And I wonder whether what she'll say will lead us to the conversation—the one we've never had, but that we need to have more than ever.

"What will *you* do?" she asks instead. "With all your money?"

"I spend all my money," I admit simply. "Apart from what I've saved for Ella, for the house, and retirement, I give it away."

"To the foundation?"

"Among other things," I say. "But, basically, yes. I've put it all back into the neighborhood."

She thinks about this for a minute, then asks, "What would you do with all *my* money?"

I have no idea how much she's worth, but I'm guessing it's in eight or nine figures. Darby's money is very old and it comes from both sides.

"With no kids to pass it on to? No inheritances to leave? I honestly don't know. But I wouldn't wait until I was dead to give it away when so many people could use it now."

Chapter Thirteen

STORMY WEATHER

"Hey, Kat?" I call out to her through the open door.

"Yeah?" she answers.

Kat and I only shout back and forth like this in the early mornings, when we're the only people in this part of the office.

"What is the Forever Floating Health Spa?" I ask.

My calendar says a car is coming to pick me up at 11:30 for an appointment I don't recognize.

When I hear her footsteps, I look up from my desk. She leans against my door, crosses her arms, and gives me a pointed look.

"You'll need to have a chat with Andrew about that."

I raise an eyebrow. Andrew rarely schedules for me anymore, and I'm surprised that he's put something on my calendar now.

"He told me to warn you that if you don't go, he's going to cut off your monthly shipment." Now it's her turn to raise an eyebrow before she turns around and goes back to her desk.

I have Andrew on speed dial.

Unsurprisingly, he sounds cheerful when he picks up. "Morning, Michael! You're in early."

But I cut to the chase. "Cutting off my candy supply? That's low."

"That's only if you don't go. So, go, and I'll keep the shipments coming. Maybe I'll even double up."

"Explain to me why I'm spending two hours of my day getting a massage at a spa that's halfway across town and another hour in a car getting there and back?"

"It's not a massage. But I should look into those, too."

"Then what the hell is it?" Curiosity piqued, I google the spa and start reading at the same time as Andrew launches into an explanation.

"It's time in a sensory deprivation tank. It induces a state of theta sleep."

"You know I'm not six, right? I don't need a $250 an hour nap."

"Darby said it's supposed to be extremely relaxing. Maybe you ought to give her a call..."

But I don't call her. I work through my to do list for the morning and decide I'll thoroughly research whatever this is on my way to the appointment. I'll lie in a ten-inch-deep pool of water that is heavily saturated with Epsom salts. The chamber will be cut off from sound and light and, in the absence of outside stimuli, I'll slip into a state of deep relaxation, so long as I can calm my mind. I'm doubtful about that last part, but more confident than I would've been a month ago. I have to admit, I am more relaxed since Darby sent those meditation head phones.

I never would have gone for either of these ideas had she bothered to ask permission, but I can't blame her for resorting to this. The idea of her treating me still makes me uncomfortable. I don't want her to think that it's her job to fix me. But it's time to stop being cryptic. I want to show her how many things I'm still willing to try.

After a brief orientation, I'm shown to my suite, where I'll shower and relax into my tank. The high concentration of saline will make my body buoyant. From what I read on the way over, this practice, called "floating", yields amazing results. But when I step into the tank, my mind is wired and I'm anxious about whether it will work. I try to use meditation techniques I've learned but I'm disheartened when my mind wanders. But it feels nice, and I think about my beach vacation with Darby and spending time with her by the side of the ocean.

"Mr. Blaine?" a voice is calling. "Your session for today has finished."

It isn't until the insistent knocking registers that I realize I was asleep. But waking up doesn't feel like it normally does. I feel rested, and even a little blissed out. I'm still in a euphoric haze, and a very good mood, twenty minutes later when I step into my car.

"Customer service," Darby says when she picks up the phone. "To leave a thank you message, stay on the line. To leave a complaint, hang up and don't call again."

"I feel like I just got a full night's sleep," I smile.

When I tried to make my next appointment at the front desk, and to pay for the visit, I learned that both had been taken care of. The appointment is a standing one, and I'm booked for the same time next week. At this point, I don't even care whether it does anything for my anxiety. The lack of sleep is catching up to me and if this can help with that, it will be worth my time.

"The results are supposed to be progressive." I can hear her shuffling papers in the background. She must be in her office. "The more you do it, the easier it is for you to slip into a prolonged theta state. And you're right—the theta state is the most restorative frequency that occurs during sleep."

"Have you ever done it before?"

"No, not personally. A friend told me about it."

She says "friend" but she means "colleague." She thinks that anxiety is my primary diagnosis. She's figured out by now that I don't want to be medicated and that I've tried the obvious things.

"Maybe you should try it," I say gently. Because I'm starting to feel a bit like roles are reversed for how stressed out and exhausted she's been. She's not a chronic insomniac with an anxiety disorder like I am, but she's been burning the candle at both ends.

"I can't think about that right now."

The paper sounds in the background stop and the joking tone from when she picked up is gone. I don't like it at all. She sounds less like herself when we talk nowadays. My trip back to Chicago can't come soon enough.

"You take such good care of me, baby," I say.

"We take care of each other," she whispers.

I am alarmed when I hear tears in her voice. A second ago we were talking about flotation tanks.

"When I get home next week," I say slowly, "We're gonna spend a lot of time together and you're gonna tell me all your problems. Okay?"

"Okay."

When she sniffles, it breaks my heart.

Chapter Fourteen

IS YOU IS OR IS YOU AIN'T MY BABY?

I'm roused from a jet-lagged slumber when I hear girly-sounding giggles. I got so little sleep on the plane that after Bex picked me up from the airport this morning, I hit the guest room and crashed.

"Is he really going to pee his pants?" I hear Ella's little voice ask.

"I guess we'll have to see." My heart begins to thunder at the realization that the second voice is Darby's.

I flex the fingers on my left hand to find that, unlike my right hand, which is cozy warm next to where I lay on my stomach under the covers, my left hand has been carefully removed. It now hangs down to the floor, not at all where I put it, and sits in a bowl of warm water below.

"You two are unbelievable," I murmur sleepily, turning toward them and prying my eyes open.

"Did you pee, uncle Michael?" Ella asks hopefully.

I flick water at her then and she giggles like a maniac. "No."

I sit up to look at Darby who is so very beautiful, and who I can hardly believe is standing, in the flesh, before me. She bites the corner of her lip and smiles at me. I can't help but smile back, despite the prank she's just pulled. I don't take my eyes off of Darby as I speak to my niece.

"Go help mommy with dinner, sweet pea. Darby and I are going to have a little talk about how it's not nice to put good little girls like you up to dirty tricks."

Ella giggles again and I hear the retreat of her feet as she runs out the door and down the hall, already yelling to Bex, "Mommy! Uncle Michael didn't pee!"

"You're hilarious," I say sarcastically, rising fully from the bed, my smiling face contradicting my words.

"You have no sense of humor," she accuses, smiling right back.

I've been anticipating this moment for the better part of three months. But the wait is over and in one fluid motion, my arms are around her waist, sweeping her into the embrace I've been craving.

"I missed you so much, cupcake," I say, my face serious as I bury it in her hair.

"I missed you, too, babe."

My hand slides up to the back of her neck and I feel her inhale deeply as she buries her face in my chest. She loves the way I smell. I've known this since the beginning. And don't think I didn't take a shower with my special soap before my nap, because I sure as hell did. She smells like herself, too—a mixture of her Molton Brown Pink Peppercorn and some expensive salon shampoo. I thread my fingers through her hair a second before I smooth it and tip her face up toward mine.

I can't help touching her like this, and it takes effort to keep my fingers from exploring her a bit more. I miss the softness of her skin, the intertwining of our fingers, my thumbs on her cheeks. I'm busy thinking of something to say other than "I love you" or "you're beautiful" when a glint from one of the diamonds in her snapdragon necklace catches my eye. It's the first time I've seen it on her. The picture didn't do it justice.

"I still get compliments on it every day."

And I know she's seen me looking. I've wondered how often she wore it. Every time we do a video call, I've noticed that she has it on.

"What do people say?"

I slide my hands down her arms and intertwine our fingers. Her face is inches from mine and looking into her tiger-eyes has already mesmerized me.

"They tell me that whoever gave it to me is a keeper." She is adorably shy.

"What do you think?"

For a split second, her face turns serious, and I think that we might actually start to have this conversation, but she shrugs.

"I don't know. He's not that cute. Dumb as a doornail. Terrible in bed. Choosing jewelry is his only redeeming quality."

"That's a shame," I play along. "Anyone who would have a piece like that made would probably move mountains for you." I tuck a stray wave of hair behind her ear, and her eyes turn serious again.

"I'm so glad you're here."

When she says it, I see all the pain she's been hiding, not over me—over other things in her life that are going wrong.

"I've got you," I say as I pull her in tight once again.

I sit on Bex's back steps, not caring how much the freezing stone beneath my ass is chilling the skin under my clothes—it's been months since I've seen a good snowfall and I've missed it. Darby commented on my tan earlier, and, indeed it's in the low eighties most days in Sydney. I've taken to running outside again and am spending more time outdoors. But the snow...I've forgotten its magic, and how I love the special quiet that seems to settle over everything as it falls.

The back door creaks open quietly, and moments later, I feel Darby's warmth next to me. Ella had begged to have her read her a bedtime story, an honor she usually reserves for me, but I don't mind.

"I think she's more excited to see you than she is to see me." From the corner of my eye, I see her smile at my lighthearted comment.

"I do better character voices than you," she baits, shrugging, "...or so I'm told."

"But can you recite *The Cat in the Hat* from memory?" I challenge, turning my head to fully look at her.

God, she's beautiful.

She nudges me playfully. "I guess you've got me there."

Now that we're alone, my impulse to hold her again, to kiss her, to declare myself to her, is becoming harder to ignore. It's only been a few hours and I'm halfway to breaking the promise I made to myself—to let her set the pace. Not that every cell in my body isn't reminding me how much I need to touch her, because each and every cell is, and I certainly do. But I can't leave Chicago without saying things that must be said.

But now we are silent in this serene, simple moment, sharing breath as we gaze to one another amid the falling snow. Her eyes lower to my lips for a long moment and a slow blush colors her pale cheeks. Two things happen at once: both my cock—and her eyes—jump up in alarm.

"It's getting late." She casts her eyes aside, toward where the back-porch light is illuminating the quickly falling snow. "The roads will be bad soon. I should get home."

"The roads will be bad now. You shouldn't drive." Saying it in response to her obvious excuse doesn't make it less true. I'd never let her drive anywhere in weather like this. "You can have the guest room."

"Afraid I'll jump you in the middle of the night?" She asks it self-deprecatingly. I hear the thread of truth, see the fiber of it in her eyes.

I fix her with a pointed look. "We haven't seen each other in three months. We wouldn't just wake up Ella—we'd wake up the whole fucking neighborhood."

And I can see her mind drift for just a second—she's picturing it—the way we fuck after we've been away from one another, the sounds both of us make when we're desperate that way. But I also see the moment when something different sobers her eyes.

"I don't know how to be around you, Michael. I don't understand the rules anymore."

"There are no rules," I say quietly. "No more agreement. No limits to what we can be."

"No more knowing how to be around you..." she fires back gently. "No knowing where I stand."

She looks out at the snow as she says it, her voice resigned as she points it out.

"It's always been up to you, where you stand with me."

The insecurity in her eyes is still there, but so is that intangible thing we share, that special knowing that passes between us when we're together. Moments like this are what I've missed—even with things unsaid, something incredible hums between us when we're this close. Even with so much to decide. I'm ten times calmer in her presence.

"You're the best hugger, do you know that?" she whispers.

I move up a step so that I'm directly behind her and situate her between my legs. She leans back into me and I wrap both arms around her. This is better—far more intimate—than the way we were sitting a few seconds ago.

"I want to hold you all night..." I whisper, my chin on her shoulder. "But I don't want to mess things up. And I know I don't have the right to ask you for anything."

It's started to snow harder, and she shivers in my arms. It's an excuse for me to hold her tighter.

"We don't have to figure everything out tonight," she says. "We have all weekend."

I kiss her temple. "We don't have to figure everything out

this weekend," I counter. "Whatever happens, I want it to happen because it's right—not because my travel schedule makes you feel like there's a deadline."

She melts into me at that moment, coming even closer, nuzzling in to rub her cheek against mine. The energy between us feels as magical as the snow.

§.

"Why aren't you in the guest room with Darby?" a six-year old voice demands in a too-loud voice that is very close to my face. "I thought she was your girlfriend," the same little voice accuses as I open my eyes.

A petulant Ella stares down at me from where I'm lying on the sofa. I sit upright and wipe a hand over my chin. Apart from the jet lag, I was up thinking half the night.

"I don't know if she wants to be my girlfriend, sweetie."

I yawn. By now, I'm a master at redirecting the attentions of first graders whose questions are better left unanswered.

"I think you should get married," Ella continues as if I haven't spoken. "I can be the flower girl and Buddy can be the ring bear."

It takes effort not to laugh. Buddy the teddy bear has been Ella's constant companion and dearest friend since she was two. "What's a ring bear?" I ask with put-on confusion, eager to hear her explanation. Ella's vast life experience means that she has an answer for everything.

"The ring bear..." my eyes whip to the stairs as I hear Darby's voice, a second before I see her feet descending the steps. "...is the bear who walks down the aisle and gives the bride and groom their rings."

Ella, who's holding the bear in question, places him on the ground and shuffles him forward in a way that makes it look like he's walking. She and Buddy make it to the stairs in time to meet Darby at the bottom.

"Why don't you want to be Uncle Michael's girlfriend?"

"Stop harassing Darby and come in here to get your waffles," Bex calls from the kitchen.

Ella's eyes light up. "Yaaay, waffles!" she nearly screams, running out of the room and forgetting about the wedding completely.

Darby is still smiling at Ella's retreating form as she makes her way into the room. It gives me a moment to just enjoy looking at her. She seems happy, luminous, even, and I feel something deep stir inside me when she finally looks my way. I rise to greet her, putting my arms around her and kissing her temple. It feels entirely natural—our warm embrace, the soft voices we use when we bid each other good morning. Like the afternoon before, a simple greeting doesn't feel like enough. Once we're in one another's arms, we spend a good long minute there.

"When do we need to go?" I ask Darby minutes later

I'm on the fourth pass of powdering my third Belgian waffle with confectioner's sugar. In a minute I'll add whipped cream and strawberry compote. God bless Bex for knowing exactly what breakfast I'd like. We'd done a lot of catching up when we'd all gone out for Ella's birthday dinner the night before, and we picked up the conversation at breakfast. Ella is long gone, having finished her waffles and abandoned us for her toys, leaving us to our boring grown-up stuff.

"I have to be in at ten if I want to escape in time for dinner." Regret colors her voice.

I reach to push the carton of half and half sitting in front of Alex to in front of an empty chair. "That works," I reply.

Darby frowns a minute, not understanding what I just did.

"The Board?" Bex asks as she breezes in.

"And Avi," I say as I move the sugar, too. "He's in town for the gala."

Bex throws me a "what happened?" look.

"New information," I say, accompanied by a look that says, "don't make me explain".

She plops into the seat where I've just placed the coffee fixings with her own steaming cup at the same time she hands me a jar of cinnamon. That's when I notice that Darby is looking wide-eyed between me and Bex.

"You get used to it," Alex says, looking up from the newspaper.

"What's up with Avi?" Darby asks in the car forty-five minutes later.

The night before, we decided that I'd return with her to the city, hang out at my place while she goes to work, and meet back up with her later. She knows I have business to take care of on the South Side, but I never filled her in on the whole story.

"He's joining my Board meeting this afternoon," I say. "He's been looking into some drug activity happening in our neighborhood."

"Yeah...I hear things are getting bad on the South Side."

Even though Darby's hospital is downtown, I realize she might actually know something about the kinds of cases they're seeing in the ER at County. "What have you heard?" I ask.

"I've gotten a few calls...mostly asking us to handle some of their overflow. They run out of beds a lot faster than we do."

"Opioid detox?"

We're turning onto Lake Shore Drive and Darby is distracted for a moment as she switches lanes. "Yeah, they've definitely seen a spike in cases. We have too."

"We think there's a new supplier,"

"How do you know?"

"The gangs are rallying. The ones who are getting cut out of the action want to take down whoever it is."

"I hope they do," she says. "The mayor's not doing shit about it. He's probably getting hush money," she mutters. "This town is so fucking crooked."

My mind is whirring as we race down the highway. "Yeah..."

Chapter Fifteen

SING ME A WALTZ

I t feels amazing to see the inside of my own apartment, and I'm sorry to leave it, if only for a few hours. I spend the late morning on the South Side catching up with my Board and tying up loose ends for tomorrow's gala. Avi and Corliss show up for the last hour of the meeting. They haven't confirmed who is behind the influx of drugs that have flooded the South Side, but they've ruled out some people it's not. The casual input from my Board members corroborates what Avi has investigated and what Corliss has observed. More of the kids in our own program are at risk. Tomorrow's gala will be key. Other important community players will be in attendance and we'll need to lean on them for information and for help.

I spend the better part of the afternoon napping in my waterbed. It is glorious and I regret that I didn't have one shipped to Sydney. They said it would take months and at the time I didn't think it was worth the trouble, but I sleep so deeply that I wish I had. I wake just in time to go shopping for groceries to make dinner for Darby and me. I considered planning a night out—maybe dinner at a restaurant or a walk in the snow. But I know that what each of us wants is for us to be some version of what we used to be. I'm indescribably grateful for this quiet night at home.

Dinner is everything I had hoped it would be, and everything that I had feared. Finally, she tells me what has been happening. I'd gotten hints, but I didn't know that things with her had gotten so bad. She's so busy managing teams of other doctors, and handling advanced patient issues, that she's become an administrator and rarely has a chance to see patients. This next phase of the research doesn't interest her as much. She wants to see her discovery yield better options for opioid addicts, but developing a new drug or discovering a natural supplement to address the chemical reaction she discovered will tether her not only the development itself, but to years of FDA approvals.

"I've been thinking about what you asked me," she confesses after she's told me everything. Our plates are empty, and we've just poured another glass of wine. "About what I want to do with all my money."

"What have you decided?"

"I don't know. But I think I'm done with traditional jobs. I want to write my own ticket. Start doing what I want to do now, but do it my way."

"Do you know what that is?"

She shakes her head. "Honestly? No."

I swirl my wine in my glass. "I'm in the same boat. I know I'm not doing what I want to do, but I don't want to trade one mediocre situation for another. I want to wait until I know what's right."

She looks me right in the eye and lets out a sigh as she smiles. "How long until I come to Sydney?"

I smile back. "I've been looking forward to it, too. Both of us need a break. We've needed one for a long time."

"Eight weeks, three days..." She looks at her watch. "...Four hours. Not that I'm counting. We can make it until then, right?"

"Yeah," I say quietly. "We can."

"So, who's going to be at this gala tomorrow night?"

"Everyone you've ever heard me talk about. You'll meet Avi, the Board, Bex and Alex are going, so's Randy..." I trail off.

"But you're leaving right after..."

I nod soberly. "I have to fly tomorrow night if I want to be back at work by Monday morning."

"Then I guess we've got tonight."

"And tomorrow morning..." I trail off. I've thought through every moment I'll spend with her.

Before long, we head to my sofa, grab a blanket and go to put a movie on. I tell her she can pick. I don't care what we watch— I just want to hold her. And I'm more than shocked when she searches on demand and hits Play on *Before Midnight*.

"I think I'm ready." She turns to look at me for a long moment before she settles into my embrace.

And so we watch it in all its tragic beauty. A relationship past its prime. The reality of building a life together. The reality of the sacrifices we make for love. This is the saddest and least forgiving of the entire trilogy. I wonder whether it's what she wanted. It's everything she feared and everything she dared to hope for. They've each lost a piece of themselves. The movie has the potential to end badly, but they've built something both of them ultimately decides is worth saving.

As the credits roll, she is still in my arms, and I wonder what she's thinking. She turns to me and buries her face in my chest, just letting me hold her, just breathing with me. The energy that's been there all along continues to swirl between us, intensified by how close our bodies are. I don't know whether it's me who lifts my fingers to tip her head up to mine, or whether it's she who looks up at me, but the next thing I know, her hands are on my face and we're kissing.

I'm slow to the uptake because I've been dreaming of this kiss. Part of me is startled that she's closed this space between us. This kiss has lingered between us in nearly every moment, silent and waiting, and maybe even a little patient, and when my sense kicks in, I step forward to claim it. My body is quick to remember the rhythm of our kisses, and the softness of her lips. I hear myself whimper from the sublime perfection of her tongue sliding against mine. It's the best thing that has ever happened to me, and I know that this isn't about pent up sexual frustration or old feelings. This is about us exploring something new.

And it does feel exploratory—as if we're trying on a new garment to see how well it fits. It feels tentative and shy and infinitely tender. We kiss for a long time before she pulls away, rests her head back on my chest, and just like that, it's over.

I'm in bed, but not sleeping, though Darby still is. The night before, she had tugged me up from where we had been lying on my couch and commanded gently that we go to my room. Her toothbrush is still in my bathroom where it belongs, and we'd exchanged shy, playful smiles as we'd washed up. It was such a simple pleasure—standing side-by-side at the double sinks, sharing the ritual of getting ready for bed.

Now, it's morning and her fingers have sought out my body in her sleep, her thumb absently stroking my chest as her nose nuzzles into my neck. So many times, I have woken up to her lightly caressing my scalp. That one was always my favorite. It's been like this from the beginning—even before we were us, her body had known how to cast a spell on mine.

I'm still tired, but my body doesn't dare let me sleep. I'm too drunk from her touch, too high on this contact I've been craving. I may start purring from touches that mean nothing to her and everything to me. Darby's touch always straddled the line between soothing my body's sensory needs and arousing me in a way that drives me wild.

When she hums a little, I know that she's starting to wake up. Discreetly, I shift my hips back. I'm already hard as a rock, and however much I want to do something about that fact, I still want her to be the one to set the pace. It's just my luck that my attempt to back off a little is foiled when her body follows mine.

"Hiding your morning wood?" she murmurs. "What are we, fifteen?"

She's smiling before she opens her eyes.

"Morning wood leads to morning sex."

My voice is playful and I'm growing harder, but when she opens her eyes, I'm filled with gratitude and awe. God, I miss waking up to her.

"C'mon, Michael. Don't be a prude."

Her smile turns from lazy to coquettish and I have to chuckle at that.

"What is this? An ABC After School Special?"

"Mm-hmm," she murmurs, bringing her lips closer to mine. "All the cool kids are doing it."

When her lips touch mine, all joking is forgotten. This kiss is nothing like the one we shared last night. It isn't tentative or exploratory—it holds everything we've always been. The whole exchange is déjà vu—shallow words that betray a current with such fathomless force that we are powerless against being pulled under.

For nearly three months, I thought my fantasies were about having her body again. I've craved the sound she makes when she comes, her mouth on me, the taste of her. But it's so much more than that. It's this feeling of being submerged, of surrendering over and over to the death of me and the birth of us.

I don't really know how we got our clothes off, but my mouth won't leave her skin. My hands explore, but for some reason, I can't stop licking her. And I do feel submerged. I hear the sounds of pleasure she's making as if I'm underwater. My brain, which is not in control, puzzles at my insanity. I can't seem to stop licking her.

My fingers find their way between her legs before my tongue does and I'm laving the divot between her hip and her belly button the first time I make her come. When she begins to pulse, my mouth finds her clit and I suck her in hard. Her soft cries escalate as I help her ride it out.

But I stay where I am, shifting my position to give me even better access. I bury my whole face in her core. She opens her legs wider, inviting me in, but before long, her thighs have tightened around my head. Her vice grip means that my ears are covered. I only feel it on my finger and taste it on my tongue a minute later when she comes again.

When I come up for air, I'm drunk, and I fall next to her on the bed, but not before I scoop her up until she's straddled my hips. I whimper with desperation a moment before I drive her down on my shaft, and now it's my own helpless cries I hear as she moves up and down on me. My eyes don't leave hers and I'm getting off as much from the magnetism that pulls our souls together as I am from the friction of our bodies.

My asshole tightens with every throb of my dick and I feel my lower back begin to tingle. I know I'm going to come, and I can barely believe it, but I think she might come again, too. Her eyes fall shut and her rhythm falters when my middle finger strokes her clit—just enough to get it wet. When I reach around to slide it into her other entrance, she tightens around me and I lose it. My orgasm feels like it lasts for minutes and I'm at the end of riding it out when her ass tightening hard on my finger signals that she's about to come, and the whole thing is the hottest thing that's ever happened to me.

We do it everywhere that morning—against my windows, in the shower, on the kitchen counter. I learn she's nursed a fantasy about me bending her over my drafting table, so we even do it there. It is everything—and I feel naïve for having wanted to wait. For whatever jumbled purpose it had once served, this had never failed to strengthen our connection. As always, it gave me the divine satisfaction of being impossibly close. I have never felt closer to her.

We eat our first ravenous meal some time after noon, lounge in bed snoozing and kissing for a while before we have each other once more. She leaves me at five to go to her place and get ready for the gala. I'll see her in fewer than two hours, but before she walks out the door, kissing her again is all I can do not to tell her how much I love her. I regret that it will be the last time we're alone together until she comes to Sydney. But I know that when she comes, we'll start something new.

·

Chapter Sixteen

SUCH GREAT HEIGHTS

"Hey, beautiful."

I answer my phone rather jovially, partially because I'm pleased to hear from Darby, partially because I'm a bit drunk.

"Hey, handsome," she comes back, and I can hear the amused smile in her voice. I know why. I rarely greet her in that way. "Where are you?" Evidently, she hears voices and music in the background.

"A few of us went out for drinks after work," I say, making my way out of the bar to the garden out back.

It's a balmy night, the winter in the southern hemisphere now behind us and the spring melting into what feels like early summer. It' been two weeks since I left Chicago, and even though we speak often, I still gladly drop whatever I'm doing whenever she calls.

"Do you want to talk later?"

"No..." I say, drawing out my "o". "I want to talk now. I always want to talk to you. You at work?"

"I got sent home—for once, I overbooked the schedule. That should tell you how tired I am. I just got back to my place. I just...missed you, so I thought I'd call."

"I miss you, too, cupcake. So much," I admit then. We don't say it to one another often, but whenever we do, it feels like relief. And we've been saying it more and more since I left Chicago. I find an empty table in the far corner of the small courtyard and sit down with my beer.

"How long again 'till Christmas?" she asks, showing me again that she does, too.

"We don't have to wait 'till Christmas," I say, voicing the thought that has been on my mind since Chicago. I'm desperate to see her again. "I've been thinking of coming home for a few days if you can get some time off."

She doesn't say anything for a minute.

"Or not..." I wonder what she's thinking.

"No—I've been thinking about it, too. Coming to Sydney sooner rather than later, I mean. It's just—what happens when we see each other again? Do we float away in our little bubble or do we actually try to figure things out?"

Her question sobers me.

"We do both," I say with perfect clarity, straightening in my seat.

Her silence makes me nervous, and I wish I could see her face. I consider whether to admit it, knowing even in the moment that liquid courage is at play. But if she doesn't understand this by now—even if it's over the phone, it has to be said.

"I'm want everything with you, Darby. This thing between us...for me, it'll always be there."

"How do you know that?"

"Have you seen yourself?" I mean for it to break the tension, but her answer is serious.

"I'm just a girl, Michael."

"You know that's not true."

I hear her sigh on the other end.

"So, should we do it?" and for some reason, her phrasing strikes my funny bone. It makes me think of notes passed in middle school. I smile at what I say next.

"Darby, do you want to be my girlfriend? Circle your answer: yes or no."

"Don't be a dick." I finally hear a smile in her voice. "You already know the answer."

"You already know the answer, too."

"This is complicated," she sighs.

"I know, baby. I'm sorry." And I mean it. "I know I messed everything up. I never meant for it to turn out like this."

"How did you think it would turn out?"

"I thought I'd be able to at least pretend that I could get over you."

She takes a shaky breath.

"I should stop talking. I'm drunk."

"No," she says quickly. "It's kind of nice, not having to pretend."

I could have ended it there, but the truth is, I want us to keep moving closer to what we're supposed to be. "There's something I want you to understand about me. Even if being together turns out to be a total disaster, even if we decide it's best if we don't, it won't change anything for me."

"What are you saying?"

"Nothing you haven't already figured out."

"I don't have anything figured out, Michael."

"I haven't figured out the how, but I've figured out the what."

She doesn't say anything for a long, long time. "I need to see you. I'm coming to Sydney."

"Tell me when. I'll take the time off."

I settle on the sofa with a bar of my favorite chocolate. After last night, it seems prudent to skip the wine. I go out so seldom nowadays that a few drinks have an effect on me. Despite my mild hangover this morning, I'm not sorry about anything that happened last night.

Apparently, all I needed to begin to tell Darby how I felt about her was a few drinks. Drinking makes me bold, and more than a little horny, and I think back to the night we met. If I hadn't drunk half a bottle of champagne, and been so drunk on Darby herself, I never would have kissed her like I did. I never would have struck up the agreement that sealed my fate. I never would have coaxed her into that first magical night.

It's been damn near eighteen months, but I still think about it. Even then I knew that it wasn't just sex, but it took me a long time to face that fact. It had been so long since I'd been with a woman, I tried to convince myself it only felt so good because I was so hard-up. That was a goddamned lie. I kept telling myself that eventually the novelty would wear off, but it never did. Every time I was with her, it only made me want her more.

And, after last night, she knows how much I want her. I'm mentally planning what we'll do when she comes to Sydney. I'll ask her on a real date and take her to the coast. I won't let her leave until we've figured it out. I'll say it all out loud, so many times she gets sick of hearing me utter the words.

But my thoughts are interrupted by my phone. Avi's calling, at a very unusual hour.

"Avi. What's going on?"

"I'm in Mexico City. We've got trouble." Avi doesn't beat around the bush. "I called off the meeting. There's new information. We need time to regroup."

Avi is supposed to be on his way back to Chicago. He's still investigating the drug kingpin and wanted to spend some time in our old neighborhood. He started the process a couple of weeks ago when he was in town for the gala. He had planned on coordinating a session with some other concerned parties—community leaders with a stake in the situation. But, for some reason he's in Mexico City and it seems the meeting is off.

"Can you talk?" I ask.

He can be skittish about saying too much over the phone.

Being a hacker himself, he knows how insecure everything digital really is. And he's never sounded so secretive.

"I'm coming to Sydney. I'll save the details for when I get there. In the meantime, think about who has cronies at the enforcement agency."

When I realize that Avi is speaking in code, I'm even more alarmed. The "enforcement agency" he's talking about has to be DEA. The fact that he didn't say it means he doesn't want our call to get flagged by a bot. And "cronies" is a signal too. He's only ever used that word when we've talked about Charlie or Frank.

"Which one?" I ask. If I'm right about this, he'll say something else in code.

"I'm not sure. I think the chief is the kingpin. But the boss definitely knows."

Charlie Sweeney is Frank Christensen's Chief of Staff. Frank is Charlie's boss. Avi has just told me that Darby's father is somehow caught up in this. But he's not done.

"And I'm pretty sure that's why they won't let go of the South Side."

Part Two

SMOOTH CRIMINAL

Chapter Seventeen

SOMETHING'S ALWAYS WRONG

"Start from the beginning."

It's been a tense thirty-six hours. Avi had to fly three legs with long layovers, and even though he was in the Mexico City airport when I spoke to him, he's just arrived in Sydney.

Avi's body takes up nearly half the width of my sofa. We're both tall but he's broad and made of pure muscle. Right now, he's giving me a look. I know what this look means. He doesn't have to say it. Frank and Sweeney are definitely involved. And I need to know everything. Because nearly everyone I live for—Darby, the kids in my program, the families on the South Side—is in jeopardy because of this.

"You have to remember," he begins, "...that the gangs are just the distributors. The product itself comes from larger syndicates. I've spent the past month checking out all the usual suspects. The Irish mob. The Italian mafia. The Russians. The Mexican cartels. Not one of them is involved."

"How can you be sure?" I don't doubt Avi, but I need to understand the nuts and bolts. I always need to understand how things work.

"They're cooperating with each other," Avi says simply.

"That's what I was doing in Mexico City. Checking out a tip about a secret meeting that brought reps from each organization. At first, each one suspected the others. It got pretty bloody for a minute, but since they figured it out, they've been talking about an alliance."

I murmur, "The enemy of my enemy is my friend."

"I found out the location of the meeting. Kept an eye on who was coming in and out...took pictures, ran IDs. The operatives who went were important enough that I recognized half of them on the spot."

"Why Mexico City? It would be dangerous for known mobsters to travel out of the country. Wouldn't these guys have warrants?"

Avi gives me a sidelong glance and his eyes are full of approval. He appreciates that I've picked up on this. "They wouldn't have traveled commercial. But they know the feds are always watching. Mexico City let them flaunt the fact that something big was going on."

The pieces start assembling themselves in my head. The meeting may have served a practical purpose, but it was also designed to be a warning.

"The FBI is watching all of them. Depending on what else they deal in, they may have DEA or ATF tailing them, too. Even though they all source from outside the U.S., the Mexicans always have Border Control and Immigrations on their backs. A meeting as big as that would make sure that every agent in every single one of the Chicago bureaus knew that something was cooking. It would put whoever's been selling seized inventory on alert."

"Seized inventory," I echo. And then I understand. Only someone inside one of the agencies would have access to drugs that had been seized. Someone on the inside was looting the confiscated product and reselling the drugs. It was a classic racket.

"How do you know it's Frank?"

"Right now, it's circumstantial," Avi admits. "He's got motive, means, and opportunity. But, you're right—he's not the only one who could pull it off."

"Motive?" I don't see it. Frank is bidding for the White House. Why wouldn't he want to keep his nose clean?

"Do you know what Senate sub-committee Sanderson chairs?"

I shake my head. Sanderson is the presumptive nominee. Frank will become Vice President of the United States if Sanderson's ticket wins.

"International Narcotics Control," Avi says gravely. "And you're right. Frank would have been in a better position to control the Chicago drug market when he was mayor. My guess is that delivering this was table stakes for becoming the running mate."

I'm quiet for a full five minutes. My mind is racing, dissecting every possibility. It's plausible. But it sounds like a stretch. If these really are confiscated drugs, any number of government employees who touch the product might have gotten greedy.

"We need evidence."

"For what? To take him down? Michael, we can't get in the middle of this. Five major crime organizations are hatching a plan we know nothing about. We'll get ourselves killed."

"I'm not thinking about that right now. I'm thinking that I can't not try to stop whatever is happening. That I can't keep a secret like this from Darby. And that I can't tell her unless I'm absolutely sure. I need to see it, Av. I need to see it with my own eyes."

Avi has known me long enough to realize that I'm not going to let this go.

"Then we'll hack our way into some evidence," he vows.

"Michael. I'm sorry. But you gotta see this."

Even though Avi's words register, my eyes are closed and my body is heavy. He's standing over my bed, shaking me hard. I sit up, disoriented. From the fact that it's still dark out, I can't have been sleeping for long.

"I found something." He looks tired, but I see a glint of excitement in his eyes. "If this is what I think it is, we've gotta move."

I follow him to my kitchen, where he's set up what looks like a mobile command center—his laptop, plus some sort of satellite connection and other electronics that let him surf on his own. He laughed openly when I asked him if he needed my wi-fi password a few hours ago. But he's not laughing now. He's pulling up a barstool for me. He has to close a few windows of pretty raw-looking code to show more recognizable screens, but I still don't understand.

"What am I looking at?"

"Frank's schedule," he begins. "A shell company he owns has been quietly acquiring steel processing plants downstate. Two of those plants just won government contracts—but not with agencies that buy steel. The contracts are with DEA, Border Control and ATF."

"Alright...so he's gonna use the plants to warehouse the drugs. That still doesn't explain how he gets the agencies to hand them over, unless he's got someone on the inside at all three."

"He doesn't need someone on the inside if he's authorized to take possession of the confiscated product."

"I don't get it," I say bluntly.

"I think he's building an empire of companies that are authorized to destroy the drugs."

"Why steel plants?"

"Government agencies have subcontracted this function out for decades. They hire crematoriums, hazardous waste disposal companies, and even steelmakers. They can incinerate thousands of pounds of drugs with molten steel."

I shake my head. "It's too obvious. Someone else has to have tried it before. There must be oversight."

"I'm guessing that's who Frank has on the inside. He would've needed someone to make sure they won the contracts and someone else to make sure the auditors look the other way. Sanderson may be helping."

This is making a lot more sense and serving up a lot more proof than whatever we had a few hours ago. Solving the puzzle is satisfying, but the idea that it really could be Frank makes me sick. Only a truly vile person would let these drugs onto the streets. But he's worse than that. This is a man whose wife over-dosed on Oxy, whose daughter has devoted her life to combat-ting addiction. I'm awake now and fantasizing about a world in which Frank Christensen is dead.

"So, instead of destroying the product, he'll sell it back to the streets. But there has to be a trail. Won't the factory workers know? It will be suspicious if the plant isn't running."

"That's what I haven't figured out yet," Avi says. Then he motions back to his computer screen. "But I had to wake you up. Frank and Charlie are both scheduled to tour one of the plants in three days' time. I think something's gonna go down.'

"Hey, baby," I say, smiling in spite of my fatigue. I'm bitter as hell about all I've found out, but Darby doesn't need to know about my foul mood.

"Hey."

Hearing the smile in her voice kills me a little. She's been in a better mood since Chicago, and since we talked about her coming to Sydney. But, when she does come, what I tell her will destroy her happiness.

"Have you booked your ticket yet?"

"No, but I've been looking at dates."

"I was wondering whether you think you can get Thanksgiving off."

"I can..." she begins with a question in her voice. "Since I worked it last year, I automatically have it off this year. I was gonna book for the first week in December. I figured that later would be better than sooner for you since you have a big deadline that week. Since it's not a holiday in Australia, I didn't think it would make a difference to you."

"The deadline was moved up," I lie. "Do you think you can come sooner?"

"Sure." And her voice is happy again. But I can't let her think it will be all sweetness and light.

"There's something else...Avi's getting closer to figuring out why Frank won't let go of the redevelopment project on the South Side."

"What's he thinking?"

"Gimme a week." I remember the first conversation we had about this on Lake Shore Drive and I don't want to lie to her. "I should know something by the time you come to visit."

❧

This time I wake up on my own. The sun is setting and I realize I'm hungry. Avi and I stayed up well past sunrise trying to figure out Frank's connection to the drugs. When I realized that he'd been up for more than twenty-four hours on top of being jet lagged from the flight, I insisted that both of us take a break.

I head to the kitchen and look in the fridge. When I see that I have a huge container of fresh basil, I pull it out. I'm pretty sure there are pine nuts in the cabinet and I decide that I'll make pesto. Cooking relaxes me. It always ties me to fond memories of cooking with my mom as a kid. I still remember the yellow stool I used to stand on when I was really little—too little to reach the countertop—and my mother let me help her fix our dinner.

Avi shuffles in as I'm draining the spaghetti and he looks at me gratefully as I set a huge plate of pasta in front of him. He is multitasking—clicking around on his computer as he eats to see whether anything else is happening, when I have a thought.

"Can you hack into the plant's computers?"

He gives me an 'are you serious?' look.

"I still don't think he can fool the employees."

"It wouldn't be a secret that the plant will stop producing steel," Avi argues.

"But if he wants the staff he keeps to go along with it, they have to think they're destroying drugs. Even if the product is fake, they have to believe the story."

"So, he opens the plant a few days a week, gets them to destroy a few hundred pounds of sugar pills..."

"Except we still don't know how he transports the real inventory to Chicago. There will be no explanation for why so many trucks are still leaving the plant."

"It's an industrial plant. Trucks could be coming in full of supplies for the destruction process and leaving empty."

"Let's at least see whether he's fired any employees."

Twenty minutes later, Avi has hacked the payroll provider used by at least three of Frank's plants. He's downloaded a bunch of data and I watch him pivot it out in Excel.

"You were right about him firing workers," Avi says as he scans through the data. "Looks like payroll expenses dropped by about seventy percent. Every week was the same for at least a year, until this week." He points at the screen. "This week, he paid out ten times the usual."

"Severance," I speculate.

"Then, the following week, it drops down to around a quarter of the original average."

"Scroll over?" I request, wanting to scan a bit farther, to look at what the average is now. "Right here," I say, as I see the average ramping up. "What's happening?"

Avi sees it too. "Good question."

Half an hour later, we've made a discovery. He's hired a new crop of employees, all living at addresses on the South Side of Chicago, a two-hour drive away. They're earning minimum wage and we ran checks on a few of them. They're mostly ex-cons, a lot of them drug felons.

"This is smart," Avi murmurs, a bit of admiration in his voice. "He gave the dealers legitimate jobs. I'm guessing these kids come down a couple times a week, clock into the factory, hand off the money, and leave with a trunk full of drugs in their own cars."

"That's why no one knows who the kingpin is," I conclude. "Instead of getting product through the crime organizations, the gangs are getting it directly from the source. If anyone comes poking around, the fake employees lie and the real employees verify that the operation is running."

"Which handles the authorities," Avi continues, "...but doesn't handle the mob. They've gotta be trailing the dealers by now. If they haven't already, they're close to finding the source."

"How often does Frank tour his facilities?" I ask, knowing that Avi's thinking what I'm thinking.

"I couldn't find anything else on their schedule that was obviously related to this. If they're going there in person, they're meeting with someone."

"Be careful," I tell Avi, regretting for the third time today that I had insisted on seeing proof.

An hour ago, I tried again to talk him out of going to Chicago. When this started, I had no idea that getting evidence would lead us down a path this dangerous. I know all I need to, and with what we've just learned, I know it's enough to tell Darby. But Avi won't relent. And I realize he's no longer working for me. Huck was for me. Sweeney was for me. But not this. The South Side belongs to both of us. And he wants to take it back.

I do, too. It's where I'm from. I care about the people who

live there. I don't want all the progress that's been made to go to shit. But it's bigger for Avi. His mother's life—and his own child-hood—were ruined by the crack epidemic. And that's what this could turn into. Through Darby, I know better than most what damage opioid addiction could cause. Letting Frank's supply flow into the South Side would have an impact for generations.

"You need to stop watching *Columbo*," Avi says with a smile. "No one does stakeouts sitting in their cars with a pair of binoc-ulars anymore. I run a high-tech operation. The surveillance van will be more than a mile away from the site."

"I know, I know." I repeat what he spent the car ride telling me about. "Drones."

His setup is astonishing. Even as we speak, Avi's got a guy who works for him in Washington—a kid named Philip—driving his van to meet him in Chicago. He'll use satellite imagery to figure out where to place the cameras. Our primary goal is to be able to confirm who attends. He'll fly the cameras in and out using drones.

This means we'll be able to get shots of individual people as they get in and out of their cars to identify who attends the meeting. Avi and Philip will arrive as early as possible, they'll land the cameras in strategic locations. On top of low roofs and underneath the large tractor trailers that satellite data tells us have been parked in the loading docks for weeks.

Despite my apprehension, I know it's a good plan. We'll see what happens as it happens and back up the feed. Just in case anyone is paying attention—not that we think anyone will be—they'll use jamming technology to mask the transmission signals. No one will even know that anyone's looking, let alone who the spy may be.

I pull up to the curb at the airport and give Avi a long look. "Be careful," I say again.

He nods and gets out of the car. Before he closes the door, he reaches into his bag and hands me a folder. "The other file you asked for," he says.

Chapter Eighteen

CAT'S IN THE CRADLE

I stare blankly at my screen as I listen to the machine whir. Before I loaded it into the scanner, I refused to look at a single page. The second I realized what it was, I called Bex. This is something she and I need to do together. That's why I'm sitting here listening, as my document feeder pulls each leaf in to slowly scan the pages. When it's done, I'll e-mail a PDF to her.

"Avi?" she guesses when she picks up my call. We're on video and I sent her a text ten minutes ago to have her check her e-mail.

I nod. "Where's Ella?"

"I called the babysitter. They went to Chuck E. Cheese"

"Good." I don't want her to be around to overhear any of this.

When I see Bex pick up a page, I realize that she's printed them. It's my cue to get started, so I do the same. The first page has the basics; legal name, age, birth date, current and previous occupations and addresses. It's a lot of information—more detail than I've ever known about this man, but there are at least thirty more pages, so I dig in.

Avi has, literally, started at the beginning. This first page is a copy of my father's birth certificate. His name is Michael Lewis Blaine and I've always hated that I was named after him. I knew my mom was twenty when she had us and that he was a few years older than her. The certificate confirms what we've always been told. I just turned thirty-two. A few weeks from now, he'll be fifty-five. That means he was twenty-six or twenty-seven when he abandoned us, some five years younger than I am now.

I recognize the town he was born in. It's a rural town downstate. You pass a sign for it on the way down to Urbana if you get off the highway and take the state roads. Now, I can't imagine that he didn't grow up poor or middle class. Nothing like the rich white guy I had always envisioned from his address. There's something else about his birth certificate. It's his mother's maiden name that is Blaine. She is listed as single—seventeen when she had him. The father is listed as unknown.

I hear the sound of pages flipping and I realize Bex is moving on. From what I can tell, she's a few pages ahead of me, so I keep going. He has no criminal record, no lawsuits, not even a speeding ticket. So far, he seems a little boring. Even his medical history is clean.

"I guess he doesn't need a kidney," I quip, but when I look up, her face is serious, and she doesn't react.

Next is his work history. He's held down steady jobs for at least the past ten years and I feel a little queasy when I see that his career relates to art. He's a dealer with an auction house I've been to before. We used to joke that my mom couldn't draw a circle with a compass. Now I know for sure where my artistic talent comes from.

The next page is another birth certificate. We've always known he left us for his second family. He got a woman pregnant when we were three. I read two more birth certificates for two more children and focus on the dates of birth. Each sibling is three or four years younger than the last, which means that the youngest is ten years younger than us.

I look up at Bex when I sense something is wrong—she's

stock still and silent, and no longer reading. But she's not looking up at me, either. Not looking anywhere, really.

"Look at the mothers' names," Bex says.

So I lay each birth certificate side by side, in chronological order. Jennifer Blaine. Heather Blaine. Daniela Blaine. We were just the first.

"You were right." Bex's voice is shaking with anger when she speaks again. "We're not getting anywhere near this."

I'm stress eating. Clean out of Kit Kat, I've defaulted to Pixy Stix and full-sugar Coke. It's so delicious. *Too* delicious I rarely let myself indulge. But I'm nervous as hell and not much help to Avi and Philip from so far away. My computer shows a split screen of rotating monitor views and they've got me by phone, on speaker, in the van.

I'm not good at waiting. I never have been, and I need some sort of distraction. I can't dwell on the danger they'll be in if they're discovered, and what will happen in four days when Darby lands in Sydney. If I don't give myself something to do while I wait for this to unfold, I'm going to think too hard about my own father, and how badly this news will hurt Darby.

"Frank's plane landed," Philip confirms. We've been waiting for this. He's hacked into air traffic control and just got information about the tail on Frank's private jet. We still don't know who he's planning to meet and Avi's stayed away from his mob informants.

A drone that we set by the side of the road, across the street from the security gate at the entrance, has been set up to capture the makes and models of the cars that enter, and their license plates. That will be our first indication of who's coming and going if we don't get good shots of men coming in and out of cars. If they're angled strangely, or wearing hats, IDs could be difficult. And since Avi's still working on hacking into the camera feeds inside the factory, this may be all we have.

The first car—the one we believe carries Charlie and Frank—is useless. It's a limo with a license plate that points to a taxi service that's headquartered forty miles away.

"He's going to be on the Republican ticket," I say. "Shouldn't he have a secret service detail or something?" I ask.

"Not until the nomination is official," Avi murmurs.

The car makes its way down a long gravel driveway that kicks dirt up around its shiny black finish. I'm holding my breath when the car stops and the doors open. I knew it was going to happen, but my heart still leaps into my throat when Charlie Sweeney steps out of the car. Frank follows, and three other men get out. Unlike Frank's lean frame and Charlie's heavyset one, these other men are wide, thick and stony-faced. These last three are obviously part of their security team.

Frank and Charlie are chatting jovially. It sickens me to see both of them, but their lightness is a good sign. It means that they feel good going into this meeting. They don't suspect they're being watched. And they're confident they have the upper hand.

I've been thinking about it. Most likely, the mob will simply want a piece of the action. Sure, Frank's operation cut into their business, but ultimately, the drug-runners win when more customers are addicted to drugs. If Frank had offered distribution to the crime families first, and tried to get them in on the racket, they may not have been inclined to negotiate a deal. But Frank's shown his power. In a way, he's got them by the balls.

We have no idea what time anyone else is set to arrive. It's speculation that anyone else is even coming. But Frank and Charlie's calendars were blocked off from three to seven. So we wait.

It's another forty-five minutes before another car slows and makes the turn into the factory gate. And it's not just one car. It's a caravan. Three black Suburbans that have windows with very dark tints. Philip is already running the plates as the cars make their way down the long driveway. We don't recognize any of the registrants specifically, but they're all Russian names.

"He's making a deal with the Russians," Avi says.

But I'm not sure. I have another theory. If the organized crime bosses were trying to form an alliance, the Russians have disincentives to make a side deal. We don't know what triggered this meeting, or who approached whom. The Russians could be just as easily be negotiating on behalf of all the other families as he could be set on cutting them out.

Time passes. I ingest an astonishing amount of candy. From all the Coke I drank, I have to pee twice. I look at my watch for the forty-third time. Philip has been crunching on a bag of Cheetos and the sound is driving me nuts. It annoys me that he and Avi look perfectly calm.

Ten minutes after they enter, Avi is into the plant's interior camera feed. The only ones he can get into are the ones that show what's going on, on the industrial floor. It doesn't have audio, and no one's on the floor anyway. It corroborates what we already knew. This is a business negotiation—not a plant tour.

"They've been in there for nearly an hour," I say when I can't take it anymore.

"They'll be out," Avi says calmly. "Let's just see what happens."

What happens next happens very quickly. The Russians who entered the building an hour earlier, leave. One of them shouts angrily over his shoulder. It earns him a glare from one of Frank's security guards, who brings up the rear in the long line of men who have just filed out of the building. Clearly, the guard is there to see them out.

Nobody looks happy. The Russians pile into their Suburbans, turn around on the pavement, and speed back up the gravel path. At the same time they turn onto the main road, Frank and Charlie emerge. This time, as they make their way back toward their waiting car, they appear to be bickering.

I watch in silence as I see the video feeds show the car speeding back up the road. Philip is clicking away at his computers and to be honest I have no idea what he's doing. When I finally turn to Avi, he's looking back at me.

"Something went wrong," he says.

I'm just walking back into my office from the break room when I hear the chime of my calendar through my computer speakers, a reminder that it's eight forty-five. It's set up as a recurring daily meeting, one designed to alert me in case I'm working late. If I don't order now from the one restaurant around here that's still delivering, I'll be stuck without food all night.

If I'm ever still in the office at this time of night, chances are I already feel like shit. I've probably been drinking coffee, eating candy and will have trouble keeping my energy up if I choose something too heavy. So even though I'm starving, I order a huge salad and a grilled salmon filet on the side. Since I will literally be pulling an all-nighter in order to get my project done by the time Darby shows up day-after-tomorrow, I'm looking forward to taking a break. I've been marking up designs for so long that my neck is getting tired.

Darby had been right. I do have a big deadline this week. Plans for the scale models of the first two Kensington hotels need to be submitted to the vendor by tomorrow. From our detailed design renderings, they make miniature models of our projects—delicate glass buildings, tiny art installations, and little acrylic trees. It's easy to look at flat drawings of a project, but it's not until clients see the model that the concept comes alive. It will be our first major deliverable—our first chance to impress the client.

My job now is to give the last round of feedback, and to itemize details I want worked into the scale model. Before I leave, I need to clear my schedule—to delegate where necessary, and to ask Kat to move whatever else can be handled after Darby leaves.

Andrew, meanwhile, coordinated an adorable rental for us in Crescent Head. Beyond this weeklong getaway, I'm hoping to convince her to come back in January, as we had originally planned. This week will be all beach, and if she wants to see more of Sydney, we can do it when she comes back there.

When I sit down at the table in my conference room a minute later, my stomach actually growls from the smell of my food. My salmon is still warm when I take a huge first bite—it lays in one piece atop my greens. I'm already craving the second bite as I reach for the remote to turn the TV on. The morning news show on CNN is telling me that last month, the economy gained 196,000 jobs when I hear the breaking news drumbeat.

For a moment, I stop wolfing down my food. When the intro screen disappears, I read the chyron at the bottom of the screen and it registers before Wolf Blitzer can say it.

"We're joining you from CNN studios in New York with breaking news. The U.S. Senator from Illinois, Frank Christensen, is dead."

Chapter Nineteen

GET HERE

I swipe my phone out of airplane mode the second my flight touches down and a full three and a half minutes before a saccharine voice over the loudspeaker invites me to. Alerts and text messages slow my progress toward checking my voicemail.

Nothing.

Backtracking, I scan my e-mail for anything from her, reviewing my texts and direct messages just in case she's sent me anything since they turned the in-flight Internet off thirty-five minutes ago. With nothing at all directly from Darby, I cycle back to what other new messages may have come through Andrew or Kat.

I don't expect much from Kat—I was supposed to be off now anyway. She still doesn't know that I left the country, or about the circumstances surrounding my departure. The lone e-mail from her holds the only thing I care about—a paraphrased message: "Darby called. She says she needs to talk to you urgently and wants a callback ASAP. She sounded upset." Andrew's text is completely the opposite.

Darby's dad is dead. You need to get here NOW. I've got you on the first flight out.

I feel a pang of regret at having been so quick to get on a plane before I had a chance to tell anyone. I'd barely packed a bag. I have clothes in Chicago and if I hadn't left right away, I would've missed the first plane. It had been morning her time, and she'd worked a late shift, and I hadn't wanted to wake her just in case she didn't know. It had seemed wrong to interrupt what might be her last decent night of sleep.

There's something most people don't know about airlines. They only let you book connections they think you can make. For international flights, they force a layover of at least two hours in case the arriving flight is late. But I'd figured out that I could make an earlier connection if I was quick enough getting to the gate. So I'd booked a separate ticket, on the earlier connecting flight, and had to literally run to make it.

If I had missed that flight, I would have called her, but now I have been unreachable for eighteen hours. I'd rather have gotten here sooner than spoken to her sooner, though achieving both would have been ideal. I feel sick at the bit of news that Kat has delivered. Darby sounds upset—of course she is—but I ache to know how she's really doing. Her relationship with Frank has been complex and unsatisfying at best, but he was still her father.

I watched the coverage on live TV on the flight from Vancouver. The networks were careful to skirt the question of his cause of death—no one wants to call anything until it is confirmed. They're spewing bullshit excuses about notifying his family and waiting for an official statement. But I'm guessing there's more to it than that.

As usual, in the absence of any real facts to report, they're repeating stale information. It's the biggest news story in months. Now that the Republican ticket is in question, they've called in political pundits to comment on who Sanderson will choose as a replacement. With this much speculation, I know that Darby will be denied the courtesy of being left to grieve privately—cameras will be on her for days.

It takes longer than usual for me to disembark from the plane—having booked so late has found me in row 35—a far cry from the comfort and convenience of First Class. Under normal circumstances I'd have been the first person off of the plane. Ignoring my stiff joints and the crick in my neck, I make haste to get through customs and walk briskly to the meeting point the driver of my Town Car has named.

Once inside, I waste no time dialing her number but as suspected, it goes directly to voicemail. An automated recording curtly informs me that her voice mail box is full, and I am relieved. What was I going to say anyway? It feels inadequate to express any sort of condolences over voicemail and I don't want to feed her the same line as everyone else. Training my eyes out the window, I wonder again about what condition I will find her in. I know enough about her older, deeper wounds to anticipate that Frank's death will unearth unwelcome memories that are better left forgotten. I'm glad he's dead, and I can't find it inside me to feel guilty about it. He can't hurt her anymore.

A sense of déjà vu washes over me as the familiar scenery creeps by at what feels like a snail's pace. I don't miss the daily gridlock on the Dan Ryan from O'Hare to the Loop, but I do feel a sense of nostalgia as I pass certain landmarks. I think of late nights and greasy food at the Wiener Circle and of Whirlyball. I think of the robata grill we both loved as we passed the corner we would normally have turned off onto. Just as the Town Car passes The Four Seasons, my phone rings.

"Darby." I say her name as I pick up on the first ring, pausing for a moment. "I heard. I'm sorry."

"This is bullshit." Her anger is a bad sign.

"I know, baby," I soothe.

"It's being televised." She is seething. "The funeral's not for another three days and the goddamned paparazzi are in front of my house."

"It'll be an even bigger story if you don't show up."

She lets out a frustrated sound between a growl and an aimless yell that tells me just how upset she is about all of this.

"I fucking hated him."

Except some part of her didn't. Because anger and sadness are parallel emotions. And I know what it's like to hate yourself for giving a shit about your low-life father.

"It's over. You never have to see him again."

"Fuck my life," she groans.

I hear her shaky breathing on the other side of the phone. The car rounds the corner of her street and there are, indeed, paparazzi outside her house. I motion to the driver to go around to the back alley.

"I wish you were coming." Her voice breaks then.

"Of course I'm coming. Someone has to make sure you wait 'til everyone's gone before you spit on his grave."

Shakily, she sighs. "I feel like shit asking you to spend 24 hours each way getting here just so you can hold my hand for half a day and suffer through disingenuous speeches and funeral bullshit."

"I already made up my mind." I motion for the car to stop.

"It's me who's supposed to be getting on a plane right now. We're supposed to be lying on a beach somewhere..."

I grab my garment bag and my duffel, key in the security code to her back gate, and shuffle up the kitchen steps.

"Are you trying to talk me out of coming?" I interrupt.

When I hear her sniffle my arms ache to hold her.

"Because I'm on the back steps. So you'd better open the door."

ॐ

I'm kissing her hair. She's been suspended in an extended slumber that is strangely deep—she's been out for fifteen hours. I slept next to her for about twelve of those, because I'm fucking exhausted, too. Now I lie awake, staring up at our butterfly painting, holding her in an attempt to make her feel engulfed. My arms pull us flush, my legs intertwine with hers, and I am attempting to offer her every comfort I can.

"I knew you would come."

Evidently, she's more awake than I thought.

"You needed me." I kiss her hair.

"I always need you." And it's a knife in my gut. I feel her tense.

"I'm sorry." We say it at the same time, her voice panicked, mine ashamed.

"Jinx," she says softly. She tips her head up to look at me, remorse in her wakeful eyes. "I didn't mean it like that."

"I know." I kiss her hair again.

"I just miss you."

"I know. I'm working on fixing that."

Her arms pull tighter around me. "I'm sorry this hijacked our vacation." It's the saddest I've heard her sound since I arrived. "You have no idea how much I was looking forward to being alone with you."

My traitorous dick stirs, but I try to shut it down. "We'll reschedule. And don't you dare apologize."

"I'm still not waiting 'till January."

I repeat what I've told her a thousand times. "The sooner, the better. Come any time you want."

We're quiet again, holding each other gently, touching each other softly. Since the moment I arrived, our bodies have been in constant contact. It's an odd exchange. I've come here to comfort her but being next to her like this has a healing effect on me. I think that's what both of us need right now—to heal. Our jobs are killing us. Being apart is hard. And things with Frank and the South Side keep dealing both of us blow after blow. We need to lick our wounds, to find comfort in one another, to leave this shit behind and build something brand new. She's right— holing ourselves up in a beach cottage in Australia can't come soon enough.

But there's no escaping the now. Even as I lie here with her, I'm playing a role. Until the sharks stop circling, I'm the gate-keeper. I'm keeping the phones and televisions silent. I'm keeping away the press, the cops and well-meaning, but distant, friends. I'm working with Frank's assistant to answer on Darby's behalf about funeral details and other inane logistics—access to the Evanston home for the repast and the reading of the will.

The only people who have penetrated this fortress are people from Darby's inner circle. People who are dear to her in some way, who have a role to play right now. Anne was by the day before I came with crass jokes and alcohol. Andrew came by with his little dog. And a sweet woman named Iris showed up with homemade comfort food and something for Darby to wear to the funeral. After we lounge for a while, I convince her to head downstairs and have something to eat. Just as we are finishing, she gets a call from Ben.

I jump on the opportunity to discreetly read what the newspapers are saying this morning. Darby doesn't need to be exposed to this right now, but I want to know what's being said about Frank's death. I pull out my laptop and angle it away from her, multitasking as I clean the kitchen. After I'm done, I go to grab my earbuds and settle onto a barstool to check out a few video news segments. When I realize Darby's talking about me, my ears perk up a little and I delay putting my earbuds in.

"Yeah...he got here yesterday. Showed up on my doorstep before I could even ask him to get on a plane...I know...I know...I know he does...yeah...this would be ten times worse if he wasn't here..."

When she says that last part, she glances over at me. Through the door that connects the two rooms, she has a clear line of sight. She knows I'm eavesdropping, but she doesn't look uncomfortable that I've heard. She even throws me a little smile.

"Well, he hated him, too. I never told you what happened. I'll tell you when you get into town...yeah...he's cute when he's worried...yeah..." She laughs at something then. "I know...he's waiting for me to start grieving." She looks over at me again.

When she walks into the kitchen a minute later, she tosses her phone on the counter. She's hung up with Ben, which means it's time for me to stop what I'm doing. I close the windows on my browser and shut my laptop. I do it casually, but with deliberate speed. I don't want her to see the headlines confirming that Frank's death has been ruled a murder. I'll have to find another quiet moment to talk to Avi about that.

"I'm not waiting for you to start grieving," I say gently.

"Yes, you are," she smiles again. "And it's okay. It's what everyone's waiting for—the mournful daughter. But you can stop worrying. I'm fine." She turns to open a cabinet above her and takes a few steps toward the fridge to fill a glass of water.

"You may have hated him, cupcake. But he was still your father."

Her hand halts in mid-air, the drink of water she was about to take temporarily forgotten.

"When someone hurts you enough...by the time they actually die, they've already been dead to you for a long time." Her eyes stay on mine as her glass completes its journey and she takes a deep swallow of the water.

I must not look convinced.

"I see grief every day, Michael. The families of addicts...they all know how it's gonna end. When the people they love die, there are only two kinds of survivors: the ones who are just starting to grieve and the ones who accepted it a long time ago."

She's telling me that she's already grieved. And in a certain respect, I know she has. But I think of my own father, who has also been dead to me for many years, and how being forced out of the blue to relive our relationship has dredged up a river of shit.

"So, what is it that you've accepted?"

"Hating him," she says simply. "Grieving for someone who has failed you is different from grieving somebody who loved you well." She's looking down at her fingers, playing with her glass in her hands a second before she places it back on the bar. She looks me straight in the eye. "Do you want to know the truth? When I got the call, I felt relief. It's all I've been feeling for the past three days. You may think I'm cold hearted for saying it, but I'm glad he's dead."

I don't think she's cold hearted, but I do worry that she's oversimplifying things. "It's not an either/or. You can be glad the shitty part of him is dead at the same time as you mourn the parts of him you loved."

She walks over to where I'm sitting and stands between my legs. My arms slide around her waist as she rests her arms on my shoulders. Her fingers stroke the short hair on the back of my head, just above my neck, and her touch feels so good.

"True…" she admits. With me sitting, she's slightly taller than me, looking down. "But I'm not avoiding my emotions, okay? Right now, relief is what I feel. Maybe I'll feel differently in a week. Who knows? So you can keep your handkerchief in your pocket. I'm still blazing mad over the media frenzy. But I won't be shedding any tears."

I study her for clues—for any tell that she's lying to herself about this, for any signs of bravado. "So, nothing more you found out about him could hurt you…" I test. "Like, if I told you he was tied up in human trafficking, or ran a child pornography ring, or that he was a drug lord or something…"

Realization dawns in her eyes and they narrow in recollection. "You were gonna tell me what was really going on, on the South Side."

"It's bad."

But nothing in her reaction shows fear or apprehension. She looks at me with something akin to pity and shakes her head. "Do you even remember how many times I tried to warn you off of crossing him? I know what he was capable of. We'd be up all night if I told you all the things I've seen him do to gain more status or make another buck. So, whatever this thing is you're not telling me...it's just details. You can't hurt me with what I already know."

Avi is here. He's been in Chicago since the meeting. It's hard to believe that everything I witnessed happened only four days ago. He stuck around to poke his other sources for information that would get us closer to knowing the truth. Piecing things together has been easier said than done. Avi's questioning can't be too obvious or direct. If it is, he'll blow his cover and get dragged into it.

We sit Darby down in her living room and start from the beginning. We tell her how it began—as an attempt to learn the identity of the kingpin. About figuring out it had to be an inside job. About the steel plants and the government contracts and all roads leading to Frank. She listens patiently, intently, asking all the right questions, and becoming convinced. When Avi pulls out his laptop and shows her video of the factory scene, she takes it better than I thought she would. It takes her a full five minutes to speak and she's still staring at the last frame of the video on Avi's screen. Her body is still, but I can see the fire, burning brighter with every passing second, in her eyes.

"I knew it." She finally turns to me. "I always knew this is how it would end for him. He's always been a bad man. He's always done business with bad people. And he's always been cocky enough to think he'd never lose." She shakes her head. The expression on her face is hard to read. "And he's still screwing me over from beyond the grave." She turns to Avi. "But I need to make it right. Will you help me?"

He says "Yes" at the same time I say "No".

"There's no need for you to get involved in this," I insist, signaling to Avi that I will deal with him later.

"She's already involved," he says gravely. And I don't like the understanding that's passing between he and Darby right now. What has he figured out that I haven't?

"I'm Frank's next of kin. Unless he cut me out of the will, I'm the new owner of those plants."

I let this sink in.

"I'm not letting those drugs on the streets. You know that, right? The businesses have legal access to confiscated drugs. The right thing to do is to destroy them."

"Now that the mobs see dollar signs, they're not gonna let this go. They may already be in cahoots with Sweeney," I say. "You can't let yourself be in danger from cleaning up a mess your father got you in, Darby. You have to get rid of those plants."

"So, find me someone." She stands up and turns to Avi. "Find me someone to sell the plants to, someone who will take them over and do the right thing. Who had the contracts before my father's company won them?"

"Different players," Avi says.

"Find out all the ones who were legitimately destroying the drugs. Get me those names, and I'll sell the plants back to them."

Chapter Twenty

WHAT GOES AROUND, COMES AROUND

She's sleeping deeply again, but I'm wide awake. I slip out of bed, take a shower, and get myself ready for the funeral. I want her to get rest, so I wait until the last possible moment to rouse her. I awaken her as I have so many times before, with my fingers combing gently through her gorgeous mane of red-brown hair.

"It's time," I say simply when her eyes open to mine.

When she closes them again, I can feel her sense of dread.

"The motorcade will be here in an hour," I explain apologetically.

An hour and fifteen minutes later, she's showered, donned the black dress and coat Iris brought her, and a ridiculously dramatic wide-brimmed black hat that I'm sure she wouldn't have worn under any other circumstance. I recognized it for the disguise that it is—it will add to the illusion that she's the appropriately mournful daughter. Never one to forget a single detail, I pass her large, stylish sunglasses that I find in her closet before sliding on a pair of my own.

It occurs to me for the first time in a long time what a striking couple we'll make, and how much attention my act of supporting her so publicly will garner. Darby is no longer just the late senator's daughter—she'll be a focal point of Frank's mysterious death, and is now the heiress to a far more notable fortune than the one she already possesses.

I take her hand then, and when I do, I get the distinct sense that the feeling of me steadying her is all that her consciousness can register. Outwardly, she is perfect, but I can hear that she is hollow inside. A motorcade complete with a police escort and all the state regalia awaits us, and after we climb into the limousine, she stares out the window, saying nothing. She seems eerily absent except for the determined grip with which she holds my hand. Despite what she says, I know that this will be hard and that I am the only thing that's grounding her. I feel grateful that I've gotten here so quickly, grateful that she has so willingly placed me in this role.

"Captain Obvious graces us with his presence."

I don't even see Anne walk up to me. I'm too busy hovering over Darby from a distance. From what I've gathered, she and Rich haven't spoken much since she fired him from her project. But he showed up and the two of them stand in the corner. It's the first time I've left her side all day, but it seems like they need to talk. I flip my eyes to Anne's for a split second before training them back on Darby. She seems fine for the moment, but I want to be ready the second that changes.

"It's written all over you, you know," she continues.

"It's not a secret." I'm not an idiot. I know what Anne is talking about.

"Then why haven't you told her?"

"How do you know I haven't?" It's useless misdirection. I have no doubt that Anne knows everything about what has or hasn't been said. I'm glad she was there for Darby, even when I wasn't, even if leaving us in more limbo than we need to be makes me kind of a dick.

"She needs to hear it. Even if it's over, she needs you to say it."

"She knows it's not over."

"No shit, Sherlock. She still needs to hear it."

I sigh heavily and look back at her. "I'm going to tell her. Soon."

"So, what's stopping you?"

"We're supposed to be on a romantic vacation together on the Great Barrier Reef. We were going to talk about things between us then."

Anne nods in understanding. "Then Frank ruined your plans by having the nerve to die."

"Among other things." I change the subject before Anne can push on that. "How bad is it at work?"

"This is a conversation you should be having with her."

"I know it is." I'm careful to soften my voice before I speak again. "But her father just died. So, can you cut me a break?"

Anne thinks this over for a minute. It doesn't take her long to spill, even though I can tell she doesn't like the idea of spreading Darby's business. When she does it's as I suspected.

"She buried herself in work as soon as you left. She thought it would pass the time. She bit off more than she could chew, then things got worse after Rich left. They also fired her boss, over the Huck thing. The new guy's okay, but it's a lot of change."

I glance back over at Darby and Rich, who seem to be chatting pleasantly enough, but my ears are listening to Anne.

"I don't think she's happy. I don't think all this is good for her."

Anne is trying not to glare at me—I know she's conflicted about whether I'm good for Darby. She blames me for Darby being unhappy and I can't be mad at her for that. For a year she leaned on me. I helped her beat Huck and all the shit her father pulled with Sweeney. We both know Darby would be better if I were still here.

"I know this looks bad." I might as well level with Anne. She can smell bullshit a thousand miles away and even though she hates me right now, we are allies to a common cause. "I know you think I abandoned her. But what we had before wasn't made to last. That arrangement was predicated on a promise that there would be no commitment. It had to die."

"You didn't have to try to kill her along with it."

Anne's words hit me hard. But I punch back. I'm not perfect, but I'm not the person she's making me out to be.

"I'd been in line for that promotion for months. She never would've let me fall on my sword. And don't forget—before I got Huck fired, Darby was looking too. I may have dealt the death blow, but it was both of our game."

Something changes in Anne's eyes and I think I'm winning her over.

"You were behind what happened with Huck?"

Shit.

"Officially? No. Unofficially? Yes," I admit. And for the first time, I see her smile. "I'm not out to break her heart. I'm out to win it. And it would be nice if you and me could be friends. Because what I want with her is permanent. And it's never good when the best friend and the boyfriend don't get along."

"You had me at 'unofficially yes'," she quips, her smile melting into an approving look. "And if you want it to be permanent, you'd better be more than her boyfriend."

"She doesn't believe in marriage."

"So, you'd marry her?"

Now Anne is testing me.

"I would propose today if I thought she'd say yes."

"Things aren't always what they seem with her," Anne says cryptically. "Being with you changed her. She's open to more than you think."

And before I can ask Anne to say more about that, the sound of a deep voice speaking Darby's name rips my eyes back over to check on her. Ben has just arrived.

❦

As I approach Darby and Ben, I don't like the stab of pain that rips through me as I witness their intimate hug. I know everything romantic between them is long since done, but it's their amazing connection that hurts. If a friend is all I can be to her right now, I selfishly want to be the best.

But I discard these thoughts as I approach, feeling guilty about them already. This will no-doubt be one of the most difficult times in her life, and I should feel grateful that so many people love her. Ben had been in some remote locale in Alaska for a story. It had taken two days to get a message to him, but when he'd received it, he'd come.

"Tami wanted to be here, but she's past her fly date," Ben is saying when I arrive. "The airlines make you stop getting on planes at around seven months."

"How's the baby?" Darby smiles a little.

"*Babies*," Ben clarifies with emphasis. "Twins." Ben shrugs in that nonchalant way of his, a second before he notices me. "Before long, I'll be calling your house to get advice from this kid."

Darby blinks. Ben is a sneaky bastard, one who knows good and well that I live in Australia. He's insinuated that "before long" Darby and I will be together. All before I've even had time to say hello.

"Hey, Man."

I step into him and we do the man hug thing, patting one another's backs and all. Rich has disappeared and for the next half hour, we are a united front, helping Darby manage a steady stream of mourners wanting to personally pay their respects. It's a mixed bag of some distant cousins, the Chicago elite and political heavy-hitters—everyone from the mayor, to a cast of Congress people from both sides of the aisle, to top leadership within the RNC. Most of them, she doesn't even know.

The mourners deliver their expected condolences, sharing

anecdotes about Frank or uttering comforting words. But, away from us, tongues wag in hushed whispers, speculating on the outcome of what is surely the political upset of the year. Sanderson himself is in attendance and is garnering at least as much attention as Darby. But I'm watching on the fringes— keeping my eyes out for Sweeney and observing who Darby pointed out as police detectives quietly eavesdrop around the room.

When I turn my full attention back to Darby, she is speaking to a woman who looks like neither a politician nor a Chicago socialite.

"Who was that?" My eyes follow the woman as she walks out the door.

"I stopped paying attention to the introductions an hour ago," Darby mutters tiredly.

I can tell her stamina is waning, and I'm seconds away from rescuing her. Before I can, Anne is there, insisting that she and Darby go for a walk. Ben is suspiciously quiet as we head to the bar.

"Did you know that Darby and I broke up five times?"

I shake my head. "I didn't."

"We officially broke up the summer before Freshman year. But then we'd see each other here and there. We kept hooking up and then we'd have to remind ourselves it wasn't a good idea."

I say nothing.

"It took me a long time to admit that it was over for real. And, to this day, letting her go was one of the hardest things I've ever had to do." He gives me a pointed look.

"This is the shittiest pep talk you've ever given me."

Neither of us cracks a smile. If he's saying what I think he's saying, he's telling me to leave her alone.

"When it was really over," he continues slowly, "I made her a promise. That I would be her best friend and her protector— that I would be the man in her life—until she met the person she was really supposed to be with. And I promised her that, on her wedding day, I would kick Frank to the curb and be the one to walk her down the aisle."

Ben takes a long sip of his drink as I set mine down. Realization is setting in. He's not warding me off. He's giving me his blessing.

"We both know you're never getting her in a white dress. And this may be the closest I'll ever get to giving her away. You've already filled my shoes in all the other ways. Now go make her happy."

❧

The second we step back into the limousine to return to her house, her head finds my chest and I wonder whether she will cry. When I kiss her hair, she squeezes my hand even harder. I get the sense that she barely heard the words spoken at the church, could not feel the cold at the cemetery, and barely registered the countless condolences offered by the other mourners. The only evidence that she was present was the fact that her hand barely left mine, that her body never failed to seek me out. I am glad that the repast is over, grateful that she is mine again.

I think back to what happened at his graveside. Frank's coffin had been lowered into his final resting place at her family's private cemetery. Form dictated that Frank be interred in the mausoleum that bore her mother's name. Her mother had been cremated, but the crypt had been built in her memory, and it was where her father was intended to be laid.

That he be buried elsewhere was the one thing Darby had insisted upon. She'd made certain that the grand sepulcher remained pristine and bore only her mother's name. She had chosen for Frank to be buried in a far corner of the cemetery with a simple tombstone, not in a vault, but deep in the ground.

The other mourners had gone. We were alone save for the limousine driver who stood, unseeing, by the empty road. Only then did Darby turn her back on Frank's grave and walk to put the single flower in her hand on her mother's tomb. The only tears I saw her cry were shed when she placed that pink rose.

Back at her house, she flops down wordlessly on her bed, still strangely catatonic, I silently remove her clothes. First one shoe, then the other, then each leg of her panty hose, then I tug down the zipper on her dress. Even like this, she is unimaginably beautiful. After running the water for a bath, I add some jasmine-scented salts before easing us inside. We sit that way for more than an hour, shoulders-deep in the just-hotter-than-warm water. I pull her against me, skin to skin, her back to my chest, my arms tight around her, and my cheek touching hers.

Chapter Twenty-One

TURN THE PAGE

I'm dreaming. Her soft breasts are pressed against my chest and her fingers stroke the back of my scalp in a way that is giving me shivers. I can feel her breath on my lips as we nuzzle our noses, and a moment later, her tongue is slow-dancing with mine. When her delicate foot runs up the length of my calf, I shiver again. It is then that I notice my arms are around her, and I pull her closer. I pull away from her juicy lips long enough to trail kisses down her jaw, and when I find that spot, I bite it and she whispers my name.

I don't have dreams like this often, but when I do, they are delicious. This is, by far, the best one yet. This is usually when I wake up a little, slide my hands down my shorts and hold on to the dream as much as I can while I let myself finish. But this feels so good—so real—that I hold off, not wanting it to end.

I whisper her name. When she echoes mine, it sounds so close by that I do open my eyes.

"Michael." This time it's not a whisper. It's a delicate moan.

My lips are, indeed, on her neck and I'm dazed and blinking to get my bearings. Then I hear her next words.

"Don't stop." It's breathy and pleading and when she says it, she wraps both of her legs around one of mine and rubs herself against me until I can feel the dampness at her core. The way she's sliding herself against me has my neglected dick rock hard. It's so good that I lose my grip. The beast I know how to restrain when I'm awake has caught me unaware and wrestled free from his leash.

I do bite her again then, harder this time, groaning as my teeth sink into her neck, some strange fury coursing through me. When she answers with her own violence—her teeth tugging my ear and her nails digging into my shoulders, I know this will be nothing like the last time.

"Now," she commands, joining me in tugging down my boxers. My free hand palms her breast through the sheer camisole she's wearing and when my boxers are off, I slip the strap off of her shoulder. I'm so impatient to get my mouth on her that I begin to suck her nipple through the fabric—but only until I can slip the neckline of the camisole down. As I suckle her bare skin, she hisses, and her fingers grip the back of my skull. I am relentless in teasing her with my lips and teeth as we fumble to get her underwear off.

She pushes me away long enough to rise onto her knees and her nipple breaks free of my mouth with a soft little pop. I mirror her motions pulling my own shirt off as I see her do the same. Before I can dive back in, she turns her back to me, catching my eyes from over her shoulder for a moment before she drops down to all fours.

It breaks me. And, a second later, I'm giving it to her the way I know she needs it. Her body guides me to that angle, to that rhythm, that will have her undone. Her breath commands me to keep her there until she aches for my permission. And when she surrenders to me in these sacred moments—rough or gentle, fast or slow, desperate or patient—she breaks me all over again.

We are insatiable. I'm hard again by the time we crawl our way into her shower, stopping on every wall, and every surface, to touch, and bite and kiss. Her soft screams match my loud moans as they echo off of her walls. No other woman has ever made me feel like this.

We don't slow down until the sun has risen. I could go again, but she'll be sore, and I want to be able to do this again later. Her lips are swollen and her hair is wild and we're both marked from nails and sucks and teeth. Before we sleep, I hear her whisper, "You're mine."

❦

On Friday, two police detectives come. They had questioned her briefly on the day I spent on the plane, but the investigation is progressing, and they seem eager to know more about Darby's personal life.

"We're sorry to bother you again, ma'am," the first detective says, "…but given the circumstances of your father's death, we need to ask you a few more questions."

"Okay," Darby says listlessly. She's been warm with me, but the detectives have turned her cold. And, despite all the sleep we've gotten, she still seems tired.

"Let me start out by saying that you're not a suspect—"

Darby interrupts with eerie calm. "So, you're ruling it a murder?"

The detectives look at one another. They're wondering why she doesn't know.

"We've been steering clear of watching the news," I explain, giving her hand a squeeze.

"Did your father have any enemies?" the first detective asks.

Darby's mouth melts into a subtle smile and she raises an eyebrow. "He was a politician," she says in a voice that indicates that fact alone should have allowed them to answer that question themselves.

"Can you name anybody in particular?"

"My father and I barely spoke to begin with. We had an agreement. He could call on me to attend social functions no more than three times a year. Several months ago, we had a falling out and stopped speaking entirely."

"What was the falling out about?"

Her lips set into a thin line and her voice fills with tension. "When I was fourteen, a colleague of his attempted to rape me. He covered it up. It was one of many reasons why we haven't been close. On the night of our falling out, he had asked me to attend a wedding to help him land some big donors for his presidential campaign. When I found out that one of the donors he wanted me to court was that old colleague of his, I told him to never talk to me again."

"I'm sorry I have to ask this, but who was his colleague?"

"Charlie Sweeney. His current Chief of Staff."

The detectives look at one another again.

"Do you know whether they had a good relationship?"

"I always assumed they did from the fact that my father kept him around. But, again, my father and I weren't close."

"Alright." Detective number one seems satisfied.

"Did he ever try to contact you after that?" the second one asks.

"My father? No."

"Did you ever contact him?"

"No. That was the last time I saw or spoke to him."

"I was a witness to the falling-out," I say then, concerned that even though they've said she's not a suspect, she's just admitted to a possible motive.

"What is your relationship?" the detective asked.

"We're dating," I say.

"Did you have any contact with the senator after that night?"

"No," I say. "That was the first and last time I ever saw him. I moved to Australia a few months after that wedding. I've been out of the country for the majority of the past five months. I came back a few days ago for the funeral."

This seems to satisfy the detectives.

"Did it strike you as peculiar that Charlie Sweeney did not attend your father's funeral?"

"I didn't notice that he wasn't there," she lies. "But I would've expected him to come." And then Darby does something I've never seen her do. She feigns innocence. "Is he a suspect?"

"We can't track him down. We're trying to figure out whether he should be."

Darby takes a breath, then hesitates. She's still acting. I can see it. But they don't. And she's brilliant. Because in that moment, I know she's trying to frame Charlie Sweeney.

"If there's something you think we should know, now's the time to tell us, Miss Christensen," the first cop says.

She shakes her head a little. "You want facts. All I have is speculation."

"Speculation about what?"

"All those years, I wondered why my father would stay friends with a man who tried to rape me. My father was not a forgiving man. He had a reputation for going farther than he needed to, to cut out people he didn't like. I always figured he couldn't cut Charlie Sweeney off because Charlie had something on him—you know—something big enough to end his political career."

"You indicated that Sweeney was a prospective campaign donor. Would your father have kept him close for his money?"

"Maybe..." Darby doesn't want to seem like she's leading them too much. "But it was more than a financial relationship. My father was always appointing Charlie to pretty high positions —you know—making him his right hand everywhere he went."

"Could Sweeney have been blackmailing him?"

"Honestly, I don't know. "I always got the impression that he enjoyed the status. But he wouldn't have been able to accept an appointment if my father made it to The White House. Charlie ran for mayor once. They dug up so many skeletons, he dropped out of the race. He was unelectable. He'd never survive a major appointment vetting."

Sweeney already had means and opportunity to kill Frank. Darby is hinting at motive.

"So, you think he approached your father for an appointment and was turned down."

"How well do you know presidential politics?", Darby asks. She's establishing her authority. "I've been around it since I was a kid. Promising appointments to certain donors is standard. Major donors with loose experience in politics rarely get appointments, but Charlie worked for Frank when he was the mayor, the governor and now the senator. He would see himself as a shoo-in for a cabinet appointment."

"Vice Presidents don't appoint cabinet members—Presidents do," the other cop observes.

"Yes, but if my father landed major donors who helped the ticket, he'd have a say. It would have been on the table for them to talk about where Frank would put him in his cabinet."

"If Sweeney was unelectable, wouldn't he know your father would be reticent to give him a prominent position?"

"A normal person would understand that." Her eyes turn cold then. "But some people are so entitled, they think they can have anything they want."

Saturday night comes too soon, and with it, my return trip to Sydney. I want her to come back with me now—if I really needed to, I could take this next week off from work and Darby could squeeze the hospital for a lot more bereavement days. But she knows I have the Kensington presentation this week and the truth is, there's still a lot more to be done with settling Frank's estate.

Once we figured out Darby might own the steel plants, we had the reading of the will moved up to yesterday. As expected,

Frank left Darby everything. Now Darby has Avi on an even bigger mission—to go beyond the steel plants and dig into all the companies Frank owned. She wants to know about all the ones that are illegitimate, then find new owners—honest ones—for those businesses too.

Sweeney still hasn't turned up, and from a longer-term surveillance system Avi put in, he knows the steel plants are closed. He has several days of footage showing employees being turned away at the gate. We had always assumed that Frank and Charlie weren't a part of everyday management, so it's not clear who would have halted operations, or why.

There are still enough unanswered questions to make me uneasy about being gone. Darby has agreed to move into my apartment for now, and to do whatever else Avi tells her to in terms of security. But I'll feel better when this is all over and she's with me in Sydney.

And so we stand again, three hours before my flight is scheduled to board, inside my entryway this time, saying our goodbyes. I don't like the déjà vu of it all. What I won't promise her yet, but what I promise myself, is that this will be our last goodbye.

"Thank you," she murmurs, leaning her forehead against mine.

"Don't thank me. This week was a total disaster." I caress her cheek. "The only good thing that came of it was seeing you."

"And taking down a major drug operation," she adds casually.

I smile. "Don't forget about the part where we framed someone for murder."

"I did the framing. You did the shutting up. He deserved it. He's not an innocent man." She looks at me like I'm going to object.

I laugh a little. "What? You're not gonna hear any opposition from me."

"Maybe it's time we put away our masters' degrees...Join Avi. Buy cool outfits. Spend the rest of our lives fighting crime...you know you love that vigilante justice shit." She's still smiling play-fully, but I'm still stuck on the part where she said 'the rest of our lives'.

"Don't tease me..." I warn.

"I'll come as soon as I can."

Chapter *Twenty-Two*

RUMORS

Apparently, we're deeply in love and getting married in June.

I hear the chime of the text come in over the sound of my music and nearly fall off of my treadmill when I read it. The Stop button decelerates my pace too quickly and it nearly causes me to wipe out. Heart racing, and not just from my run, I rip my earbuds out and begin toweling off my face. I look back at the text, blinking hard, and wonder what the hell Darby is talking about.

A second later, a photo comes through. I can see her slender hand on the edge of the newspaper, holding up a section that contains the picture she wants me to see. It's an article on Page Six, the salacious and obviously speculative gossip column in the Daily News, and we are the feature. Another text comes in This time she's quoting something.

"Despite earlier claims that they were just friends, Darby Christensen and Michael Blaine confirmed suspicions that they are a couple when Blaine, a partner at Dewey and Rowe and a current resident of Sydney, Australia, appeared at her side on Thursday to escort her to the late Governor Frank Christensen's funeral. Sources tell us that, not only have the two quietly nursed a passionate long-distance romance, but are secretly scheduled to be married in Chicago in June."

Good Lord.

I dial her number, and don't wait for her to talk before she speaks.

"You'd better avoid baggy clothes. Next thing we know you'll be pregnant and it'll be spun as a shotgun wedding."

"Shit. I guess I ought to throw out that muumuu I was going to wear tomorrow. As big as that thing, is, they'd say we were having twins."

"And you'd better get some diamonds on your finger—at least five carats, or I'm the cheap bastard who didn't get you a decent ring. They'll rip me apart for that."

"I can't wear the ring, Michael. I'm already super-bloated from the pregnancy. Or wasn't that obvious from the pictures?"

I relax a little, relieved that my levity worked, or at least that she doesn't seem unhinged by the situation. I, however, am unhinged, though I hope I'm doing a fine job of hiding it.

"So, I guess this means the paps aren't off your back?"

"Not even close. But I guess I shouldn't complain. Dodging questions about this is better than dodging questions about Frank's murder..."

I cringe. "How are they treating you at work?"

"They're handling me with kid gloves," she admits. "They think I've been busy mourning."

"Do you feel any differently? Now that it's been a few days?"

I'm hesitant to mention again that she hasn't shown any outward signs of actual mourning. I know she is convinced that she's done with grieving, but I also know that it could take her months, if not years, to fully process what has happened. She thinks her tumultuous relationship with Frank will make it easier, but in the long run, it will only make things harder.

Darby sighs and I feel a little guilty. I don't want to push her too far.

"You're 10,000 miles away. You know I worry about you. I know you think it's stupid."

"It's not stupid—it's sweet." She's defending me now.

"Well, whatever you're thinking about Frank, it's not stupid either, so tell me, okay?"

"Okay," she acquiesces. "You're a pain in the ass," she grouses a second later.

"Not as big of a pain as you. Any news from the detectives?"

"No."

"What do you think happened?" Our theory about the Russians has been a dead end, and we've all been rethinking the possibilities.

"I dunno. Maybe one of the other cartels? Either way, he messed with the wrong person. And he got what he had coming."

Charlie Sweeney has been arrested for my father's murder.

I feel the text come in on the phone in my pocket. In meetings, I have it on Do Not Disturb mode. It's set to notify me in the event that only five people reach out. The most important is Darby—even if she only wants to reach me for something trivial, I want to know right away. The other four are Bex, Alex, Ella's school, and Dale.

But this isn't trivial. They've found Charlie. The man Darby tried to frame. The man who had been on the run.

Where'd they find him?

They didn't have to. He turned himself in and confessed to the whole thing this morning.

I excuse myself from the meeting. It's bad form. The client is here, and as Managing Partner, I'm expected to lend my attention. But my woman's in trouble and I couldn't care less.

"Tell me," I say, not waiting for her to speak when she picks up. My heart breaks a little when I realize she's been crying.

"I saw his confession. The detectives called me in. Charlie told them about the contracts and admitted that they were both involved in reselling the confiscated drugs—he said they argued about what to do when they started receiving threats from the mob, and that when they did, Frank pulled out a gun. He said that Frank's death was accidental."

"He's going for manslaughter," I conclude.

"That's Plan B," she says. "Plan A is to make a deal. I'm betting he wants to trade information about other crimes for a lesser sentence—maybe just racketeering. He knows every skeleton in Frank's closet. They need me to cooperate by giving them access to information about the illegitimate businesses I inherited."

I sigh.

"What do you think?", I ask her.

"He was definitely there. He gave them details about the crime that checked out—where it happened, where on his body Frank was shot…"

"But you don't think he did it."

"No."

I think about this. About why he would turn himself in. If he was resourceful about it, a man of his means and shady connections could have disappeared.

"Why?"

"If he can see his way into a white-collar prison instead of maximum security, he'll be safer in there than out here."

And now I get it. She thinks the mob is after him. That Sweeney is afraid they'll do the same thing to him as they did to Frank. And that making a deal is a better option to getting killed.

"Is that enough for you?" She knows what I'm asking. She cares more about justice than she cares about truth. And we share the opinion that Charlie Sweeney deserves to be locked up for the rest of his life.

"He'll get off, Michael." And I hear the bitterness in her

voice. "Reduced charges will have him out in five years. But now that he's close to being punished for at least some of his crimes... I don't want to see him win."

"You shouldn't be alone. I'm coming," I say with determination.

I'm already back at my desk and I begin to log onto my computer. I can't remember whether Kat was at her desk when I passed just seconds ago. I'll find her, wherever she is, and have her book the next ticket.

"No," Darby protests immediately. "It hit the press an hour ago. The paparazzi will be relentless. Please...let me come there. You were right before. I need to get out of this place."

My fingers still. *Thank fuck.* "I'll book you on the next flight."

She actually chuckles at that. "I think I can afford a ticket."

"Then tell me when you're coming. I'll pick you up from the airport. I'll take time off. It'll just be you and me."

She sniffles yet again, and her voice is weak again the next time she speaks. "Okay."

Chapter Twenty-Three

REUNITED (AND IT FEELS SO GOOD)

I push the refresh button on the browser on my phone for the tenth time in so many minutes. The app keeps telling me that her flight is on time, but I'm waiting for the status to change to 'landed'. I know the Sydney airport like the back of my hand. I know exactly where to wait for her the second she clears customs. My body hums with anticipation. I know it's real, but I can't wrap my head around the fact that in a few minutes she'll be in my arms. I've waited for this moment—for time for just the two of us—for so long.

No sooner do I see what I've been hoping for on my phone than do I look up to the sliding automatic doors. She's among the flood of people emerging, and all I can think is that she's beautiful. Seeing her in the flesh, her reddish hair forming a flowing halo around her face as she scans the crowd for me, stirs me in all the expected ways. I can see the instant she spots me, her face brightening involuntarily as her lips melt into a relieved smile. When her clear ochre eyes meet mine, it's everything.

I begin walking toward her then, my body taking over without me making the conscious decision for it to do so. At some point, I realize that I'm smiling, too, and it feels like relief when she practically jumps into my arms. We hug for a long time, saying nothing, my fingers in her fragrant hair and my kiss returning over and over to her lips. The reunion is so fierce, so desperate, that any bystander watching would not have believed that we saw one another just two weeks before.

"Take me home," she says in a way that feels loaded with meaning.

So I do. I carry her bags and usher her to my car. It's an Audi Spyder convertible that I can't wait to drive with the top down when I take her to the coast. I hold her hand every moment that I'm not shifting gears.

I can't seem to keep my hands off of her—even in the elevator—and I press another soft kiss to her forehead as we are whisked up to my high-rise apartment. The code I use to gain entry to this penthouse is the same code I use to get into the one in Chicago. I wonder whether she's ever caught on to the fact that 3-2-7-2-9 spells out D-A-R-B-Y.

I give her a brief tour and soon enough, we end up in my bedroom. I can see that this space is her favorite and I like the way she runs her fingers across my shirts when we enter my closet. When I set her suitcase down on my dressing bench, I am irrationally eager for her to unpack it. I don't want her to live out of her suitcase for the next two weeks—I want any space that belongs to me to be ours.

It's just past 11PM in Sydney, which means that it's around 8AM in Chicago. Though she must have slept on the plane, she's spent the past twenty-one hours traveling. What worries me more than jet lag, though is her obvious exhaustion from all she's been through. Her father's death, and Sweeney's resurfacing has given her the one-two punch. And it's clear to me now that she's in front of me that she is completely drained.

"Tell me what sounds good," I say, turning her around so that her back is to my chest and we're looking at each other in the large dressing mirror in my closet. "Dinner, movie, shower or sleep?"

"I'm not really hungry." I let my eyes scan over the reflection of her body. I noticed in Chicago that she's looking gaunt and wondered how well she was eating. I hate when she doesn't eat. "But a shower and a movie sounds nice."

When I show her into my bathroom, she actually smiles, motioning toward my rainfall shower and Japanese toilet.

"Please tell me this isn't why you picked this apartment."

I shrug, unable to stop myself from smiling now that she has. "I had them installed."

"You're ridiculous."

I let her shower then, trying not to focus on the fact that there is a naked Darby twenty-five feet away from me. While she dresses, I take off my street clothes and put on pair of pajama pants and an undershirt. I sit on my bed with my back against the headboard pretending to read the book I've plucked off of my bedside table. But I can't concentrate. She's finally here and I'm determined to comfort her, but I'm not sure yet what she needs.

My heartbeat quickens when I hear the shower shut off, and a minute later, the pad of her footsteps on my closet floor. I don't dare look, but I know when she unzips her suitcase and rummages around. When she emerges, she's wearing the Tufts Crew t-shirt I'd slipped into her closet before I left, and a pair of panties. Nothing more.

I would have had trouble not staring, not dwelling on this, if I hadn't noticed something else. Tears are in her eyes and she looks like she's going to break down. Setting my book down on the bed, I go to her, seeing that she's trying desperately not to cry.

My arms around her is all it takes. In an instant, she's sobbing. It is so raw, so heartbreaking, so wracking as her body shakes that it seems like she'll never stop. But I don't want to placate her. I want her to let it out. She can cry for days if she wants to. This isn't only about Sweeney and she's been holding it back for a very long time. She clings to me fiercely, as if I'm her lifeline.

"I'm so scared," I hear her sob finally.

"I know, baby," I soothe.

"I don't know what to do."

"We'll figure it out."

This makes her cry some more.

"Will you hold me?" she asks finally, after she's cried for a bit.

"I'll hold you all night long."

A minute later, we're in my bed, her cheek to my chest, and my arms are around her again. She's still sniffling, but her sobs have subsided. And so I wait, knowing that she's gathering her courage, knowing there's much that she has to say.

"It's like he's haunting me."

I kiss her temple. I don't know whether she's talking about her father or Charlie Sweeney. She can't seem to be rid of either of them.

"Why couldn't I have had a normal father? Not even a great father. Just one who cared enough about me to leave me out of the messy parts of his life?"

There's not a single word I can say in Frank Christensen's defense. He'd starved her of love and kindness. He'd used her all his life. He'd left her his money, which was the one thing she didn't care about. And, by leaving her all of his criminal enterprises, he left her with a huge mess.

I've never really told Darby about my father. Even now, part of me doesn't want to compare a standard issue deadbeat dad with the epically evil Frank. Still, maybe hearing what a piece of shit my own dad was will help Darby feel less alone.

"My dad had a second family," I reveal. "That's why he left us. He fell in love with another woman, and she got pregnant."

She's quiet for a few minutes, and I'm stroking her hair and enjoying the feeling of her in my arms. I'm supposed to be comforting her, but, as always, she has a relaxing effect on me.

"When was the last time you saw him?"

"He showed up at my mother's funeral. I made sure he knew he wasn't welcome."

She squeezes me a little then and I kiss her hair and hold tighter to her.

"A few months after that, he sent me a graduation card right after I got my Master's."

She brings her hand up to my chest and tips her head up to me then. "What did it say?"

"That he was proud of me. That he remembered what a smart kid I was. That he'd always known I'd do well. That he hoped to have a chance to get to know me."

Darby begins rubbing calming circles on my chest with her thumb. She can feel the emotion this is bringing up. I bring her fingers to my lips and kiss them to let her know that I'm okay.

"What got me was his return address. It was for a street on the Gold Coast. I looked his house up on Zillow. He lived in a million-dollar brownstone. I grew up in a tenement." I shake my head at the memory. "I snapped. I hadn't felt hatred like that for him since I was eight years old. But at twenty-one, I could do something about it. I was halfway across town, on my way to beat his ass, when Bex called. She knew that something was up."

"I take it you didn't kick his ass."

"No. Bex wisely reminded me that starting my professional career with a felony assault charge is not recommended. She graduated from SSA the same year as me, and she got a similar card in the mail a few weeks later. So we sat down and wrote him a letter."

"We told him off pretty good. To say that he'd always known we would do well, and to credit our success to how smart we were, without even mentioning my mother...it was just so insulting. We were middle class before he left. Because of him, we lived in poverty. A single mother raising twins on her own in a dangerous neighborhood? We told him the only card he should have ever written to any of us was a thank you card to our mother for raising his children, for doing whatever she had to, to make sure we could survive."

When I finish, Darby is still looking at me, some mix of surprise and respect in her eyes.

"Did you ever hear back from him?"

I sigh, working to calm myself down. Darby's in my arms and I want to focus on that feeling. "A few months after that, he sent a response letter. Neither of us wanted anything to do with it. It's never even been opened."

"Wow..."

"But he contacted Bex a couple months ago. He wants to be in Ella's life."

She sits up a little then. "That's big news...now I really can't believe you haven't told me any of this."

But I only shrug a little. "I didn't think there was anything to tell. I thought I'd grieved for him—that he'd been dead to me for a long time. But having all those old feelings dredged up showed me that I was wrong." I'm laying it on thick and both of us know it.

Darby raises an eyebrow. "So, basically, in Chicago, you were projecting displaced feelings about grieving for your own father onto me." She's using a joking tone to gently call me out.

"I'll admit to that if you admit you're not as resolved with all this as you thought you'd be."

"Touché." She settles back into my arms.

"So, what is Bex gonna do?"

"Avi ran a check on him and confirmed that he's not a psychopath or a criminal. But he *is* a serial cheater. Turns out my mother was the first of four wives he left only when he'd gotten the next one pregnant."

"Shit."

"Bex wants nothing to do with him, and there's no way in hell she's letting him around Ella."

"What about you?"

"I never even wanted to consider it in the first place. He skipped all the shitty parts," I say finally. Because that's what's really been bothering me. "And now that life is great for us, he wants in. We waded through shit for half of our lives. Now he wants to make amends and play with his grandkids."

"He wanted to make amends before," she says softly. "Now he's just trying again. I'm sure he wants a relationship with Ella, but maybe it doubles as a reason to get to know you."

I hadn't thought of this, but I can see she might be right.

"What would you do?" I ask.

"I don't know. But he's coming to you on his knees and giving you a shot at something that people with dads like ours almost never get." She looks up at me then. "Answers."

I settle back into her then, and we hold each other a little tighter. I wonder what it would have meant to her if Frank had ever once been willing to level with her. I think back to the one time I met him—how, after fifteen years of secrecy and shame—he still couldn't have a naked conversation, let alone had he ever tried to make amends. Darby is right, and it makes me feel petty, like I'm squandering something that I should treat as a gift. I don't have to let him back in, but maybe I've been wrong to dismiss whatever it is he has to say.

Thoughts of my father are replaced with thoughts of Darby and I see how much I've needed this. She's been a confidante to me in more ways than she knows. I miss our pillow talk, and holding her like this reminds me how starved I am for human contact, and for her unique companionship. It feels good not to be alone in Sydney anymore.

When we are out of greater Sydney and breathing the air of the countryside, I begin to taste the freedom I've been craving all these weeks. We are finally making our journey to Crescent Head. Darby hasn't spoken much since last night, but the silence between us is easy. I can see the drive is doing her good. For all the city living she's done, she relaxes into natural settings and loves things that are peaceful and remote.

The scenery is beautiful, and I enjoy the transition to every new terrain. The drive up the Pacific Highway takes us through verdant national parks that are punctuated with intermittent farming communities and small towns. From the way Darby opens her window, I can tell she is enjoying the smell of the salt air. She perks up a little, sitting straighter in her seat to take in the town when we enter it. She recognizes the name from the sign: Crescent Head - population 1,586.

"Wanna come with?" I ask, parking outside the general store. I've brought plenty of food and wine to stock our kitchen, but I want eggs and milk and other things that wouldn't have kept well on the journey. I'd have opted to buy them here anyway—there is no comparison between what you get in the city to this farm fresh goodness.

Inside, I leave her to her own devices as I navigate the store. I gather some nice-looking steaks and some really fresh fish and the accoutrements that will go with them. She's my favorite person to cook for and I want to indulge her every night with rich, savory dinners and amazing wine. When I find her again, she is shyly ordering some local cheese from a woman behind the counter. When she sees me approaching, the light returns to her eyes, and it fills me with hope and courage.

I can tell she will adore the cottage before we even park the car. It is idyllic, a small but utterly well-kept house on a stunning private beach. Wordlessly, I hand her the keys. I've seen pictures online and know what to expect but I want her to have a look. I watch with deep satisfaction as I observe her taking it all in from where I lag behind. The living room that looks more like a library, with its inlaid floor-to-ceiling bookshelves and bay window, the breakfast nook that sits in its own small turret with an ocean view, a cozy and inviting bedroom done in whites and grays. I see her delight compound with every moment.

After I've put away the groceries, whipped together a marinade for the steak I'll grill us tonight, and gotten our luggage inside, I go looking for her. Her shoes sit, abandoned on the back porch and she's left a trail of footprints between the cottage and the ocean. I follow them. She is knee-deep in water that is crystal clear and bathwater warm. I shift her hair to fall over one shoulder so that I can rest my chin on the opposite one. By the time I do, my hands are already around her waist.

"Watch the sunset with me?"

It's a redundant question. Because we're already watching the sunset together. I've already joined my body to hers and everything already feels right. There is no other place in the world we are meant to be, other than here. And I don't care if we never leave.

Chapter Twenty-Four

COME SAIL AWAY

I am astounded to see that the clock on the bedside table tells me that it's quarter past ten. Darby's gone, but It's always a jarring surprise to remember how well I sleep when she's next to me. I have no idea how long it's been since she got up. It could have been hours by now. Her body clock is still screwed up from being on Chicago time.

The smell of what I don't dare to hope are cinnamon rolls draws me to the kitchen. It's been so many months since I've had her cooking that I would gladly eat anything she's baked. I locate the plate next to the oven. They're some sort of bars with a topping that's kind of thick and too cohesive for me to think it's streusel. The truth is, I don't know what the hell they are, and I don't care. They're buttery and sweet and still a little warm and I wash three of them down with two glasses of milk.

As I achieve some strange balance between savoring this treat and shoveling them in as quickly as possible, I watch her through the kitchen window. She sits, unmoving, under the thatch-roofed cabana and part of me doesn't want to disturb her. It's ironic—how I've imagined all these months that she was painfully alone. But maybe she never felt that way—maybe the pressures of work and the paparazzi and real life were crowding her. Maybe what she needs right now is solitude.

It's getting hot already, so I squeeze some grapefruit juice with the citrus press and make a tray to take outside. The bucket of ice, pitchers of juice and water, and the bottle of vodka will be perfect for a brunch favorite of hers—greyhounds. I don't care if it's barely noon—with all that's happened, she's earned drink and either way, she's on vacation.

I set everything down on the small table next to the canvas-topped bed she's reclining on. Her back is propped up on pillows and she's looking toward the ocean. I place my hand on her neck, standing next to her, saying nothing, just being with her in that moment.

"I love this place," she breathes, leaning into my touch.

"We can stay here as long as you want."

"Sit with me?"

And I take the invitation, walking around to sit on the opposite side, and settle us so that her head sits on my shoulder. Having her in my arms again is bliss and I close my eyes. Between her calming effect on me and the sounds of the ocean, I could sleep again. And I almost do. She hasn't spoken again, and I'm convinced by then that she's lost in thought.

"Why does hating him hurt so much?"

I know the answer to this question, and she does too. She just needs it to be said.

"Because the part of you that hates him only hates him because some other part of you loves him."

"I want to resurrect him from the dead and kill him again."

"I want that too," I admit bitterly.

She's quiet for another long while.

"The shit with his estate...it could take months to settle. Every time I think I find a way to delegate it, something new comes up."

"You know I'll help you, baby," I say, squeezing her a little tighter.

"I envy you, Michael" she whispers finally. "You have Bex and Ella and Alex, but I've been by myself for five years. When my mom died, that was the end of my family.

I pull back well enough to bring my hands to cup her face in both of mine, angling it upward until she looks at me.

"I'm your family. Ben is your family. Anne is your family. All family means is the people who you love, and who love you...you have to know how much I love you, Darby. I didn't want to say it over the phone or lump it in with all the funeral and crime-fighting shit that was going on."

My heart begins to thunder, and I know she can feel it.

"But now I'm saying it officially. For the record. In case there was any doubt. Because it's way past time." I brush a thumb over her bottom lip. "I love you. Darby," I repeat. "You're everything to me. Everyone knows it."

And now both of our hearts together are making enough noise to start a marching band. But she hasn't pulled away yet and she's not foreshadowing her next words with the pitying look of a woman who's about to break my heart.

"Everybody?"

"Anne's started calling me Captain Obvious."

But she doesn't crack a smile. She closes her eyes, and takes a deep breath, and her body appears to be trembling. I don't expect such a visceral reaction.

"I didn't leave my house for a week after you left." she whispers. The pain in her voice surpasses anything I've heard since she arrived. "I didn't leave my bed for three days. Anne came over when no one had heard from me. She nearly called my father. That's how messed up I was. When she started threatening to call you...that's when I pulled myself together. I knew I had to move forward then. That if I didn't get my shit together, I might never come back."

Shit.

"How messed up you were?" I ask it as evenly as possible.

"I'd had a little to drink."

The moment has long since passed but my instinct to protect her still takes over.

"You texted me. You sent a picture. You were *smiling* in the picture," I grind out. "I thought—"

"You thought what I wanted you to think, Michael. I wanted to be the only woman who never tried to pin you down. I knew that if I fell in love with you like all the others..."

"You were nothing like the others."

She shakes her head and looks out at the water. "I kept thinking about what you said, that first night on the beach, how it wouldn't feel transactional, how it would feel intimate, how I couldn't ever confuse what we did with love. So, I told myself it wasn't love for you, even though it was for me."

I close my eyes and rest my forehead against hers, regretting how long I let her believe that was still true. "God, I fucked things up."

"We both did. I could've told you too. Even though it was obvious, I could have been the one to say it."

"Do you regret it? You know? The way all of this has happened?"

She shakes her head. "I think everything happened exactly like it was supposed to. And you were right. I did know it. As soon as you left, I was sure. And even though things have been up in the air, you've taken care of me like someone who loved me would."

"I'll always take care of you, Darby," I murmur back, turning her so that her back is to my chest.

"I'll hold you to that," she whispers.

⁊☙

I'm finishing up my second glass of wine—a Marlborough Sauvignon Blanc I opened for the occasion. I've been here for nearly an hour, unmoving, staring at the old envelope. Darby is upstairs, napping. We spent all morning playing in the waves and drinking champagne in the cabana. She's been sleeping a lot and I'm still not sure whether it has more to do with recovering from emotional exhaustion or the sun sucking the energy out of her. Everything about being here has been relaxing to me with the exception of this.

I found the letter in a box in my storage unit when I was in town for the funeral. After Bex and I started looking into him, I found myself thinking about it more and more. The fact that I still dug it up even after we read Avi's file should have been a sign that I still had unfinished business. Still, I wasn't sure that I would have done anything about it until last night.

I never would have read this.

I turn this thought over and over in my mind. If him reaching out again hadn't been a catalyst, it would have remained forgotten. If Darby hadn't made me think about things differently, I might have set the thing on fire. But the more I witness her grief, the more I see how much these answers will mean to me.

There have always been reasons why my wounds were deeper than Bex's. She had our mother to teach her to be a woman, but I had no one to teach me to be a man. For a long time, I was a kid who got picked on, and who didn't have many friends and didn't know how to be around other boys. Some part of me that I thought had died still needs to understand why.

"You're gonna need more wine if you plan to stare at it like that for another ten years."

I look up at the sound of Darby's gentle voice and I see her, leaning against the wall, at the top of the stairs, watching me hesitate.

"You know what you're afraid of, right?" She begins to slowly descend. "You're afraid that whatever you find in there will force you to reconsider hating him."

She comes up from behind me and wraps her arms around my chest. My devotion to hating him with the vitriol that I do is only justified if he is truly a monster.

"Will you read it to me?" I ask. Because my hands won't travel the ten inches they need to in order to open it. And maybe it will be better if I just listen and try to take it all in.

Darby picks up the letter and leads me to the sofa. She sits down first, and I cuddle into her, laying my head on her chest. She's holding the letter above me. And when I tell her I'm ready, she slowly begins to read what it says.

Dear Michael and Rebecca,

Thank you for your candid letter. Your truth is more than I deserve. It forced me to come to terms with things I've avoided thinking about for a long time. I see my mistake. I thought it would gratify you to know that I've kept tabs on you all these years. I thought it would matter for you to know that I've always loved you and to finally hear that you've made me proud. It is only now that I realized how differently we've experienced my absence.

You've never stopped meaning something to me. But I know now that I mean much less to you. I had been optimistic that I would be able to wear down your resentment and eventually earn your love. I took for granted that you would come around without thinking through why you might not. You were right in your letter. Tara deserves all the credit. And I deserve nothing.

Your hopes and dreams for me may be dead, but I still have hopes and dreams for you, mainly that you break a cycle that needs to die. Michael, I don't want you to become a deadbeat dad. Rebecca, I don't want you to marry one. So, I'll offer you something that took me a lifetime to learn: don't be better than, be good.

My own father beat my mother and all of us kids. He cheated on her openly and didn't come home for days. Sometimes he blew his check at the racetrack and we had to steal to feed ourselves. I thought being better than him was good enough. I cheated, but I came home every night and I didn't flaunt it in Tara's face. When my cheating meant that I had two families to support, I chose to live with Jen, but I sent money to Tara. It was my justification for everything. Compared to my own father, I was a stand-up guy. But compared to what all you kids deserved, I was garbage.

There are two things you should know. The first is that I haven't had a happy life. I was too damaged to do anything other than repeat my own mistakes. I never made anything good of my marriages, and my relationships with my children failed over and over again. At forty-five, I'm estranged from everyone I've ever loved, and I am alone.

But the two of you aren't. You have half-siblings. I'm enclosing some personal details that will help you track them down. If you ever change your mind and want to see me, my door is open.

Love Always,

Dad

Darby sets the letter down and links our hands together on her chest.

"That explains some things," I admit quietly. "But not everything."

"Welcome to the shitty father club," she replies just as quietly. "Membership has its privileges."

"It's been a study in human nature, huh? Why people do the things they do. Why they tell lies and do bad things to the people they're supposed to love. His advice was decent, though," I admit.

"Will you ever call your siblings?"

I honestly don't know. "I'll talk to Bex," I say. "Alex was an only child and Ella's starting to get jealous of kids who have cousins. Letting them back in wouldn't be the same thing as starting something with our father."

Darby hums in agreement. And now it's me who's tired from all that's happened today. I bring her hand up and plant a soft kiss on her wrist. And all I can think is that I'm glad that we're moving on, and that some of what's been holding both of us back feels lighter.

But hours later, I'm still thinking of unanswered questions. He never explained why he cut us off. His letter said he sent money to our mother, but I never heard about her receiving a dime. I still wanted to know how he ended up buying a fancy house when my mother was still raising me and Bex. And by the time I go to bed, I'm sure of something new: the letter was not enough.

I'm holding her again. We've been here for three days and every moment our bodies aren't occupied doing something mundane, we've been intertwined. The books we brought out here to read have been abandoned for half an hour and she's settled between my legs, her back to my front as we look out at the ocean, watching the day go by.

She's far from all right, but I can tell she's healing. She's still quiet, but some of the fog has lifted from her eyes and I know her thoughts are shifting. From stolen glances and blushes, I know she's thinking more about us.

I'm thinking more about us, too. I brought her here with the intention of giving her respite, of being whatever she needs to get through all the insanity of the past few months. At some point I realized how clearly she sees the hurt and broken parts of me. I am awestruck to discover a part of her that is fiercely protective, unflappably strong, and infinitely gentle and I find myself falling even more deeply in love.

It's caught me by surprise—how these quiet days on the beach feel more intimate than anything we've had before. Her touch is magic, and it heals me. Her tiger eyes see into the depths of my soul. I've never loved or been loved by anyone like this. For all the agonizing I did over how to say it, I barely feel I need to anymore. It resounds in our every touch, our every breath, our every unspoken thought.

I love you.

I love you.

I love you.

When she turns her head toward me, I think she means to say something and I look down at her, waiting for her to talk. But as those clear amber eyes look up at me with something I haven't seen since she got here, my brain doesn't register her intention until her lips touch mine. Our kiss is interminable and I'm too drunk with ecstasy to know whether she's on my lap because I've pulled her on top of me or because she's climbed there on her own.

"Closer."

Her breathless plea holds a desperation I don't expect. Darby is begging and it takes me a second to put together what she's asking for. She's climbing on top of me now—practically mounting me—and her hands are trembling as her fingers work at the ties on my board shorts. I've been unaware of how my own body was moving. I'll make a slow meal of her later. In this moment, I'm desperate to deepen the connection I feel with her.

Everything that happens next, I experience in flashes. Our bathing suit bottoms are suddenly off and she's letting out a wobbly moan as she sinks down onto me. I can barely breathe for how right it feels and at some point, I realize that neither of us is moving. Not only am I inside her, I'm wrapped around her and she around me, our bodies tied in the most perfect knot.

A lump forms in my throat and my eyes blur with tears and she's still trembling as the first one crawls down my cheek. My face is buried in her neck and I know I will never forget this moment—not the soundtrack of the ocean, nor the feeling of how tightly we're locked together, nor the smell of sunshine on her skin. I throb inside her, making a desperate plea of my own and her body responds by gripping me tighter. I don't command myself to move, but I do and every part of me is touching every part of her as we slide together. The orgasm her body is about to rip from mine is secondary to the other energy between us that is building to an unfathomable climax: unconditional forgiveness, fierce devotion, undying love.

The tingling in my back foreshadows my imminent release and I begin to remember how it feels to come like this. The sound she makes a second before she does is a combination of a scream and a sob. When she pulses hard around me and digs her nails into my arm, I see stars. My whole world tilts as I erupt inside her and I go off for so long that before I'm finished, I feel my own semen gushing out of her and sliding down my balls.

When we finally pull apart minutes later, tears are streaming down both of our cheeks. But for the first time I'm not worried about her. Because she's smiling through her tears and relief is in her eyes. For the first time, she's shedding them because something is right.

Ten minutes later, we've slathered each other with more sunscreen and waded into the water. We're supposed to be cleaning up, but we can't stop kissing so we're letting the waves do the work.

I won't keep her out here for long. She can't take as much sun as I can and even though the water is cool and comforting, it's hot out here, we've been drinking, and it's been awhile since she's had anything to eat. But I won't let this moment pass before I say the thing I've known since she walked into a room full of snapdragons.

"I can't be apart from you."

I murmur it into her lips between kisses and I hold my breath as I feel her pull back. But she's smiling again, and her eyes are bright and full of joy and my heart swells as she speaks the words I prayed I would one day hear.

"Let's move in together."

Chapter Twenty-Five

THE BEST IS YET TO COME

The sublime bliss of being in love overcomes us for the following two days. We spend halcyon moments window shopping in town, cooking together, strolling on the beach, and making love. We have both grown to adore this place. The town is large enough to have everything we might want—a few great restaurants, two cute boutiques, and a theater that shows indie films. But it's small enough to feel private and secluded, and the people who live here are nice.

When Darby's footsteps slow as we pass the lone real estate office, I know she's thinking the same thing I am—that we should buy a place here. We haven't talked about it yet, but I know that both of us are thinking about how to build a future.

Reality sets in the day before we're set to go back to Sydney. We've been off the grid for a week and when she powers up her laptop, she tells me her lawyers have been reaching out. There's still much to do to clean up Frank's mess. Not only is she dealing with his estate, and the detectives—she has a lot of actual labor to do in relation to settling her affairs.

His house—the house she'd grown up in—has to be cleared of his things and she'll have to decide whether to put it on the market. Because he was a high government official, there is some urgency around making sure any sensitive files he might have retained in any home of his are destroyed. There's pressure from his administrative office in the Senate to get this done.

I've already agreed to spend several days during the holiday breaks helping her. Christmas is in a little over two weeks, but her progress will be halting. The FBI's murder investigation conflicts with some of the document disposal protocols of the Senate administrative office. And it's unclear which of the inherited assets Darby will be able to claim and deal with, until the issue of their legitimacy resolves.

After my shower, I walk into the kitchen to find her on the phone. A brief eavesdrop reveals that she is talking to Avi, and that Darby is being walked through a document that he's sent. I wait patiently for her to hang up, listening in as I begin to fix us brunch.

"How's he coming on prospective buyers?" I ask when she hangs up, remembering that Avi is helping her find ethical buyers for all of Frank's businesses.

The FBI is verifying information Sweeney has provided them about Frank's dirty dealings, but he hasn't given them everything. As Sweeney's stories check out, the FBI is seizing the illegal business assets. This actually makes things much easier for Darby. With some of Frank's holdings off of her plate, Avi is helping her with the remaining list of companies. Once she has unrestricted access, she'll sell.

"That's not what he called about, actually..."

I look up to see that she's smiling a little.

"He called me for advice on a case he's working on. Turns out he was so impressed by my political knowledge when we were working on the Sweeney thing that he wants me to do a little consulting to his team."

"So, you're, like, a Washington D.C. fixer now?"

"Just call me Olivia Pope."

I have no idea who that is, but she's grinning now and so am I.

"You are so badass, babe."

On our way back to Sydney, Darby is a different person. The top on my convertible is down, and the head scarf she is wearing to control her hair paired with large sunglasses make her look like a movie star. She's smiling and humming to the playlist I've put on and her fair skin has a healthy tan. The long stretches of road before us prevent me from having to shift gears too often and we spend much of the ride hand in hand.

She thinks we're driving straight back to the city, but there's something I want her to see. She'll be on a plane two days from now and even though we haven't figured out how to make things between us work, I want her to know I'm in. If we're going to think seriously about what comes next, I want her to understand where my heart is.

"Are you up for a stop?" I ask her, when we're twenty minutes out.

"Sure..." she smiles over me. "Where are we going?"

"Just a little place I heard about," I say casually, squeezing her hand.

There's something I've learned about her on this trip. For all the time she spends indoors—at her job, at her house, in dark movie theaters and hiding from paparazzi—something in Darby comes alive when she's out in the open. For a long time, I thought it was because she's never had the freedom that privacy affords—the chance to roam anonymously—the same freedom others take for granted. But I'm starting to think it's more than anonymity that has her feeling free. She has a real wanderlust.

I don't know what this means for the two of us yet. For so long, I've treated it as a given that I'd find my way back to Chicago. I've always dreamed of building my mother's house and I know that, with Darby's job, we'll be there for at least a while longer. But I can't help but notice the way something inside her opens up whenever we're away.

"A butterfly sanctuary..." she smiles with delight after we've wended our way into the little town I diverted us to. A dirt road just past the wooden sign advertises our destination.

"You love butterflies," I say, knowing she'll take it as an explanation for why we're here. She's right to assume that most of the places I take her are chosen with the intention to delight her. She has no idea why I'm really bringing her here.

The place is unnaturally empty. It's a Saturday during moderate tourist season, but ours is the only car in the parking lot. I've rented the place out. I want us to have it to ourselves. I don't want interruptions when I tell her what I have to say.

The habitat inside the sanctuary reminds me of a greenhouse —the entire space is enclosed in an elegant dome of glass and foliage springs from every corner. It feels like a tiny forest and even though it's enclosed, it feels airy and holds some kind of magic. It has a dirt and gravel floor and winding pathways are bordered by small, colorful stones. We're in there for only a few minutes before we can't see the glass walls to the outside. It feels as if we're in another world.

It is quiet, save for the water that moves through the manmade streams. Flashes of brightness catch my eye with every glance—it's the flutter of butterfly wings. We stop every few steps, to admire this or that species, to laugh as some of them play while they fly. I recognize the monarchs and swallowtails but most of them I don't know. I'm scanning in hopes that I'll see a blue tiger or malachite breed and point them out to Darby. The teal from the former and the chartreuse from the latter inspired the painting she loves—the butterfly I invented for my painting is a mixture of both.

I can tell that she is already bewitched by the beauty around her—that this is enough for her, and that she will remember this for a long time. We reach a sectioned-off area that is perfectly in the middle of the space—this is what I've come here for. A custom-constructed wooden shelf is painted in light gray and is lined in stones on the bottom. Hanging from the top are dozens and dozens of pupas. They are green and white, and a few colorful butterflies are hanging around.

"Do you know the difference between a chrysalis and a cocoon?"

She's cocked her head to get a better look. It is a unique sight to see so many pupas in such a small space, and one you would never see in nature—only in a sanctuary such as this. She shakes her head to answer, then continues looking at the shelf. She thinks I'm just being geeky and most of the time when I ask her questions like this, I am.

I take a step closer to her. "Caterpillars don't make cocoons. Moths and other insects do. Cocoons are spun from silk. They protect what's inside, but they're vulnerable." When I take yet another step, she looks up. Now I've got her attention. "But a chrysalis is harder. Only caterpillars make them. They build an exoskeleton to protect themselves after they're done shedding their caterpillar skin. Before they go inside, they spin a silken button and attach themselves to a leaf. And so they hang, for as long as they need to. It's in the chrysalis that the metamorphosis happens."

"The painting that hangs in your bedroom? I told you before that I painted it when I was fifteen. What I didn't tell you was that I was suicidal. That kid, dressed in black, in front of Heroes and Villains...wanted it all to end. It was the lowest point in my life. I wasn't sure about anything. I honestly didn't know whether I was going to make it. But my mother saved my life. She taught me the one lesson I needed to give me hope."

Her hand finds mine and we thread our fingers and her hold on me is strong. My fear all along was that knowing how broken I once was would elicit pity, but all I feel from her now is love.

"Do you remember that book? *The Very Hungry Caterpillar*?"

"I loved that book."

"It was my favorite book when I was a little kid. My mom

dug it up from god-knows-where. It was the same copy I had read ten years before. And when she put the book in my hand, she said this proverb: just when the caterpillar thought the world was over, he became a butterfly. She said the reason why I was hurting so badly was because I was transforming."

"This is our Chrysalis, Darby. I know it's been painful—me here and you there—but it's temporary. It's not how our story ends. What we'll become is permanent and what's happening now is all part of the process. And I want you to know what I know. That when this is all over, we're going to emerge from this transformed and become the beautiful thing we were always meant to be."

Part Three

THINKING OUT LOUD

Chapter Twenty-Six

TURN THE PAGE

"W hen was the last time you were here? Before the repast?"

Darby is staring out of the car window as we drive through the gates of her childhood home in Evanston. It is one of the grander houses in the lakefront Chicago suburb and the place where her father had lived.

"Maybe my mother's funeral? Sometime around then." She speaks quietly as the house comes into view.

The eight-car garage around the side is closed and the car-lover in me wonders what's inside. A BMW and a van that says AAA Locksmiths are out front. A uniformed man who is clearly Mr. Adjani, the locksmith, chats with a suited woman who must be Frank's assistant, Anita.

Darby is the picture of calm regality as she steps out of the car to greet the locksmith with a handshake. Anita gets a hug. Betty, the housekeeper also receives a warm hug from Darby when the door swings open and all of us are let inside. I think again about how different her upbringing was from mine. Whereas I grew up in a tiny apartment filled to the brim with the love of my family, Darby was surrounded with staff. She's talked about Betty before, who, like Roberta from her lake house, was like another mother to her. Now that we have met officially, I remember having seen her at the funeral.

We start in Frank's office. That's where Adjani needs to begin. Locked drawers and safes need to be opened and the biggest is in here. Another truck is scheduled to arrive later in the day—a shredding service that will get rid of sensitive documents. A government designee from Washington will come at the end of the week to collect the documents that need official treatment. Today, Darby will go through the safes and his office.

We get the locksmith to work and leave Anita to sift through papers. Her directive is to separate anything that looks like personal business from anything that looks like it belongs to the state. In a short while, Darby and I will begin sorting through the former. I'm here to help Darby through the emotions that are bound to come up. But I have an ulterior motive. If there's anything related to what Charlie Sweeney's giving the feds, I want to have a look. If Avi and I can eliminate the FBI's need for his testimony, they'll have enough to send him away for good.

While things are getting started downstairs, Darby gives me the tour I didn't get two weeks ago. The house is gorgeously appointed if not a little cold. The antique furniture is perfectly coordinated but it feels a little like touring a landmark home— perfectly pristine, and utterly un-lived-in.

Darby's bedroom is the exception. It's the one room I've wanted to see. I didn't expect posters of New Kids on the Block or old issues of Tiger Beat, but I smile when I enter—it's definitely a teenager's room. Unlike the rest of the house, it's full of colorful elements that contrast the fine white furniture that serves as its base. The vintage canopy bed with its matching vanity and chests of drawers are complemented by brightly colored beanbag chairs, a stylish CD stand, and a 90s era stereo system. There's a guitar on a stand in the corner and another instrument case I recognize.

"You play violin?"

We both smile. She shakes her head. "Viola."

She climbs up on the king-sized bed and I expect her to sit, but she crawls to the headboard and rifles around for something between the edge of the bed and the bedside table in one corner. She whips an object I don't recognize at first from some hidden place and when I look at her face, she's smiling.

"It's still here!" She's waving a half-empty bottle of Jack Daniels triumphantly.

She's just shown me her liquor stash and I laugh. I walk to her vanity, which is mostly clear on top, save for a dozen or more bottles of perfume. She follows me and I can see she's smiling as she picks up a bottle. She opens the lid and takes a whiff then offers it to me. I haven't smelled this in fifteen years, but I remember the once-popular scent: Calvin Klein Escape. Now we're both grinning, content to be together on this trip down memory lane.

"Close your eyes," she commands, and I do. I hear a drawer open and close. "Brownie points if you can guess this one."

I hear the soft hiss of a sprayer being depressed and a masculine fragrance fills the room. I recognize it immediately.

"Is that Cool Water?" I laugh as I open my eyes. "What are you doing with that one?"

"Benji used to wear it. He thought he was hot shit.'

"Apparently, you did too," I point out. We're quiet for a beat before we both burst into laughter.

"I've always loved perfumes," she offers after our laughter subsides. I'm following her out of her room and down a long hallway that will lead us to a different wing. "When I was little—like, Ella's age—when we would visit my grandmother, I'd always disappear off to her bedroom and try on all her perfumes. They were always in fancy bottles—you know the ones; with those big tasseled bulbs you squeeze?"

I nod.

"I would play up there for hours—I'd get into her makeups and powders, too. Whenever I resurfaced, she'd joke that I looked—and smelled—like a French whore."

I like the joy I see in her eyes as she tells the story. It reminds me that her childhood had happy moments, probably many when her mother was still alive. I've agonized over the dark parts, but it does me good to remember there were light parts too.

As we walk through the hallways, the one thing I find that I love is the well-curated collection of paintings and sculptures. They're not famous pieces—most art in private collections aren't known. But I can recognize from the distinctive artistic styles that there are some huge names adorning these walls. I understand better why elements of her father's estate can't simply be auctioned off to the highest bidder. She wants to know that it won't fall in unappreciative hands.

She slows as we reach a certain door, and from her hesitation, I'm guessing it has to do with her mother. I take her hand, and she squeezes mine. I let her lead me in and her reaction reminds me of the one she had when I took her to the Art Institute last year. She is transported and I give her the space she needs. We spend a few minutes inside—sometimes, she's just standing, lost in thought. At other times, she approaches the adornments, lets her hands touch her mother's things. The smell of cedar assaults us as she opens the door to the enormous closet in which her mother's clothes and shoes are preserved. Once inside, she walks to her mother's dressing table.

I'm not surprised now when she's drawn to the perfume. Unlike Darby's vanity which had many perfume bottles, her mother's has only one. She picks it up but doesn't smell it. And just when I'm sure she's lost in memories once again, she turns her eyes to me and, with perfect clarity, holds it out.

"Will you put this in your pocket please? I want to take this one home."

§

When we return downstairs, I'm surprised by how much progress has been made and a glance at my watch tells me that Darby and I have been gone for two hours. I don't mind that Darby's taking her time. She's much stronger than she was a few weeks ago, but there's still a lot of emotional bullshit to work through. Taking it slow confirms that she's letting herself process a few things.

We set up a system. Anita created two piles for Darby and me. One are things she is almost sure are insignificant—things that I should be able to screen—and another that she thinks might have sentimental value. That pile is for Darby. Her third pile—the pile of papers she believes relate to government business and should be shredded—is being placed in bins. We only have Anita for half a day, a detail that was deliberate on my part. I want Darby to have privacy as she starts wading through all of this.

"Miss Christensen?"

Mr. Adjani calls her a few minutes after we enter. I don't know much about lock breaking, but apparently her father has a difficult vault. The older man who looks like he's been doing this job for fifty years sits in front of what must be a 1,000-pound safe with instruments fanned around him. As we approach, he informs us that he's about to make the final tweak that will crack the safe.

He has a system, too. Since there are a number of safes in the house, he will allow Darby to personally witness him opening them one-by-one. She must then transfer their contents to a set of new lock boxes he's brought. Because there's not enough time for him to reconstruct all of the safes and give them new combinations, the focus right now is on getting the contents out.

I'm surprised by the emphasis on maintaining her privacy, but I suppose it makes sense. The vaults of powerful people are full of secrets, and discretion is part of the job. When Adjani places a fine instrument in some critical spot on the disassembled lock, the heavy door opens with a dull thud. The man collects his instruments swiftly and steps away. The new lock box has been placed on the cabinet over top.

"Anita..." Darby asks calmly. "Would you mind showing Mr. Adjani the safe in the dining room?"

The two of them leave us, and it's just Darby and me. We look at each other.

"I mean...what could he have been hiding, right?" Her voice is appropriately unconvinced. Because this is Frank Christensen. And we both know he's hiding a lot more.

She steps forward to open it. Its walls are six inches thick, and the space inside is around two by two by one. It's huge for a vault, and what's inside isn't a total shock. Piles of cash, some envelopes and folders that clearly contain documents, and a couple of guns.

Darby surprises the hell out of me by going straight for one of the two pistols. In a second, she's released the clip and begins emptying the magazine of what look like 9mm bullets into her hand. She places a palm full on the desk next to her, pops the final bullet out of the chamber, and puts the clip back in. All of this is done in less than 20 seconds. That unloaded pistol is the first thing she places into the new lock box.

"That was hot as hell." The words spill out of my mouth before I have time to remind myself what a serious moment this is. She looks back and cracks an impish smile, then picks up the second pistol that's buried in the vault.

"Want to make yourself useful?"

I nod. She hands me the gun, which I don't handle nearly as elegantly as she did. This one's a .22 revolver and even though it's loaded and ready to be used, it's finely made with a pearl handle and intricate details carved on the barrel. It looks more like a collector's item than a deadly weapon. Unloading it, I place the smaller bullets next to the ones Darby has already set on the desk and place the pistol gingerly in the box.

She's already loading stacks of hundreds and I quickly do some math in my head. A stack of hundred-dollar bills adds to

$10,000 and if I'm eyeballing it right Frank had about $250,000 in cash just lying around. It's more money than I've ever seen in one single place and it's difficult for some part of me to comprehend. But Darby seems unfazed. I think about all the things she must have seen growing up. If nothing else, being a bystander is helping me see her more clearly. She herself has been a bystander to white collar crime and political dealings at a level that few people can fathom. She said nothing Frank did could surprise her. I believe that now.

Two hours later, I've learned that the Christensen home has an astounding number of safes. They're behind paintings and in closets. There's even one behind a bookshelf that conceals a hidden wall. It's as if Frank had expected that at some point his house would be raided and searched. Then I remember the police came just over a month before. All day, I've been chalking up Darby's mood to being forced to remember an unhappy childhood. Now I realize she's been anticipating something I'm not. Today, we may discover something she doesn't want anyone else to find.

We've been at it for three hours. It's tedious work that yields very little, mostly ancient files related to maintaining the house. We reduce them to several folders of things that would be financially prudent to keep. Purchase receipts and appraisals for valuables. Insurance documentation. Years and years' worth of tax returns. Deeds to the houses Frank owned and proof of authenticity for the art.

When we're through sorting the papers, it's time to start in on the lockboxes. The first three are full of expensive jewels. Darby chooses a few pieces she remembers her mother and grandmother wearing, as well as a few pair of cufflinks that she remembers as her grandfather's and puts the rest aside. It's starting to get confusing, so she finds Post-It notes and labels three of the ones she's sorting the items into. The first says "Darby", the second is "Cousins", the third says "Auction".

There's something peculiar about the contents from each of the smaller safes, however. Most of them hold heirlooms but every single one has a manila envelope with a different name. Darby recognizes them as the surnames of some of Frank's closest associates. I even recognize a few. I raise my eyebrow when I see Darby putting them in a pile. She shrugs.

"It's evidence against them."

I shake my head.

"I'm sorry...what?"

"That's the reason why there are so many safes. So that if he ever got arrested and wanted to take someone down with him, he could direct investigators to a specific hidden vault. That way, he'd be able to give up one of them without giving up all of them. It's the oldest trick in the book."

For as much as I hate Frank, I'm impressed.

More family heirlooms and smaller stashes of cash reveal themselves from the smaller lock boxes, and what we find in unmarked folders ranges from turn of the century photographs of her great-grandparents to records of her family's accomplishments. She finds everything from her great-grandfather's college degree, to purchase receipts for early issue shares of U.S. Steel, to a hand-drawn family tree that began in Denmark and ended a generation before Darby was born. These heirlooms tell the story of how the two families she came from emigrated to the U.S. and built their fortunes.

As she inspects each item slowly, I see something inside her open up. She's told me before that she dislikes the way both sides of her family made their money. The first generations pulled themselves up from their bootstraps, but later generations hoarded money and built wealth on the backs of others. On her mother's side, they'd been slumlords. Her father's family owned factories during the industrial revolution. Darby wasn't ashamed of how they'd *gotten* rich—she was ashamed of how they'd stayed that way.

But right now, she's touching things that belonged to those from the generations before. We chat about it a little. She tells me stories about these people—what she knows from what she's been told. Even if it's ancient history, I'm glad she's finding something to admire about her family.

Soon, a fourth box is marked. On the Post-It, she writes "Duplicate".

"Things I'll have copied for all of my cousins," she explains quietly.

"I'm sure they'd love to see these," I say with a small smile.

When we open the cylinders that had been hidden in the vault behind a bookcase, we find some truly amazing, and quite valuable, paintings on canvas.

"How did the cops miss all this?" I ask as I put the second-to-last lock box away. Right now, we have only the boxes we're sorting into—and the one with the important stuff—open.

"There's a decoy safe," she slips in as if it's the most obvious thing in the world. "Everyone knew that if the cops ever came, to take them to the one over there."

She motions behind her head. I open a cabinet that is the twin of the one concealing the safe that we just had cracked. This one is unlocked and empty.

"What was in this one?"

"Money. Jewelry. Birth certificates and shit. Everyone in the family knew the rule: righty, tighty, lefty loosie. It meant the one on the right was the one to keep tight and the left one was the one they were allowed to know about."

This explains it. I say what I've been suspecting. "You thought of telling the cops about this."

"Yup." She pops her 'p' unapologetically.

"But you didn't."

"Nope."

It's at times like this, I'm reminded that my woman is

shrewd. I think back to her interview with the detectives and know that, once again, I've underestimated her.

"Easiest one first?" I ask.

She nods and picks up the one labeled 'Cavendish'. It's one of the manila envelopes that was found in the smaller safes. What's inside are items we can't decipher. Documents that mean nothing to us, but that align with Darby's theory that they're Frank's insurance policy.

"God forbid Frank Christensen go down alone," she mumbles as she replaces what we've found. We go through the next set of manila envelopes until we reach the final five from the big safe. She picks up the one labeled 'McCormick'

"Do you have any idea what that means?" I ask as she uses her fingers to pinch the tiny metal closers together, allowing the nine by eleven manila envelope to open.

"I'm pretty sure it was the shell company he used to move money he wasn't supposed to have to places it wasn't supposed to go," she says drily, turning the envelope upside-down to slide papers out. "Since he held office, his tax returns and business interests were public. Anything he needed to do that wasn't above board had to be done some other way."

"Sounds like he was pretty open about it."

"You can't imagine the shit he used to teach me with the idea that one day, I'd go into the family business. He took pride in teaching me how to be corrupt. The man taught me how to count cards in single-deck blackjack when I was six."

We both smile at that.

"And anything he didn't tell me, I figured out on my own. I was an only child with no one to play with," she points out. "I hid everywhere and overheard everything. How do you think I know where all the safes are?"

She turns her attention to the papers in her hands. I try to be patient as she scans her eyes over whatever she's looking at. After she finishes the first page, she hands it to me.

It's some sort of org chart. As I keep reading, I see that it's a roster for the Board of Directors. Frank is named, and the other names I see are those of his lackeys. Some of them are identical to the names of the men on the envelopes from the other safes. I scan for Charlie Sweeney's name, but I don't find it. Just as I finish scanning this first document, she's handing me a key vendor list. The final two papers she gives over are an annualized grid of Board Director earnings and a similar chart showing a year-by-year account of each vendor's Tax ID number, and how much each was paid.

"Is this...?" I can't even finish. If I'm seeing what I think I'm seeing, Frank has created a file of evidence that would incriminate himself and everyone he knows for money laundering in the hundreds of millions.

Darby nods. "It's legal for companies to pay their Board members a salary for lending their expertise to the business. But their Board salaries came from whatever revenue was earned from illegal acts."

"What does McCormic Corp do?" I ask.

"Financial services and consulting." This earns me an ironic look.

"Which is code for insider trading—"

"And a ton of other shit we don't want to know about," she says.

"And the vendors?"

"Probably fixers, hit men, people like that, with shell companies of their own."

Holy shit.

By the time we finish, it's nine at night and both of us are exhausted. She's gotten what she came here for. There's such a pandora's box of evidence against various characters, that Darby decides against giving these files to the cops. But she has taken a liking to Avi, and she wants to see whether he can comb through any of it and get more dirt on Sweeney. Even if he can't, she likes the idea that he'd use the information in other ways she would approve of. Before we head to the car, she hands me the bin with all these files.

"And you say I'm the one who's obsessed with vigilante justice..." I tease.

She shrugs, but I see something in her eyes. "I guess not."

Chapter Twenty-Seven

MELE KALIKIMAKA

"I think Bex is pregnant."

Darby looks sideways at me as we drive up Lake Shore Drive. We spent the night having a steamy reunion in my waterbed and now we're on our way to Bex's house for dinner. Since it's almost Christmas, we've decided to stay up north for the next couple of days. Bex lives closer to Evanston than either of us do, and Evanston is where Darby is still busy going through her father's house.

Being away from Bex and Ella is something I've been thinking about lately. Darby wasn't the only one I've been missing. The more I think about where I belong, the more I know that Sydney—or any place as far away from my family as Sydney—is not where I should be long-term. Darby and I are no closer to resolving the "where" and the "when" of living together, but there has been some basic relief in knowing that we're both committed to a plan.

"Isn't that what Ella wants for Christmas?" Darby asks smiling.

"It is," I say. "Did I tell you I knew Bex was pregnant with Ella before anyone else?"

Darby laughs. She thinks the twin thing is adorable and I

know that she loves Bex. They're on track to become great friends. Bex already thinks of Darby as a sister.

When we arrive, all it takes is a look to know my theory is correct. Bex looks tired and she nods when I look at her stomach, confirming what I've suspected before I have to say a word.

"Twins," I whisper in her ear as I hug her, and she gapes.

"It's too early for a heartbeat," she hisses after confirming that Ella is busy kidnapping Darby to go play with her.

"When it's time...mark my words, you'll hear two."

Bex just shakes her head.

We spend the afternoon building snowmen, playing good guys vs. bad guys, and after Darby and Ella bake cookies together, we eat them at the table while Ella and I draw. I've trained my little pupil well and at the tender age of seven, she already has good taste in comic books, and she likes to draw her own stories.

Alex arrives from the airport just before dinner, which I'm cooking as Darby drinks wine and "helps" me by tasting along the way. We leave Alex, Bex, and Ella to their reunion, and when she arrives at dinner, I know Bex is grateful for the help.

Dinner is spent catching up on everything that's happened. Between vacationing with Darby and catching up at work, I've barely talked to Bex over the past few weeks. Darby gives everyone the short version of what happened with Frank. After Ella's gone to bed, I relay vague details about what was contained in the letter from our father, but I've brought it with me, and I hand it off to Bex. I also let her know that I've contacted him and that I'll be visiting him tomorrow. Bex gets that this is something I need to do, and to do alone.

Darby and I insist upon doing the dishes and letting Bex go to bed early. It's the day before Christmas Eve, but even without the holiday here yet, this feels as warm and cozy as Christmas itself. When everyone else is upstairs in bed, Darby and I spike some store-bought egg nog with brandy and I build a fire in the fireplace. We sit on the loveseat in the living room with our feet up, enjoying the fire, the drinks, and the smell of the fresh-cut tree.

"So, Bex is pregnant, huh?" Darby asks casually after she takes a long sip of her drink

"What gave her away? The dark circles under her eyes, or her three-hour nap?"

"She had to leave the kitchen when she walked in and smelled the cookies."

I chuckle at that. "It's twins," I say.

She looks at me.

"For real?"

"All her life she's known she had an increased chance."

"But you're fraternal twins," she observes.

"Coincidence," I say.

Darby gets a little quiet and I figure she's just as relaxed as I am. The house still smells like cookies, Bing Crosby is playing, and all's right in the world.

"Tell me the truth, Michael. Do you want this?"

My eyes open and I look at her.

"Life in the suburbs. Getting married. Having kids."

"I know you don't want to get married or have kids, Darby. I would never ask you to."

"I'm asking what you want."

"I told you the first night we met that I don't want to have kids."

"You told me you didn't think you'd have time for them. That's not the same thing as not wanting them."

"If it happened, I'd figure the universe was guiding us towards having kids. But, no, I don't think I'll ever want to try."

"It's not just that I don't want kids, Michael. It's that I can't have them."

I don't say anything for a minute. "So...is it that you don't want them?" I ask gently. "Or have you just given up on ever having them?"

"I really don't want them," she admits. And she still looks apprehensive. She's afraid this is a deal breaker for me.

"Do you want the truth?" I say, needing to crush this before it becomes an issue. "I could be happy in a lot of situations. If you wanted ten kids, I'd seriously consider it. If you only wanted one, we'd have one. But since you don't want any, we'll get a dog and give him his own room and buy clothes for him."

She laughs then, and I smile for having created it.

"What kind of dog?" she wants to know.

"A Labradoodle named Corky."

"You've given this a lot of thought," she observes, her voice still thick with mirth.

"Maybe."

"So, it's less about the kids and more about the woman?"

"It's about what's right for both of us. If kids aren't right for what we want from our lives and our relationship, let's not have them."

She's thinking about this, but I feel that some of the worry has left her body.

"It's not like we don't have plenty of kids in our lives," I point out, set on bringing the idea home. "Ella's six. Bex's twins aren't even born. I'm sure Tami and Ben would take us up on an offer to babysit their kids so they can get away for a while. I think we're going to be able to get our fix."

"I want to give you your Christmas present." She says it abruptly.

"It's not Christmas yet."

"I want to give it to you sooner rather than later." There's something strange in her tone.

"Should I give you yours now, too?"

"It's not something that will fit under the tree," she says cryptically, and then shakes her head. "Sorry, I'm not explaining this well. I can't give it to you now. And I have to go in for a few hours in the morning tomorrow, but how about afternoon?"

❧

I don't even remember what he looks like, I realize as I stand, nearly shivering, on the front steps of his house. Despite being back here for a few days already, I still haven't adjusted to the cold. When I realized my father lives only five blocks from Darby, I walk. A restaurant she and I used to go to for brunch is at the corner of his block. When I was younger, I used to think about what I would do if I ran into him. Now, I wonder whether I've seen him around the neighborhood before and didn't realize who he was.

It takes me a full five minutes to gather the courage to ring the doorbell, but the cold gets the best of me and I feel like an idiot standing on someone's doorstep in a neighborhood like this in broad daylight. My heart is loud in my chest, though I'm not sure it's from nerves. I'm surprised by how much animosity I still feel toward this man. I entertain a brief fantasy of punching him as soon as he opens the door.

When he does open the door, I see blue eyes that mirror mine staring back at me, and I'm not sure whether this immediate recognition stems from a memory or his likeness to me and Bex. This man is definitely my father. And I I've never seen him around here before. The resemblance is so strong that I'm sure that I—or even Darby—would have known.

He's tall like me, at least six feet, but ghostly pale. I've always known that Blaine is a Scottish name, and his extremely fair coloring further explains how Bex and I look as white as we do. Unlike us, he is freckled. He looks older than I expected—older than the fifty-five I know him to be—and I think about what his letter said, about having a difficult life.

But despite his letter, I have never pictured his life as difficult. And, no matter the burden I see from his face, I doubt any words he could say would make me believe it. If nothing he says will sway me, maybe coming here was a mistake.

"Michael," he says.

I'm not going to call him Dad.

"Please...come in," he says after seconds have passed without me offering a greeting.

As I walk inside, my brain processes the details of his home. From the exterior, I can tell it was built around the turn of the century. Inside, I'm surprised to find a number of original details, though some of the interior structure has been redone. The decor is classic and masculine, and I wonder whether he lives alone. From the unique paintings on his walls, I know that Avi's intel about him being an art dealer is true. Even though it's Christmas Eve, I see no evidence of a tree.

"Thank you for coming."

Once I'm in his entryway, he looks me squarely in the eye. I've never held such strong resemblance to anyone and It's still a little creepy. Looking at him leaves me with the eerie sense that I'm staring at what I myself will look like thirty years from now.

"Will you sit with me?" he asks.

Even without knowing him, I can read his gratitude. I like to think of myself as a gracious person but I'm having trouble finding compassion for this man. I have yet to utter a word. I mutter a "yes" as he leads me into some sort of living room.

"Can I offer you a drink?"

"No, thank you." I say politely, relieved that my manners haven't abandoned me completely.

I don't say that I'll only be staying long enough to have my questions answered. I'm about to start interrogating him—to press him to explain how he ended up with four wives and five kids all in the span of fifteen years, when his face falls a little and he speaks.

"I'm sorry, Michael. All you kids deserved a lot better than me."

But I don't want him to launch into his sob story. I read all of that in his letter.

"I didn't come here to hear your apology." I say it with as little bite as possible.

"Then I'm sure you must have questions."

And I think of them then. Whether he let us struggle more than we had to. What he was thinking by leaving all of those wives with small kids. What he was thinking by doing it four times. But, in this moment, I realize the answers are meaningless, and the questions past their prime. And that my real reason for coming is to say what I have to say to him.

"Once upon a time I did," I concede. "By now, they don't really matter. But I did come here to find something out."

"What do you want to know?" He's more cautious now. I've set fire to his script.

"I want to know whether you ever learned to be a good father," I say simply. "Maybe you screwed up with me and Bex, but I want to know whether you ever took the time to learn from your mistakes and mastered the art of being a dad."

It's not a trick question, but I can see he is caught off guard and doesn't know how to answer. When he does, he speaks very carefully.

"Once I realized how badly I had screwed up with my own kids...my kids weren't kids anymore. By the time I knew what being a good father meant, I'd missed my chance."

Strike one.

"Fatherhood doesn't end when your kids grow up. You say you've learned to be a good father...so what makes you feel right about approaching us now?"

I notice the tone of my voice—it's quiet calm smooths over more intense notes—it's the same voice I use when I interview people.

"I know the day has passed for me to be a father to you, but I could still be a good influence on Ella. I'm trying to make amends. This is my chance, for once, to do the right thing by all of you."

Strike two.

"So, you're doing this for Ella?"

"It could be a great relationship for both of us."

"What's in it for her?"

"Love," he says simply.

"What makes you think she doesn't have enough of that, or that you're uniquely positioned to provide it for her?"

"What Ella needs is the love of her family. And I'm her grandfather."

Strike three.

"Here's the thing. You may not have been around, but I had surrogate fathers. I'm kind of a surrogate father to Ella. And one thing I know is that good parents do what's best for their kids. But in order to give someone what's best for them, you have to see them clearly. That means seeing past yourself."

My façade of calm slips a little and I pause, but I can see his expression change as he lets the words sink in. For a second, he does not look repentant—he looks resentful. And, in that moment I understand. He thinks he's done his penance. He thinks he deserves this, deserves us. He thinks I'm punishing him because I'm angry. I am angry, but I'm not punishing him. I'm doing what has to be done.

"You don't know what Ella needs," I continue. "Just like you don't know what we need. Because you don't know us. And you haven't even bothered to ask what's best for anyone other than you in this situation. You could have done that before asking what you wanted. You haven't thought through how we'll explain to Ella why you don't have a relationship with me and Bex."

He quiets at this.

"Do you remember the advice in your letter? 'Don't be better —be good?'" I ask. "I appreciate what you're trying to do, and I appreciate that it's more stand-up than anything else you may have done on the parenting front, but it's just not enough. You may be better at this than you've ever been, but you're still not good at this. So, please, respect our wishes and leave all of us alone."

Chapter Twenty-Eight
OUR HOUSE

I'm blindfolded. Darby insisted on that fact and, amused, I've gone along with her. She's been uncommonly quiet for the first part of the ride and has seemed a bit nervous all morning. All I know so far is that driving to wherever she's taking me has something to do with my Christmas gift. We're scheduled to be at Bex's house in about two hours and I'd been eager to know what she had in store since she mentioned it to me.

I gave her her gift this morning after I served her breakfast in my bed. I love that she never bothered to move back into her brownstone. I came home to half the closet taken over by her girly things. It's crowded now, and less orderly, but I can't help but to love it.

For her present, I had some of the old family records that she'd had Anita duplicate bound into a gorgeous leather book. I wanted her to have a memento of all she'd learned about her family—but one that left a sweet taste in her mouth. I'd also let her know that I was having a lab recreate the bottle of perfume her mother gave me, and I'm pleased to see that she loves them both.

But I have no idea about the kind of gift she'll get me. She's only ever given me simple things before, but whatever this is, I've figured out it isn't simple.

We've been driving for a good hour and I have no idea where we are by the time she stops the car. From what I can surmise, we've driven on traffic light roads as well as highways, but from Chicago that could have put us anywhere between Wisconsin and Indiana. I expect her to relieve my suspense right then, to finally remove my blindfold, but she lets the engine idle, and I hear her shifting it into Park. She takes a few deeper-than usual breaths and my heart quickens a bit. I can tell that she feels vulnerable, and I want to know why. We're still in the car. I hear the hum of the engine and wait for the sound of her voice.

"This thing that I got you..." she begins softly, her voice almost shaky. 'I'm pretty sure you'll like it and I hope that you love it, but I'm afraid you won't accept it, or that you'll say it's too much. I've never bought someone something like this before, but when I saw this, I thought that it could be perfect for you. So, remember that, okay? And before your analytical brain starts working out how much it cost, or how outrageous something like this is for one person to give another, remind yourself that I can afford it and think back to how I have graciously accepted, and treasured, every single gift that you have ever given me. If you're mad about the money, remember the Harry Winston necklace and the private investigator I'm sure didn't come cheap and the $5,000 a night weekend at the Drake."

"None of those things were about the money, Darby."

"I know," she replies. "This isn't about the money either. Do you trust me?"

"More than anyone."

"Good," she says, and I hear her get out of the car. She opens the passenger door and pulls me out of my side, blindfold still on as she leads me to the front of the car, turning me around so that I'm facing the hood.

"Then take off your blindfold and sign your deed."

Before I can touch my blindfold, she places one of my hands upon something flat, something I immediately recognize as some sort of folder. Slowly taking off my blindfold with the other hand, I look down at it and recognize the Sotheby's name. It's a high-end real-estate firm.

"Open it!" she implores nervously, biting her lip.

She bought me property.

I've figured out as much by then—and when I open the folder to read the first of many papers, my suspicions are confirmed. The address is 200 Lakewood Drive, Glencoe. The town where my mother always wanted to live. The town where I've always known I would build Tara. She wants me to build my house.

My own tears immediately blur my vision, yet I continue to stare, dumbly, toward the papers on the hood, despite the fact that I can no longer see them well anymore. I blink then, my tears falling, and turn to find that we're parked on a long, tree-lined driveway, which, in the distance, reveals the very beginnings of the frame of a house.

"It was in foreclosure," Darby begins to explain, and my wide eyes swing back to hers. "They had gotten far enough to tear down the old house and start to build the new one, but they couldn't afford to finish it. I thought you would like it, so I bought you the land."

I feel so many things for her in that moment that I know I cannot speak. No stringing together of words is sufficient to tell her everything I wish she knows. I can barely even hold the folder steady in my hand. Letting it fall, I raise my arms to pull her, fiercely, to my body.

"I love it so much," I say with effort. "Thank you, baby. Thank you..." I'm whispering by the end. I feel her body relax a bit against mine and after a moment, I tip up her face so I can look into her eyes. They're so luminous in the afternoon sun. "Thank you," I say again.

"I expect to be invited to the housewarming party." She

smiles a bit then, and even though we plan to move in together, I realize she still thinks of this as my house.

"You'll be co-hosting," I say.

"Show me around," I command gently, and with that I take her hand.

And she does, and I'm amazed by just how perfect this property is. I learn that it sits on six acres, a gargantuan plot for this town, with thick woods from the west to add privacy, a large clearing of ample size to build the house, and Lake Michigan on the eastern border of the property line. It's better than even I had ever dreamed, and grander than my mother ever had as well. Property in Glencoe rarely goes up for sale, let alone property that's on the lake.

The foundation of the house had been planned and laid, and what little frame had been built can easily be torn down. We'll have a new foundation dug up for me to start over. If I need another sign that it's time to make a change in my life, this is it. Tara has to be built, even if it ends up being a weekend home. I know my place is with Darby.

When we return to her car, she recovers the folder, opens it, turns to a flagged page. She fishes into her pocket before retrieving an elegant pen.

"Sign here, Michael," she smiles. "Now it belongs to you."

And even though I've taken so many leaps over the past six weeks, over what I had once believed was the biggest hurdle, I know that my next big hurdle is drawing near. With the promise of this house being built, I feel myself begin to wiggle my way out of the chrysalis. Now all I have to do is get her to want to spend the rest of her life with me.

By the time we return to our place after spending several days with Bex, the sun is setting, and I can see Darby's exhaustion. I expect us to fall in bed with a movie, order takeout, and fall asleep. We do order takeout, but only after she's surprised me with a flawless seduction—a shower turned naughty followed by two hours of slow lovemaking in our opulent bed. I'll never get tired of the way she makes me feel when our bodies are connected. Our lovemaking is as intense as ever, and it shuts out anything else that may be happening in our world.

"I don't want to go back."

I hear her whispered words through the fog of quasi-sleep. It's well into the next morning, but what feels like perpetual fatigue finds us still in bed, talking quietly in between brief rounds of dozing.

"You can make it another two weeks," I reply sleepily.

She'll return to work for a couple weeks—admittedly, a busy couple of weeks given her patient load through the holidays. Then, she'll fly back to Sydney for our planned January vacation.

"That's not what I meant."

Something in her voice wakes me up a little more and I angle my head down to her to find that she's already looking up at me.

"I meant that I don't want to ever go back. I don't want to be chief anymore. I don't want to continue my research. I want to take time off...and after I do, maybe do something else."

We talked about this—back in November when I came the weekend of Ella's birthday. I knew she would reach this conclusion, but I want her to be sure.

"I've done what I set out to do with my research. And every reason why I started this—they aren't good enough reasons anymore. I never even wanted to be a doctor. Did you know that?"

"You wanted to be a writer," I recall aloud.

"I want more out of life than seventy-hour weeks for a payoff that's lost its luster. Just because I'm great at something isn't a reason to keep doing it."

And it strikes a chord in me. Because I know in that moment that she's not just talking about herself—she's talking about both of us.

"Are you happy?" she asks.

And it's such a loaded question. It doesn't seem right to complain given the way I've accomplished everything I ever set out to achieve. Financial stability and a career that lets me do so many things I love are meaningful to me. But is what I'm doing my life's purpose?

"No."

I say it aloud before I have time to let the weight of the confession sink in.

"What did you want to be?"

"A comic book artist."

I was sure a lot of kids like me had wanted to be that. And I'd done it—even though it was my side hustle, I'd been successful even at that.

"Do you ever think about that?"

"I haven't thought about doing it as a career in years."

"Yet, you find time for it and you're wildly successful at it, maybe in spite of yourself."

But I haven't had time for it. I'm a year and a half late on delivering my next graphic novel. For the first time, this part of my life is slipping from my grasp.

"It doesn't feel like work."

"That's what I want. To find something I'm so passionate about that it doesn't feel like work. Then, whatever it is, I want to go work at that."

Softly, I kiss her lips.

"I want that for you, too, baby."

"But I want more free time, too." She's picking up steam. "I don't want whatever I'm passionate about to consume me anymore—I want to see more movies and to travel and to cultivate this amazing love I have with you."

I want that, too. Though, for some reason, my mouth can't form the words. Because I still don't know what that looks like for us. We're lucky enough to have the kind of money that will let us leave everything behind. But I've never been good at not having a solid plan.

"The world is your oyster," I tell her. Because even if I don't know what I want yet, I want her to know that the possibilities are endless for her. "I'll follow you wherever you go."

"I don't want you to give anything up for me," she whispers, and I remember the promises that used to define our relationship.

"The only thing I refuse to give up is you."

Chapter Twenty-Nine

FAITHFULLY

This time it's Darby who takes me to the airport. She's driven me here in her old car and I think of the last time—the only time—that we were here together. This morning, I sat next to her on a barstool in the kitchen of my apartment as she made the call to her boss. The hospital was quick to offer to grant her a leave of absence. Darby politely declined.

What will come next is beyond my wildest dreams. Darby will wrap up the last of her affairs that she has to handle personally and, in less than two weeks, will board a plane to Sydney on a ticket that is one way. We're going to be together. No more planning visits. No more agonizing over whether we can make something work. She's following me to Sydney now and I'll follow her to wherever she decides to go next if that's what it takes for us to stay this way.

All along, I've been opposed to the idea of her giving up her career to be with me, and I have to remind myself constantly that she needs this. Quitting her job isn't about me—it's about her redefining her life, and it occurs to me that we may spend much longer than I thought in our chrysalis.

My fears are different this time around. As she rediscovers

herself, I know there is a possibility that she will envision a future that has nothing to do with me. This has become about more than us finding a way to be together. My only job is to help her find her place in this world, even if that place isn't next to me.

But I'm willing to take that chance, and if I'm honest, I have a lot of my own figuring out to do. We are both transforming, and my dearest hope is that, whatever flight we take, we'll take together. I'm more committed than ever to sharing our lives.

I spend the majority of the plane ride working on the logistics of her arrival—looking into long-term visas for her and booking the beach house again for our vacation. Since we had always planned on her visiting in January, I've planned for the time off. She made it clear that she wants our vacation to involve what we both know has become our special place. I'm hoping that we'll keep getting closer to finding where we belong while we're there.

Somewhere over the pacific, reality sets in and I shift into all that I've missed at work over the past week since I've been gone. For the first time in my life, I have trouble focusing on the demands of my job. It's not just that I have a lot on my mind—I come to the candid realization that I am unmotivated to work on my pending projects. Unlike Darby's, whose epiphany came quickly, mine has been building for many months. But the part of me that likes to know what's coming next is painfully uncomfortable without a plan.

"Dale," I say, picking up after Kat has put the call through. It's January 4th and I'm in time for our usual one-on-one.

I pulled an all-nighter getting back up to speed on what's going on and I'm ready to brief him fully. It helps that everyone is also just returning from holiday vacation, and that December is always a little slow.

But January will ramp up quickly. The Kensington presentation went so well that we're approved for the next phase; my team pitched a new prospect; and we just broke ground on a project that pre-dated my arrival.

"How's Darby?" Dale wants to know before we hang up the phone.

He's got a soft spot for her, even though they've never met. When Frank was killed, he had Andrew sent a gorgeous bouquet directly to her house. I fight the compulsion to give him my pat answer—to tell him that she's doing as well as can be expected. He doesn't need the whole sordid truth about Frank and Charlie, but I want to tell him something real.

"The whole thing is a total shit show," I admit, glad in this moment to be able to say this to someone other than Bex. "The murder...the mysterious circumstances...even inheriting all that money...it's a lot. And it's worse with her father's dirty laundry spread all over the news."

Dale commiserates, calling the paparazzi vultures, and recounting a tale from when, earlier in his career, he himself had some negative attention. Though I've never directly copped to the fact that Darby and I are together, he mentions again that I have whatever leeway I want to be flexible. He reminds me that I can split my time between the Sydney and Chicago offices if that's what I need to do.

"She's moving here," I reveal. "She decided to quit her job. She's not happy anymore and she needs time to regroup, given all that's happened. It's not like she needs the money. The time's more important to her than anything else."

"Smart woman," Dale says. "Most people wait until the job is killing them before they decide to get out. If you ask me, it's much better to have your fun when you're young."

"Sixty is the new thirty," I quip, remembering the huge birthday party we threw for him last year. "Besides, I don't see you in any rush to retire any time soon."

"Most days it feels like sixty is the new fifty-five," he grouses. "I'd pay good money to be able to keep up with these younger women. They make them different these days."

I laugh but keep my mouth shut. "So, you know I'm taking more time in January," I remind him. "It's the vacation I've had planned for a while. Darby loves Crescent Head. I took her there in November."

"That's a great spot," Dale agrees. "You're managing the office beautifully, despite all the time you've been taking off. You must be burning the candle at both ends," he observes.

"I am," I admit.

"Don't let yourself burn out."

Darby lets out a loud hoot as she guns the engine. We're going so fast that wisps of her pulled back hair have loosened and are flying in the wind. We switched places after I got us out of Sydney—she's now the driver, and I'm now the passenger, and all that's before us on this stretch is empty, open road. Despite seeing each other more frequently than we were even when I was based in Chicago, and traveling all the time, each absence feels longer. I've missed Darby in the two weeks since I've seen her and all I want right now is another week in what I've come to think of in my mind as our house.

I can't help but to smile at her happiness. In the few weeks since she quit her job, I've seen a new Darby emerge. But the part of me that is grateful for her newfound joy is subdued beneath my own angst. The first time we made this journey, Darby was the one who was lost and confused and feeling like she needed an eternity to sort out all that was nagging her brain. Now I'm the only one burdened by doubt.

Even with the question of our physical separation resolved, the time for change is coming near. She'd be content for a long while to wait things out with me in Sydney, for us to both take time to decide what we want. I see a lot of wisdom in taking the pressure off of ourselves for a while, to recover from all that's happened so we can regroup, but it feels like backwards progress. I've spent these past six months in Sydney preparing myself to leave here. But now that she's here, I'm realizing how many of my own reasons I had to want to go back home. And I don't really want to stay.

So, I do what she did back in December. I spend three days intermittently sleeping off my physical and mental exhaustion. I spend endless hours staring, from the cabana, out at the sea. I let Darby sit in solidarity with me, every single day. I let her gentle touch and her quiet presence soothe me. I let her give me time and space, even though the kind of space I need involves her being there beside me.

For the first time in what feels like months, I draw. At first, it's stress relief. Three days into the trip, I become inspired. I sketch out our beautiful beach, draw new pictures of her— smiling and happy and with the ocean breeze in her hair, and I even come up with a story I'm excited about for a new graphic novel.

Darby, meanwhile, is blossoming under the sun of her own new creative pursuits. In addition to baking like crazy for me, she's letting me teach her how to cook savory food. She's been an eager pupil and doing simple things together, like cutting vegetables, walking to the market, and picking herbs in the garden, feels rich. Avi was serious about wanting her to consult on some of his cases and I can see already that she shares his zeal for investigation. The other day I caught her writing. She could have been journaling, but I hope it's a story.

With every passing day, she becomes more confident, more like a version of herself I've never met but who I really want to know. Quitting her job has reminded her that there are other things she's good at, broader value she has to add to the world, new things to learn and new ways to grow. It is a combination of watching her and coming to some of my own conclusions that the puzzle pieces finally come together in my mind. And when they do, I've never been clearer about my purpose.

"I don't want it anymore."

The sun is setting and we're walking on the beach. I've worked up to saying this out loud all day.

"I don't want what's waiting for me at the top of the ladder. I still want to be an architect, but only part time. And under circumstances that are nothing like this."

She doesn't say anything at first. I'm waiting for her to challenge me. Not to disagree or talk me down—just to chime in with one of her smart insights that would help me think it through. When I look over at her, she's smiling and looking at our feet as we walk in the sand, the surf lapping up to our ankles.

"Took you long enough," she quips.

I bump her playfully with my hip.

"Took *you* long enough," I retort. "And now look at you. You're all...happy."

She takes my arm and we continue to walk. I'll never get tired of her being this close to me.

"So, tell me about your happy place," she gently commands.

The air is becoming cool and the breeze is picking up and it reminds me of that first night we spent together at the beach. Some part of me is afraid to voice the dream I've been nursing for the better part of two days. The more I roll it around, the more it feels like a dream I've always had.

"A tiny shop—a partnership between me and someone else, with just a few people under us. No plans to grow. No goals to get bigger or richer. We'd cherry-pick a few amazing projects each year. And not just local projects we take based on wherever we set up shop. I'd want the projects to be all over the world."

"I love that idea." Her voice is quiet and calm. "What are you gonna do with the rest of your time?"

This part won't surprise her. "I want more time for my community work. And I want more time to draw—not just my graphic novels. I think I want a studio, and to go back to studying art."

She stops when she hears this. When she looks up at me her

eyes are even more gorgeous than usual, in the setting sun. It's highlighting the red in her hair and she is smiling beatifically.

"I love that idea most of all."

I wrap my arms around her shoulders, and she wraps hers around my waist and we hold each other in the breeze.

"But we both know you could have done something like this a long time ago. So, what's stopping you?"

Telling the truth about this scares me more than finally voicing my innermost dream. Because I know the answer and it's so core to my personality that it's been with me all my life.

"I don't want to disappoint anyone," I say.

And I wonder who—not what—I've been doing this for. Where these dreams I've chased for what seems like half of my life really came from. And how many of them even matter anymore. I made my mother proud. I got the last laugh on kids who hated on me. I've become a role model to several cohorts of kids who came up after me in my neighborhood. Once upon a time, succeeding had even been about proving something to my father. Financial success was so tied up in all of this, that I'd traded what had probably been my truest desire—to become an artist of some kind—for the practicality of becoming an architect.

But as I look at my life now, at the people I really don't want to disappoint, the only ones left are Bex, Ella, Darby, and Randy. I know that anything I decide to do with my life would be embraced by both women and that the only thing that has disappointed Ella is me being so far away.

The only person that leaves is Dale. I know I'm his star performer. I know he's got a lot riding on me and that I've made him promises. I feel like I owe it to him to finish what I started here, but I can't think of a good time or circumstance to tag myself out.

"I fought for this, Darby...for more than a year, I did everything to place myself in a position to take over this office. It seems like the wrong thing to do—to just quit and leave him in the lurch. And not just because it would be unprofessional. Dale has had my back in more ways than you know."

"So, give him a few months runway," she gently suggests, and I know it's the most logical thing in the world.

"I feel like I owe him more than a few months."

"Pick a number, then. Six months. A year. Whatever you think you owe him, give it to him. But after that, do what you want and promise yourself you'll never tether yourself to anything that makes you feel this trapped again."

Chapter Thirty

LANDSLIDE

I'm nervous as I walk into the restaurant, early for my meeting with Dale. I'm never nervous when I meet with him, a fact that only puts me more on edge. He's come all the way to Sydney, which means he's got something on his mind. I don't think I'm fucking anything up, though, no matter how badly I did, I have no doubt we'd get through it. My shit's getting done—I've just been less available.

Fushi is one of the hottest lunch restaurants in Sydney right now. It's a place I want to bring Darby to, but we've only been back in the city for three weeks. The cuisine is sushi and I know she'd love it. I've been working a fair bit—catching up on all I've missed, and quietly moving the chess pieces that will set the office up for success once I quit. I haven't had the conversation with Dale yet. Before I do, I want to have thoroughly crafted my exit plan.

But there is no sense of urgency. Darby is enjoying this part of the world and we've already planned half a dozen long weekend adventures for the next several months. From Australia, it's a short jump to dozens of island nations. She's already planning itineraries for us in New Zealand, Fiji, Papua New Guinea and Indonesia. We'll also return to the beach house and see more areas of Australia. I was right about her wanderlust. At the end of each day, she is bright-eyed and smiling when she tells me about what sights she's seen.

"How's Darby liking Sydney?" he asks just after we've ordered our hard liquor drinks. Dale is old-school. He's all about the three-martini lunch.

"So far, so good," I reply. "She loves the warm weather. I think I've mentioned that she loves art, too. She's been hitting all the museums. The move's been good for her."

"I'm glad," he says genuinely. "Like I said, she's a smart woman for getting out of the rat race. Good for her."

A more serious look comes over his face and I expect him to get down to business. I stayed up half the night last night making sure to be prepared. The briefing I'm about to give him has been carefully crafted to assure him that I'm completely in control. But he doesn't bring up the Sydney office. He brings up something for which I'm wholly unprepared.

"You remember Lena, right? Remind me...what year did you join the firm?"

"November of 2010," I say, already perplexed.

"That's right," he recalls with uncommon wistfulness. "She raved about you after the office Christmas party. You made quite an impression on her."

I don't know what I'm supposed to say. Lena is his ex-wife. She was a lovely woman, but they've been apart for years. He spares me the need to respond by speaking again.

"Two weeks after that party—on the day after New Year's— she filed for divorce."

We're about to have a sentimental conversation. We *are* having a sentimental conversation. The problem is, I have no idea why.

"What I should've done," he begins slowly, "...was let someone else run the company and beg for her to take me back. She was the love of my life, and I should've gone after her. She's remarried now. To a forty-year old French guy."

Our drinks arrive and he pauses from his story long enough to thank the waitress and take a long sip of his cocktail.

"I'm happy that she's happy. I don't want her to be miserable. But I'm miserable," he reveals. "And I miss her every minute. Most days I can't look myself in the mirror for how much this job has cost me." He takes another sip. "Can you?"

And in that moment, I know he's had me pegged all along. I shake my head, and in doing so I shake off the persona I had planned to present today.

"No," I admit. And confessing it feels good.

"Good." He nods approvingly.

It is then that I realize that part of him expected me to deny it. And, why wouldn't he? I've been brushing him off for months.

"When you came here...I always knew it would be temporary. I had you slated for Managing Partner in Chicago."

I'm floored. Chicago is his territory. He's founder and CEO and it's the backbone of the firm.

"I had planned on announcing my retirement next year, but I realized I wouldn't mind accelerating it if I wanted to keep you. I've been grooming you, Michael. Truth is, I always thought you would be my successor."

He leans back in his seat.

"I knew you could have gone anywhere you wanted, but I've been doing everything I had to all these years, to make you want to be here. But as much as I want you to fill my shoes, I don't want you to end up like me. And if I let you stay here, no matter how much rope I gave you, I know you would. Because that's the job. And doing the job is who you are."

I don't know what to say.

"This has nothing to do with your performance. Despite everything that's going on, you're still running circles around the MPs in every other office. And I'm not pushing you out the door right away. You can have as much time as you want, and I'll do whatever you want me to do to preserve the optics of whatever you decide. I'll expect you at work tomorrow. I know you'll lead a good transition. I know you won't let me down. But this isn't what you're supposed to be doing right now. And if you don't know it already, you will. So, Michael..."

He straightens up and looks me dead in the eye.

"You're fired."

Chapter Thirty-One

THINKING OUT LOUD

A month after Dale fires me, I'm on a plane to meet Darby in Chicago. I'll spend more time on planes getting there and back than I'll spend in the city, but I wouldn't have missed this for the world. Darby has finally accepted The Art Institute's offer to name one of its newest wings for her family—The Christensen Gallery. It will be the newest expansion of the modern art wing. Darby's been here for two days working with the museum and preparing her speech for the event.

My cheeks hurt from how hard I'm smiling and my hands ring from the force of my applause at the close of her gracious speech. She cuts the ribbon to let the hundred or so cocktail-attired VIPs come inside. My hand is in hers all night as she chats with the patrons. Her eyes are alight with excitement. The art community is her tribe as much as it is mine and events like this let her network her way into attractive projects. Since leaving the hospital, she's been thinking more about how to spend her money and her time.

We stay until the last of the champagne has been drunk and until after the last stragglers have filtered out. The Executive Director bade us goodbye fifteen minutes ago and we are utterly alone. I took precautions to make sure we'd stay this way. I've arranged for a guard to be posted at the door, and for the cleanup crew to wait until we're gone. I know that having this place to ourselves again—even though we had not yet visited this wing—reminds Darby of that night I brought her here nearly a year ago.

"You know how we're in this together..." I turn to face her and take her other hand in mine.

She nods through a small smile that blooms on her face, a mixture of amusement and curiosity. She has no idea where I'm going with this. She's tickled and maybe a little drunk from the champagne, but I'm nervous as hell.

"I'm devoted to you for the rest of my life. Even if we decide not to be together, I will always have your back. Through rich or poor. Through thick and thin. You know all of that, right?"

She nods, hesitantly now.

I drop down on one knee. Realization dawns in her eyes. I look down to fish the box out of my pocket—it's not the blue of Harry Winston, but the red of Cartier. When I bring my eyes back up to hers, I can see that she recognizes the packaging, but doesn't know what's inside. It's not the telltale cube that she's expecting, the one that would indicate a ring. She's trying to figure out what could be inside a box that is rectangular and wide.

"Darby Nicole Christensen..."

Her hand flies up to cover her mouth.

"I don't need to marry you to love you forever. And I'll never, ever pressure you to wear my ring. But married people have rights that we don't. If you're sick, I want to have the right to sit by your bedside. If you're in trouble, I want the legal rights that any husband or wife would have. And I want you to have the same rights when it comes to me."

With my eyes on her face, I open the box.

"I'm giving you this pen today as a token of my undying love.

Will you use it to sign documentation that would entitle us to that?"

She doesn't answer right away. She's too busy admiring the stunning fountain pen. The entire barrel is covered in pave diamonds set in eighteen-carat white gold. There is a larger diamond at the base of the stylus and when she opens the cap, she'll find an elegant sterling silver nib. It's a vintage piece. No more than ten are believed to remain anywhere in the world.

She's transfixed, but I'm impatient. It is obvious that she loves the pen. But I'm nervous about how much she likes this idea. I'm about to continue making my case when her eyes meet mine again and her face lights up in a brilliant smile.

"Yes."

❦

"Let's get dressed up," Darby says between kisses in bed. We've been lazing around all morning. This past month has been the first time since I was ten that I didn't have a job. I've repaid years' worth of sleep debt, found time to work on my foundation, and made love to Darby in every square inch of our apartment. At first, I was ambivalent about getting fired, but so far, I haven't had a single regret.

Since I left Dewey and Rowe, I flew back to Chicago just once—to talk to some builders about Tara. I know who delivers and who doesn't, and I want to lock down firms I like. A lot goes into building a house if you want it built right. And I've been making modifications to the plans. With Darby's input, we've added a movie theater, doubled the size of the library, and killed a guest bedroom to triple the size of the master closet. We've even created a small room for a sensory deprivation tank.

But today is a special day. And I've looked forward to it. We've flown in our lawyers from Chicago. This month, we've also made decisions about all of the legal rights we've decided to give. We'll give one another medical and financial power of attorney so that we can make critical decisions on one another's behalf. I'll officially install her as Vice President on the Board of Directors on my non-profit. If anything happens to either of us, the other one is in charge, and will be completely covered.

Thinking through things like this has also given me the opportunity to rework my affairs as they relate to Bex. Since I started making real money, she's always been in charge of anything related to my estate. The way we've worked it, Darby has the power to make financial decisions on my behalf if I'm incapacitated for as long as I'm alive. But if I die, there's no way she'll ever need a penny of my money. I've left everything except items that mean something special to Darby to Ella, her little brothers, and Bex. The way we structured it is much smarter than what the law would have provided had we decided to marry.

"Dressed up like how?" I ask, wondering what Darby has in mind.

"You know...make a day out of it. Maybe go to dinner afterward. We've barely put clothes on for the past month, but today...why don't you dust off one of those sexy suits?"

Darby likes me in a suit and tie. And she's right—I have been spending a lot of time in t-shirts and boxers. I don't mind getting dressed up for her and I'm looking forward to when we'll take it all off, later.

It's only when she walks into the kitchen just under an hour later that I know that I've been tricked. She is wearing a gorgeous white dress. It is cream-colored lace that falls off of her shoulder and a white sheath beneath it to modestly hide what would have otherwise been a scandalous showing of skin. She's got on white satin shoes with cute bejeweled bows and she's clutching a small sequined purse in her hand.

"Can't forget my pen," she says casually, waving the purse a little as she meets my eye. "Let's go not get married," she smiles, and I know she knows she's got me.

But I'm too choked up to respond. Because Darby's giving

me the wedding she knows I would have preferred, and I can't imagine a more beautiful bride.

§

The signing of the papers barely takes half an hour. We've read over everything in advance. We sit in a glass-walled conference room with a beautiful view of the bay beneath us, turning to the pages with flags on them, signing and dating on thick black lines.

Darby has planned a special dinner for us, and she must think we'll get a little drunk, because when we went to leave the apartment, she had already booked a car. On the ride over, she presented me with a beautiful pen of my own. Another vintage Cartier that is the understated match for the one I got her.

The final document we sign had nothing to do with our non-wedding. They are the closing documents for our beachfront house. It was owned by a New Yorker who rarely went there anymore and had taken to renting it out on Air B 'n B. The price we offered him made it attractive for him to part with. Accepting the deed to that house is the most gratifying part of the event. It is the first and only asset that Darby and I own together. We still don't have a solid plan, but I like the way I'm settling into ceasing to need one. None of this could be turning out better.

As we pull up to a restaurant called Riverrun—one of my favorites—I begin to get suspicious when I see a sign that says it's closed for a private party. It's a small place, but I am almost certain that it has some sort of party room and I don't know why Darby would book it.

When I walk inside, I don't see the empty tables I expect. I see the only faces that could possibly make this day better.

"Uncle Michael!" Ella runs up to me and nearly knocks me down, because by now I'm weak on my feet. The restaurant has been transformed and glows softly in candlelight. In the room is everyone the both of us love.

I am dazed as I shake hands and receive hugs from Bex and Alex, from Ben and Tami and their tiny babies who can't be more than four months old. I get a whispered "It's about time" from Anne before I'm introduced to her new girlfriend, Meghann. I get an exuberant hug from Andrew and congratulations from his boyfriend Ken. I am floored when I see Avi, smiling for me even as I see on his face that he is still raw over Jasmine and that being here is bittersweet. I get a hard pat on the back from Dale and am thoroughly choked up when Randy pulls me in for a hug.

Darby has given me some amazing nights, but this night—the night of our non-wedding—replaces everything that came before it as the best night I've ever had. This is my family. These people are my life and I'm finally going to live it.

OVERJOYED

DARBY

"**T**en bucks says you get through, no problem."

Michael's breath is warm near my ear. He's speaking too quietly for the TSA agent we just passed, let alone anyone else, to hear. We're shuffling forward, toward the x-ray, in the Pre-Check security line at JFK. His hand has slid up from where it had rested on the small of my back to gently cuff the back of my neck from beneath my hair.

"I think you might lose this one," I reply, just as quietly, more focused on the stroke of his fingers on my skin and the smell of leather from his jacket than I am on what trouble I might be in if the TSA doesn't like what's in my bag.

"It's not contraband, cupcake. If they ask any questions, we'll just tell them all the kick-ass things you did to win that award."

He stops walking to gaze down at me.

"*Dr. Darby Christensen, Living Legend, For Excellence in Medical Research*'...you know how proud I am of you, right?"

"I do know." I smile back up at him, thinking back to the moment I stood on stage accepting the honor. The standing ovation I received had filled the room with resounding applause, but I swear when I caught Michael beaming at me, I could hear him clapping louder than anyone else.

"Worst they'll do is confiscate it," Michael murmurs as he sets the bag which contains it, gently, into one of the white security screening bins. It is a tall glass pyramid that stands about a foot high and, if the TSA decides to make something of it, could be considered to be a deadly weapon.

"No…" I say slowly. "Worst they'll do is escort me to a back room and do a body cavity search."

"You know I'd never let that happen," he says a little more seriously.

I resist the urge to roll my eyes. If Michael thinks he's any match for airport security, he's mistaken. But he likes being the man, and his instinct to protect me is genuine, and sweet. Since I started working with Avi, it's me who's become a force to be reckoned with. Avi does the hacking. Philip does the surveillance. And I'm the brains behind the deal-making and political maneuvering. Taking down men like my father—the bad apples of American politics—is fairly hands-off and strategic, but every once in a while, it requires a little brawn.

After we sail through security with no incident, Michael gives me an 'I told you so' look and I don't hold back from rolling my eyes this time. We stop at Hudson News to buy twenty dollars' worth of candy because, according to Michael, they "never have anything good on the plane". When I browse the area around the cash register to look for a trashy magazine, I can see that most newspapers are still running yesterday's story.

"They say good things happen in threes," Michael murmurs a minute later as we exit the store and begin making our way to the gate. I know then that he saw me eyeing the news. Avi found enough in my father's snitch files to gather evidence that devalued the FBI's need for Charlie Sweeney's testimony. In police custody with no bargaining chip for a reduced sentence, the manslaughter charges stuck. Despite a fast conviction on that front, he avoided a maximum-security prison for the first three years. Evidence from my father's files put him on the hot seat for nearly a dozen other charges.

He did time in an Illinois jail during that period. With so many pending lawsuits, they needed him close so that he could attend proceedings in court. We made sure that the leaked evidence couldn't be traced back to what Frank had known— primarily for my safety. But I'm sure my father's other associates figured it out, and, wisely, laid low.

By the time we were done with him, he had a total of forty-two years with no chance for parole. Fifteen for manslaughter, and eighteen for the racketeering, election tampering, and securities fraud charges our efforts brought. The other nine had nothing to do with us. Once the train started rolling, new people started to pile on. His enemies came right out of the woodwork.

What we read in yesterday's news had been only a matter of time. Fox River Federal Penitentiary housed hardened criminals. We'd always figured that if Charlie didn't get killed in a skirmish with other inmates, he would take his own life. He did the latter.

"What's number three?" I ask. The first good thing is the award. The second is these things with Charlie being over. From the look in his eye, I can tell that Michael's got something in store.

"Paris is always a good thing," he points out.

It's been a short walk to our gate. We're on Air France Flight 52, JFK to CDG. It's our seventh time riding the Concorde since they brought a new version of the aircraft online and did runway extensions. Michael was too risk-averse to take us on its maiden voyage, but after six months without incident, it's been a convenient shuttle. A three-and-a-half hour hop to Paris is hard to beat. We spent the time cuddling together, watching a movie in roomy seats, drinking champagne and snacking on candy and warm nuts.

"Look at this."

Michael is smiling as he gazes down at his phone. We've just touched down at Charles DeGaulle and he's powering it back up for the first time. When he passes the device to me, I break into a grin when I see the video, courtesy of our favorite nephews and best pet-sitters.

"Aww, look...they're having such a great time."

For the past month, Frederick and Paul have been obsessed with dressing up our adorable mutt. Ever the good sport, our little Lucy is indulging them. This time they've got her in a yellow raincoat, matching hat, and four tiny galoshes cover her paws. In the video, she's flanked by Frederick and Paul, also dressed in raincoats and galoshes. Ten-year-old Ella is instructing her little brothers to look at the camera, but the twins are too busy cooing at Lucy, who sits contentedly, as calm and gentle as she was the day we brought her home from the pound.

Paris, meanwhile, is sunny, and I'm glad to be headed to our apartment. Even though we rotate, every place feels like home. We spend part of the winter at our beach house in Sydney, part of the spring in Paris, and the rest of the year in Chicago, though we were so excited when our house in Glencoe was finally ready that we've spent the greater part of the past year in Chicago.

I love that house. I know it started out as Michael's monument to his mother, but as we worked together on planning it, it began to belong to us both. The weather was good this year, and we've loved making use of the outdoor kitchen and fire pit out back. There's room enough (and then some) for Bex's family to come and stay the weekend. But it's not just Bex we've hosted— all our friends love to come, too. For someone who never wanted kids, I'm surprised by how much I love a full house.

"Shit," Michael says a minute later, after I've handed him back his phone.

They've just opened the door and they're about to let us off the plane. He's rapt with concentration, reading through what- ever e-mail is worrying him, and I let him. When he throws me an apologetic look while other passengers in rows behind us disembark, I know that something is about to get in the way of our romantic plans.

"There's a problem with the lumber order," he says gravely.

Because, when you're Michael, when someone gets the lumber order for your treehouse wrong, you've got a major problem. Now that he's not working as much, pet projects around the house are his obsession. What he's building 'for the kids' can barely be called a treehouse. Trust me—I've seen the plans. The multi-room structure, complete with a library, a playroom, bunk beds, plumbing and electricity, will put the houses most of the world lives in to shame. He's trying to finish it by summer. Next on his list is a small cabin in the woods for us. He refuses to show me the plans for that one.

"Do you mind if I stop at the office?" he asks, looking at his watch. "I'll only be gone for an hour. If I shower quickly, I'll be able to make dinner on time."

We have a tradition. The first time we come back to any of our homes after being away for a while, Michael carries me over the threshold. I'm disappointed, but I acquiesce, knowing how much this treehouse means to him. And since we both work hard not to bring our work home, I'm sure that whatever he needs to get things back on track is in his Paris office.

When we pass through customs and make our way to the exit, I'm not surprised to see a proper-looking driver dressed in a dark suit holding up an iPad with the name "Blaine/Christensen" printed upon it. We walk toward the man, who is tall and slender and looks very welcoming.

"How was your flight, Miss Christensen?" The older man addresses me kindly.

"Restful," I smile.

"Wonderful, Madam. Welcome to Paris," he says, as he relieves me of my bag. Michael places his hand on the small of my back as we walk out. I don't notice until a moment too late that the driver has placed my suitcase in the trunk and left

Michael's. I'm not surprised when Michael ushers me into the limousine first, but when he leans in and casts me another apologetic glance, I know that something is amiss.

"See you in a bit, love." he says then, casting me another apologetic glance before pressing a half letter-sized envelope into my hand.

He kisses the knuckles of my free hand and squeezes lightly before he lets me go, stepping back as he lets the driver close the door. It's not until the car is pulling away, until I'm watching Michael disappear slowly from my view that I realize what is happening.

I cast my gaze down toward the small ivory envelope that displays Michael's elegant handwriting. 'Darby' is all it says. I open it slowly. Inside are two items—an official-looking train ticket that has the Eurostar logo printed up top. It tells me that at 14:22, I'll be boarding a train at Paris Gare Du Nord. The second is a book, in French: *À la Recherche du Temps Perdu* by Marcel Proust.

"In Search of Lost Time," I say out loud. I studied enough French literature to know that it is a classic work about a forbidden, and unrequited love that follows the internal struggles of the male hero. Having little else to do, and desperate to find out why Michael has chosen this particular book, which I'm sure is not a mistake, I make myself comfortable and begin to read. In just over an hour, we reached the station, having travelled from DeGaulle in what I know is good time. The driver refuses my tip, assuring me it's been taken care of.

I step into the busy station with my suitcase in tow. Normally, I would have been charmed by the scene—by the voice over the loudspeaker communicating news in French, and the distinctly European signage—by the candies at the newsstand, and the coffee kiosks, so different from the Starbuck's at home. But I can't help scanning for Michael. He's here somewhere—I know it. Yet, when the time comes without him making an appearance, I board my train.

I settle into my modern seat in business class, which is the car into which I've been booked. It's not a private cabin, rather a seat on an open car. I spend twenty minutes staring out the window as the train moves, watching the countryside rolling by. At some point, I become engrossed once again in my book.

My French is rusty after having been away for so long, but I can easily follow the story. Forty-five minutes into the ride, I'm rapt with attention when the voices of a couple in front of me become louder. They're German, I realize, and they seemed to be arguing. For half a minute, I turn my attention back to my book and think to mind my own business. But their words are strangely familiar, and I realize in an instant what Michael has done.

As my mind catches up to what my heart knows, I cast my eyes off to my right. Michael sits in the seat across the aisle from mine, staring at me as the arguing couple gets up and storms off.

"Do you have any idea what they were arguing about?"

My heart thunders, because Michael has recreated the first scene in *Before Sunrise*. He just recited Ethan Hawke's line—the Jesse character's. And I'm intended to be the Julie Delpy character, Celine.

"Do you—do you speak English?" he continues with perfect intonation. That's my cue, and I stammer through it with equal authenticity.

"Yeah. No, I'm sorry, my German is not very good."

He looks at me expectantly. If I'd had to think about the line, I wouldn't have been able to form it. I'm flabbergasted by what is happening, but I've seen the movie fifty times. So I continue.

"Have you ever heard that as couples get older, they lose their ability to hear each other?" I manage.

"No," he replies right on cue, but it takes me a breathless moment to reply.

"Well, supposedly, men lose the ability to hear higher-pitched sounds, and women eventually lose hearing in the low end. I guess they sort of nullify each other, or something."

He stands then, an action that doesn't happen in the movie. He comes right to me but I'm still so amazed that I have no idea what to do.

"I guess," he says smoothly. "Nature's way of allowing couples to grow old together without killing each other."

I beam at him then, realizing without a doubt that the best date of my life has just begun. I wouldn't have thought it possible, for all the amazing dates Michael has orchestrated for me. But in the five years since he walked into my life, Michael has never stopped serving up astonishing surprises and true romance.

"Don't worry," he assures. "I won't hold you to a recitation of the entire script."

We've broken character, and now we're just two lovers on a train, with me tucked under his arm.

"What *will* you hold me to?"

His gorgeous eyes reflect a love so unimaginable that I'm already swept away, even though our date has barely begun.

"A night spent walking around Vienna, letting our own story take shape...and letting me fall in love with you all over again."

❧

Thank you so much for reading *Chrysalis*! A tremendous amount of TLC went into writing Darby and Michael's story and I would appreciate hearing your thoughts in a review! If you read out of order, the first book, *Snapdragon*, covers the beginning of Michael and Darby's story and is told from Darby's point of view.

As you've figured out by now, there's a whole lot more to Michael's story. He and Avi are involved in a vigilante crime fighting organization, and, now, so is Darby. Avi has his own story, too.

The next book, *Vertical,* finds Avi leaving Darby and Michael's non-wedding reception to race halfway across the world to help his ex out of a predicament—the same ex who left him at the altar. The last place Avi saw Jasmine was in the front of the church, six months ago, right before she walked out of his life. Well...almost the last time. They still work on opposite ends of the same social justice organization. Can he answer her distress beacon and get to Nevada in time to save her from a human trafficking bust gone wrong?

" Thrilling combination of suspense, intrigue, and romance,
Nice backstory on Avi and Jasmine. "
-Barbara B, Amazon Reviewer

"This book is in your face right from the first page...he will
move heaven and earth to get to her. "
-Merry Jelks- Emmanuel, Amazon Reviewer

"Strong female lead who wants to right the wrongs done to
her by saving other women and girls. Couldn't put it down. "
-JLynn, Amazon Reviewer

AUTHOR'S NOTE

I loved so many things about writing *Chrysalis*. The non-wedding ending may be my favorite conclusion of any of my romances. My favorite thing about Darby and Michael is how they never marched to the beat of anyone else's drum.

I draw a lot from my real life and put personal details into my books. I put a lot of heart into my books and I say a lot about the stories behind the stories on my hidden bonus materials page: https://www.kilbyblades.com/chrysalis-bonus-materials.

Whether you loved or hated *Chrysalis*, I humbly ask and encourage you to leave a review with whatever book store you like to use. Reviews mean a lot to authors and they really do tell prospective readers what elements they might like or dislike about a book.

Finally, I would be remiss in closing without saying a huge thanks to my pro team, Tasha, Britta, Jen, Stacey and Jada, and for my beta team (who also doubled as my sanity team), Nicole and Liz. Special thanks to Lyndal for fact-checking all of my Australia details, and to Leslie and Rose for moral support. I couldn't have done this without all of you!

ABOUT KILBY BLADES

Kilby Blades is a *USA Today* Bestselling author of Romance and Women's Fiction and a fifty-time award-winning author. Her debut novel, *Snapdragon*, was a HOLT Medallion finalist, a Publisher's Weekly BookLife Prize Semi-Finalist, and an IPPY Award medalist. Kilby was honored with an RSJ Emma Award for Best Debut Author in 2018, and has been lauded by critics for "easing feminism and equality into her novels" (IndieReader) and "writing characters who complement each other like a fine wine does a good meal" (Publisher's Weekly).

When she's not writing, Kilby goes to movie matinees alone, where she eats Chocolate Pocky and buttered popcorn and usually smuggles in not-a-little-bit of red wine. She procrastinates from the difficult process of writing by oversharing on Facebook and Instagram and giving away cool stuff related to her fiction novels to her newsletter subscribers.

amazon.com/author/kilbyblades

instagram.com/kilbyblades

goodreads.com/kilbyblades

facebook.com/kilbybladesauthor

twitter.com/kilbyblades

BOOKS BY KILBY BLADES

The Gilded Love Series

BOOK 1: *SNAPDRAGON*

BOOK 2: *CHRYSALIS*

BOOK 3: *VERTICAL*

BOOK 4: *LOADED: A HOLIDAY ROMANCE*

The Hot in the Kitchen Series

BOOK 1: *THE SECRET INGREDIENT*

BOOK 2: *SPOONING LEADS TO FORKING*

Romancing the Stove *(Coming in 2022)*

The Green Valley Heroes Series

(Green Valley Chronicles, Penny Reid Book Universe)

BOOK 1: *FORREST FOR THE TREES*

The Modern Love Series

BOOK 1: *FRIENDED*

Friended eBook | Friended Audiobook

BOOK 2: *ENDED?*

Standalone Contemporary Romance

The *Worst Holiday Ever* Anthology Series

BOOK 1: *WORST HOLIDAY EVER*

BOOK 2: *WORST VALENTINE'S DAY EVER*

Non-Fiction Author Guides